The Blue Guide

A lump appears in my throat. I step up to her, drape myself over her from behind, feeling my bush against the satin skin of her buttocks, my breasts against her slender back. I reach around her and fumble for a moment, secure her hands together then pull out the ends of the tie and wind each around an arm of the chair, knot it. When I'm done, I stand back up, waiting for her command. She seems to have some pretty definite ideas about what she wants.

'Over there,' she says, turning her head over her shoulder and jerking her chin. 'My bag.'

I go back over to the bed, open her capacious Balenciaga hobo handbag. Inside are all the accoutrements the modern girl needs for her day-to-day life — mobile, hairbrush, cigarettes, tampons, Chanel sunglasses, lipstick. And amidst them all is a pink strap-on.

The Blue Guide
Carrie Williams

BLACK LACE

Black Lace books contain sexual fantasies.
In real life, always practise safe sex.

First published in 2007 by
Black Lace
Thames Wharf Studios
Rainville Rd
London W6 9HA

www.black-lace-books.com

Typeset by SetSystems Ltd, Saffron Walden, Essex

Printed in the UK by CPI Bookmarque, Croydon, CR0 4TD

The paper used in this book is a natural, recyclable product made
from wood grown in sustainable forests. The manufacturing process
conforms to the regulations of the country of origin.

ISBN 978 0 352 34131 0

To Nuala Devel
muse and partner in crime

1

The telephone by my bed rings, shrill against the muffled traffic sounds from the street below. I open one eye to check the time on the LED display, then roll away with a groan. Nine o'clock is far too early to be hauling myself out of bed on a Monday morning after working all weekend. Especially when I haven't been feeling my usual breezy self these last few months.

Sleep is already trying to suck me back down into its seductive depths when the answering machine kicks into life.

'Hello,' I hear myself say. 'This is Alicia Shaw, professional tour guide. For more information about my individually tailored tours of London, either leave your name and number after the tone, or email me via my website, www.theblueguide.com.'

I smile wryly in my half-sleep, still proud of my little joke. Not so long ago, I was entitled to sport a Blue Badge, the mark of a guide approved by the official tourist body. Then I got struck off. My new designation is a form of revenge, as well as a way of poking fun at myself, at some of the little adventures I've had of late.

The beep on the machine startles me out of my reverie, as does the brisk voice that follows it.

'Hello Alicia, this is Fenella Hamilton-Jones of Papaya Performing Artistes. I'm calling on behalf of one of my clients, who's been recommended your services. The trouble is, it's very short notice – he's arriving this afternoon, and would want to meet you for dinner to discuss an itinerary for the next couple of weeks. That said, I've been looking at your website, and I can safely say that Paco would be more than happy to double your rates if you could clear the decks for him.'

I sit up in bed, staring at the answerphone. Only yesterday I read in the weekend glossies that heartthrob flamenco dancer Paco Manchega is coming to town for a series of shows. It can't be a coincidence. And now he wants to pay me exorbitant amounts of money to show him around town. My gloomy thoughts are cast away, at least for the moment, and it's all I can do to stop myself punching the air in jubilation.

I don't waste a minute in returning Fenella's call and confirming the booking and arrangements for the evening's meeting. Then I pad into the kitchen in my dressing gown and whizz myself an energising smoothie in the blender before sitting down at the breakfast bar, opening my diary, and working my way through appointments I need to cancel.

By four o'clock, I've taken a taxi to Harvey Nics and had a cut and colour, a manicure and pedicure, and a facial. I wouldn't normally indulge myself like this, but Paco Manchega is one of the world's most gorgeous men. Not that I fancy my chances. But it wouldn't feel right being in his presence with a hair out of place, or the merest suggestion of a zit. Letting my credit card take the strain in anticipation of the almost obscenely huge cheque that Fenella's putting in the mail today, I check my watch and see that I have a couple of hours to spare. Good. That gives me time for a cocktail or two at Claridge's Bar.

Over the driest of martinis, my thoughts return, in spite of myself, to Daniel Lubowski, and a dark mood threatens to descend on me again. It must be five months since I first heard the movie producer's gravelly West Coast drawl on my message machine, enquiring about the possibility of a bespoke tour of London film locations. As I listened to him speak, I pictured a tall lean man oozing with the self-confidence that comes with money and worldly success. In his fifties, I decided, he was handsome and boyish-faced enough to have let his hair go a distinguished grey, à la Richard Gere. He was the kind of guy who teamed an Armani jacket with vintage Levi's.

I called him right back, and quickly established that though he was making great shakes in Hollywood, he was actually a connoisseur of 1960s and 70s British films, and wanted something a little more offbeat than the usual Bridget Jones in Borough Market or James Bond in Mayfair tours. He talked fondly about Alfred Hitchcock, James Fox and Dirk Bogarde in *The Servant*, Michael Caine and others, and we agreed that I would devise a few mini-tours that he would be able to slot into his busy schedule of meetings.

After we'd talked fees and timings, I hung up and logged onto the internet. A couple of hours' surfing gave me plenty of material with which to sit down and plot a handful of possible tours with the help of an *A to Z*.

Daniel flew in a few days later, and lived up to my every expectation, except that the jeans were Juicy Couture, he was in his early forties, and he was far, far sexier than Richard Gere. He had that same roguish twinkle in his eye, but there was less cocksureness about him, less swagger.

He'd asked me to book dinner somewhere 'hot', so that we might get to know each other a little before the first tour, as well as to fine tune the details together, and I'd managed to pull a few strings and secure a table at The Wolseley, which had just opened on Piccadilly. It didn't get much classier than that. Daniel approved – the decor (Japanese lacquer screens, original art deco features, marble floors) was stylish, the food faultless, and the company illustrious: we spotted Hugh Grant snuggling up to Jemima Khan, as well as Gwyneth Paltrow, with whom, it turned out, Daniel was on nodding terms.

We got on from the word go; Daniel was charming without being smarmy, and full of pithy anecdotes about his life in Los Angeles, without being boastful. The wine (an unspeakably delicious Pouilly Fuissé) flowed freely, and before long we'd moved on to more intimate matters. In my defence, it was Daniel who started it.

'So Ally,' he'd said, leaning in to me over the table, fixing me with those cobalt-blue eyes that reflected the light from the chandeliers. 'You don't mind if I call you that?'

I shook my head, trying not to let my cheeks colour. All of a sudden I'd come over all starstruck.

'What do you get up to when you're not a tour guide?' he continued.

'Well, work doesn't leave me much time for myself,' I said rather evasively, all too aware of how empty and grey my life would seem to someone who mixed with Hollywood's elite. 'I always seem to be so busy – researching, devising new walks, keeping up with the latest openings and new attractions, exploring London from different angles.'

I tried to decipher his expression, but his face was momentarily obscured by his hand as he lit a cigarette. I shook my head as he offered me one.

'And you?' I ventured.

'Nah, I don't have a boyfriend right now either,' he

said, exhaling a plume of smoke. His face was deeply serious.

Damn it, I thought as we finished our coffees and Daniel settled the bill. How could I have misread him so badly? Not only had I not clocked on that he was gay, but I'd even, for a moment, been deluded enough to imagine that he was flirting with me. Suddenly I was in a hurry to get home. Confirming that I'd collect him from his hotel at two o'clock the next day, I bade him goodnight, stepped out into the throng and neon glare of Piccadilly, and took the tube home.

2

I was armed with my usual clipboard, covered with pages of notes of names, addresses and dates that I wasn't likely to remember off the top of my head. I'd also printed off some photographs and film stills from the internet. We were in Covent Garden, where Hitchcock had shot much of *Frenzy* in 1972, in and around what was then London's main wholesale fruit and veg market. We'd decided to start with that because it was the nearest to Daniel's hotel on Aldwych.

I'd hired the movie the night before, never having seen it, and been shocked by its sheer viciousness, by the cold offhand way in which the brutal murders of a succession of women are portrayed. I wasn't surprised, when subsequently reading up on it, to discover that it had been the only Hitchcock film to garner an X-certificate, probably because it was his first one to feature nude scenes.

Daniel was dressed casually, in an eggshell-blue Ralph Lauren shirt and some DKNY jeans that fit his firm buttocks snugly. Still stinging from my misunderstanding of the previous evening, I tried to focus my mind on the tour and not on the contents of his trousers.

We started in the market itself, where, I told Daniel, Hitchcock's father had once sold produce. We compared stills from the film to the present prettified building with its touristy shops and cafés. Then we wandered into Henrietta Street, where I pointed out number three, a building that had once belonged to a writer called Clemence Dane, whose novel had inspired Hitchcock's early film *Murder*. The ground floor was currently occupied by a book distributor's office; above that was the window of the bachelor pad of the 'necktie murderer' in *Frenzy*, Bob Rusk. Daniel immediately identified it as the location of an astonishing scene in which the camera follows the killer as he leads a fresh victim up the stairs to his flat, then pulls back into the market itself, as if recoiling from the sight.

It was easy money, really. All Daniel needed me to do was show him the present-day locations, and he put the rest together from his intimate knowledge of the film. I must admit, I was impressed – he seemed to know every line of dialogue, every camera angle that had been used. We had lots of fun holding up my printouts of old photos against the buildings and spotting in which ways they'd changed and how they had stayed the same, and Daniel spoke so passionately about *Frenzy* that I told him that although I'd found it, in many ways, repellent on first viewing, I intended watching it again that night in the light of what I'd seen and what he'd told me.

'Then why not come back to my hotel and watch it with me?' he suggested. 'They have a private screening room we could use if it's free. I have a DVD of the film with me.'

We were sitting outside the Nell of Old Drury on Catherine Street, in which the man who will become the prime suspect, Richard Blaney, listens in on some city gents discussing the sex killings with obvious relish. The late April sunshine warmed us as we enjoyed a couple of beers.

Daniel raised an eyebrow. 'Unless you have other plans for the evening?' he said.

I shook my head. I wasn't about to tell him that even if I had had plans, I'd cancel them without a second thought. I'd got over my humiliation of the night before and was actually now just enjoying myself in a very straightforward way. Daniel, I had realised, was just an extraordinarily interesting – and *nice* – guy.

We walked back to his hotel. He'd called ahead, and a couple of margaritas and a trayful of canapés were waiting for us in the little cinema. I whistled as we walked in: the 30-odd seats were clad in soft baby-blue leather, and each had its own small table for a cocktail glass.

'Cool, isn't it?' said Daniel, handing me a margarita and clinking his glass gently against mine.

'It's seriously swanky,' I said, looking around.

Daniel eased himself into a seat on the front row, and I followed suit. Then he signalled the projectionist to start the DVD and we sat watching in the darkness, exchanging the odd observation and getting as excited as little kids whenever we recognized a locale that we'd visited that day. A couple more cocktails arrived, seemingly unbidden, adding to our good humour. Finally, just as the end credits were rolling and I was contemplating whether to splash out on a taxi home, and wondering whether there was anything in my fridge or whether I ought to stop off for a takeout pizza, I realised with a shiver of utter, and unutterable, pleasure that Daniel's hand was on my thigh.

I must have let out an involuntary gasp, for he retracted it slightly and said in an almost plaintive voice: 'Sorry, does that bother you?'

'No,' I moaned. 'God, no.' And to reinforce my point I grabbed his hand and placed it back on my thigh, only a little higher this time.

As he turned in his seat and nuzzled his face in my

neck, I murmured, 'It's just that I thought you were gay.'

Daniel sat up, a bemused expression on his face. 'What the hell gave you that idea?' he said.

'Last night,' I reminded him. 'When you told me you don't have a boyfriend at the moment.'

He chuckled, bringing his face back to my neck and nibbling at me – a move guaranteed to have me in paroxysms of delight in minutes. His lips grazed the tender flesh of my earlobe as he whispered, 'I said I don't have a boyfriend. Not now, not ever. I was pulling your leg, as I think you Brits say.'

In one fluid movement, he pushed my skirt up around my hips, parted my legs and hooked them over the arms of my seat, then lowered himself to his knees. Pulling the lacy fabric of my knickers aside, he brought his face to me.

'God, you're wet,' he exclaimed. 'And you smell – mmm – just great.'

I swooned back, closed my eyes and gave myself up to the feel of Daniel's expert mouth on me, listening to my skin squeaking against the leather as I writhed with pleasure. His tongue flicked at my clitoris, teasing me, and then roamed the little folds and creases of my lips as if trying to locate a mother of pearl within its shell.

'I could eat you all night,' he said when he finally came up for air. In the dim light I could see the lower half of his face glistening with my fluids. Suddenly self-conscious, I sat up.

As if reading my thoughts, Daniel whispered, 'How about if we go somewhere more private?'

I nodded and, after I'd straightened up my clothes, we took the lift. A couple got in at the ground floor, and I was more than a little relieved not to have to make inane conversation with Daniel, as I was sure I would have done. At the top floor we followed the couple out, then Daniel led me through the corridors to his suite. Swiping his card, he held the door open and ushered me into the hallway. I walked down it towards a large sitting room filled with sleek sofas, vases of orchids and tasteful artworks. Through a door to my left I glimpsed a huge bed invitingly covered with white linen.

The mood had lost its edge on the silent journey up from the screening room, and I think both of us were feeling a little shy about setting things in motion again. Reaching into the mini-bar and uncorking a bottle of white wine, Daniel suggested that, since we hadn't eaten, we order in room service. I agreed, suddenly aware that I was ravenous.

By the time our food arrived half an hour later, we had polished off the Pinot Grigio and were naked on the sofa, in what's commonly referred to as a sixty-niner. Daniel's cock was pale and smooth, and felt cool as a pebble in my mouth. And I just loved the obvious enjoyment he was getting from my pussy. We'd totally forgotten about the food, in fact, when the rap on the door came.

Daniel hotfooted it into the bathroom and came out in his fluffy bathrobe, throwing me a similar one and waiting until I'd slipped it on before opening the door. The waiter rumbled in with a trolley laden with crisp napkins, glittering cutlery and white porcelain plates covered with silver dishes.

'Where would you like it, sir?' he asked.

'In the dome room, I think,' Daniel said, turning to me. 'This is really something.'

The waiter advanced through the sitting room at a stately pace, halting before a set of double doors that I'd scarcely noticed up to that point. Opening them with somewhat of a flourish, he stood back and I saw beyond them a sumptuous circular room, the centrepiece of which was a gleaming round table.

'What on earth is that?' I said.

Daniel smiled indulgently. 'This used to be a newspaper HQ,' he said, 'and this was the boardroom.' He stepped inside and pulled back one of the chairs. 'Come in and take a seat,' he said as the waiter laid our places on the table.

When the latter retreated, Daniel signed his bill and handed the man a generous tip. Then he turned back to me, poured me a glass of wine from a fresh bottle set in an ice bucket, and, before I had chance to protest, slipped my bathrobe off my shoulders. It fell around me on the chair, leaving me naked at the table.

Bursting out laughing at my shout of surprise, Daniel took his off too, then leaned forwards, swept me up in his arms and laid me out on the table, as if I were part of the meal. Now I was laughing too.

Resting my head back against the table, I looked up at the painted inner dome of the ceiling and thought of all the high-falutin' meetings that must have taken place here over the years. Daniel, meanwhile, had got to work on the starter: he was busy dismantling a neat little dish of tiger prawns and arranging a number of them in a line down from my breasts to the top of my pussy. Bringing his mouth to me, he wound his tongue around and between the glossy crustacea. Then he cupped my ribs with his hands and, crouched over me, took the prawns into his mouth, one by one, clearly savouring the satinesque skin of them before biting into the meaty flesh.

'Now for the main course,' he announced, looking up into my eyes, and again I felt an immense thrill ripple up through my body as he began jabbing at my labia with his tongue, probing them with his mouth as he had the seafood. I closed my eyes and envisaged my own vulva, its pinks and purples recalling the flesh tones of the prawns, its juices winking like shellfish on a fishmonger's slab.

I was startled from my weird vision by a sudden icy blast, and opened my eyes to see that Daniel had drenched my pussy with half a glass of Chablis. I sat up, giggling, and pulled him up towards me. Understanding, he rolled over onto his back and this time it was my turn to smear him with butter, which I delved out of the little bowl and massaged slowly, deeply, into his chest, working each muscle group with my fingers until they began to soften like the butter. Then, taking another pat of the creamy yellow substance between my palms, I began to coat his cock thoroughly, thickly, leaving not a square millimetre uncovered. I slathered it around his balls, across his perineum and around his arsehole too. His hips were grinding away as if the sensations were becoming almost too intense for him, and low moans escaped from between his parted lips. His head was thrown back, but I could see that his eyes were open and that he was staring through one of the little round windows that gave onto the night.

As he pleaded with me to straddle him, I thrust one finger up his arse, as far as it would go, in one clean motion. He yelped, and torrents of come began pumping out of him, splashing onto his upper belly and trickling down his sides onto the polished wood of the table.

When he was done, and lay gasping, I brought my mouth to him and slowly coaxed his cock back to life, caressing his flesh with the tip of my tongue until I felt him begin to tighten and strain for me again. Then I sat up and lowered myself onto him, and his hands closed around my hips. My pussy devoured him so avidly that

I was afraid for a moment I was going to suck him up whole. I rocked back and forth, eyes closed, hands clasping my breasts, trying to establish a quiet, measured rhythm, to keep hold of the moment. His hands on each side of me steadied me, were complicit in attempting to maintain the momentum, to stave off what was inevitable – what was desired but perhaps, in some part of us, feared. But the vigour of his climax had excited me too much, and each time my clit ground against him, I came a step closer to losing it. Before long, I couldn't hold my climax back. I came violently, howling up into the empty space of that lovely dome like a she-wolf calling out into the dark.

'Jesus,' I heard him mutter as we lay spent in each others' arms, amidst the remnants of our barely eaten meal and all the posh crockery and gleaming silver. Then, after a while, Daniel rose and, sliding into his bathrobe, went off into the bedroom. He returned to tell me he'd run me a deep hot bath.

I soaked for an hour or so, letting the water caress my skin that still tingled from Daniel's touch and the frenzy that he had unleashed in me. A little television stuck on a bendy stalk was tuned into CNN news but the sound was down and the disasters and dramas that were being recounted by its coiffed presenters might as well have been taking place on the moon for all they impinged on me. I felt completely unconnected with reality.

When I climbed out, Daniel was in bed, propped up against a pile of pillows, hopping through the channels on a larger TV set.

'I'm looking for a decent old movie we can watch,' he said. 'Here,' he added, passing me a mug from the bedside table. 'I had some hot chocolate brought up for us.'

I was asleep before I had chance to drink it, and I'm not sure whether he found a good film to watch or not. All I know is that when I woke in his arms in the grey light of dawn, I had fallen more than a little for Daniel Lubowski.

3

We shared breakfast in bed, laughing as we smeared each other with fresh berries and Greek yogurt, as we stained the pristine white sheets with a mixture of crushed raspberries and our own liquors. Dan marvelled as I lay back and spread myself wide for him, holding my pussy open as if for his inspection. Exclaiming at its juiciness, he brought his hand slowly to me, slid three fingers in and and then moved them in and out slowly, entering me a little more deeply each time until I was trying to sit up, reaching for his cock, begging him to come into me. Knowing that I was on the brink, he carried on teasing me until I couldn't take any more and was up and pushing him back onto the bed. Turning around, I lowered myself onto his dick with my back to him, taking him up to the hilt, then leaning forwards so that he had a close-up view of my arse. He grabbed my cheeks violently, began pushing me forwards and then pulling me back. When it seemed we were both on the cusp of an orgasm, he sat up and pushed me forwards at the same time as he maneouvred himself onto his knees. As if repaying me for the compliment of the previous evening, he inserted his thumb into my sphincter.

With one hand outspread on the leather headboard to steady myself against his onslaught, I reached between my legs and pressed my clitoris, letting my fingers remain still for a few moments, for as long as I could bear it, knowing that the second I began strumming at myself the fireworks would flash through me, searing me. But even before I began, Dan had reached around me and removed my fingers, replacing them with his own. For a minute or two he peppered my clit with the lightest and most fleeting of touches, as if a butterfly was swooping in on me and then away. Then he mashed his fingertips into me, and as he massaged my clit up and down along my pubic bone, one finger on each side of the little pink nub, I could tell he was listening for my verbal cues, working out what best pleased me. When he hit the spot, his index and middle fingers jiggling me from side to side, he re-intensified the plunging action of his cock and it was as if, in my climax, I was being carried away by some primeval force, as if a tornado or hurricane was sweeping through the room, ravaging me.

Yelling, Dan pulled back and out of me, and I fell forwards onto the bed, tears in my eyes. The feeling was almost mystical, that of being one with the universe – a Buddhist sense, I suppose, of blending in with everything around one, of being an indissoluble part of a greater whole. I let myself float for a while, not even stirring when I felt Dan lean forwards and stroke my hair, plant a kiss on my cheek, pull the duvet up around my shoulders.

When I woke it was ten o'clock, and a note on the bedside cabinet informed me that he had gone to a meeting and would pick me up in a taxi downstairs at one o'clock to take us on our second tour. In the meantime, I was to relax and order whatever I wanted from room service.

I switched the TV on but barely watched as I flicked through the hotel directory, where I noticed that there was a swimming pool on site. After ringing down to check that they sold swimsuits for guests who had forgotten theirs, I slipped into my bathrobe and waffle slippers and headed down to the basement in the lift. There I spent an hour alternating between lap swimming and just drifting about, the classical music that was being piped underwater helping to sustain the sense of otherworldliness that had taken hold of me.

After another bath and some coffee in the Dome Suite, I was in the lobby ready for Daniel, who soon pulled up in a taxi outside and waved me to join him. As we headed west, he told me he'd been in a meeting with an up-and-coming young director who had worked on music videos for Björk and some other Icelandic artists and whom he was trying to lure into working on something a little more mainstream. He was pleased with the outcome, thought he'd made a breakthrough with the guy. Doodling on the window with his finger as we rounded Hyde Park Corner and I pointed out the majestic Wellington Arch, he explained to me that his dream was to subvert Hollywood from within, to attract the kind of avant-garde overseas talent that would put a halt to the creeping blandness of commercial American film making.

We slipped along the southern edge of Hyde Park, past the Royal Albert Hall and Albert Memorial, and then traced a course through various minor streets of Kensington to reach Earl's Court. It's a run-down area of backpackers' hotels and Australian themed bars, and we lingered only long enough to take a look at Kensington Mansions on Trebovir Road, which Roman Polanski had used as the exterior for Catherine Deneuve's flat in his film *Repulsion* in 1965. I didn't need to tell Daniel that the amazing expanding apartment itself was actually a studio set.

We headed back through South Kensington to Thurloe Place, where a number of locations used in the film have remained remarkably unchanged, including the beauty salon where Deneuve's character Carol works, still a hairdresser and beauty therapist's, the Hoop & Toy pub, and Dino's Italian café, where we went and ordered fish and chips in homage to the scene where Carol eats with her would-be boyfriend. When the waitress jotted down what we wanted, Dan asked her a few questions and was touchingly pleased to find out that the French actress also used to come here to eat during breaks from shooting.

'Imagine that,' he said dreamily. 'Catherine Deneuve might have sat at this very table.' I looked at his faraway gaze and realised that even Hollywood producers can be starry-eyed.

As we waited for our food, we chatted about the movie, which I had watched a few nights before in preparation for the tour. Conversely to the Hitchcock film, this deals with a woman murdering men, but the repulsion of the title is not the viewer's so much as Carol's, who, it is insinuated, has been abused and is thus unable to deal with sexual advances by men. The most fascinating thing for him, Dan explained, was how different viewers came to such different conclusions about Carol and her motivations. Most agree that she is sexually repressed because of childhood events, but where many people say that she is entirely sexless, Dan believed that, on the contrary, she is consumed by sexual urges that she just doesn't know how to handle because of her fear of men.

'Everything points to her being both disgusted and turned on by the same things,' he explained as he lit a cigarette and took a swig of the cheap red wine we'd ordered. I was surprised but strangely pleased to note that he didn't feel he had to spend money to impress me, that he wasn't a snob.

'Like with the boyfriend's razor and toothbrush, and the vest that she sniffs,' he continued. He leaned in towards me, lowered his voice a little. 'I'm interested – do you think she masturbates in the movie?'

I cast my mind back, tried to think. 'Not that it jumped out at me,' I replied. 'Why, do you?'

'Almost certainly,' he said. 'Right after when she walks in on her sister's boyfriend shaving. It's very subtle, very ambiguous. You just see her face, trembling a little, and then her face pucker a bit as if in distaste, and then the camera pans out and she makes a weird movement with her hand and flicks her fingers as if shaking water away, as if trying to wash away her feelings of being dirty. In fact, I think it's implied numerous times throughout the film.'

Huge platefuls of fish and chips arrived and we ate with gusto, continuing to discuss the many layers and ambiguities of the film, and then talking about other Polanski films, from classics such as *Rosemary's Baby* and *The Tenant* to the execrable if diverting *Bitter Moon* and *The Ninth Gate*. When we'd finished the food and the carafe of wine, Dan blew his cheeks out and rolled his eyes.

'I think I need a few tours round the block,' he said. 'I'm stuffed.'

I laughed. 'Me too,' I said. 'How about a walk in Hyde Park? It's just a couple of minutes away.'

'Sounds great,' he replied, standing up and pushing his seat back, signalling to the waitress that we needed our bill.

Outside, we crossed the thundering Cromwell Road and walked up past the Natural History Museum and Science Museum I'd visited with so many American teenagers. At the top of Exhibition Road, we entered the park. I was half inclined to take Dan to the Serpentine

Gallery: his talk about films enthralled me and I suspected he might be equally fascinating and insightful when it came to art, especially contemporary art. But he seemed to be enjoying being outdoors, so I let it go and we carried on down to the Serpentine lake at the heart of the park. Although it wasn't yet the summer season, a number of people were out on the water, in paddle boats or rowing boats. Dan looked at me.

'How about we go for spin?' he said.

I smiled. I'm ashamed to say that in all my years in London, in all my time as a tour guide, I had never yet boated on the Serpentine. How could I refuse?

We crossed to the other side of the lake, to the boathouses, where we paid a small deposit and set out in our craft. Daniel insisted on rowing, peeling off his navy-blue John Smedley sweater to reveal his powerful, lightly tanned arms.

'Just relax and enjoy yourself,' he said, and I lay back and let the mild late spring air caress me, watching the clouds thread their way across a luminescent sky. This, I said to myself, was bliss.

I must have dozed off, for the next thing I knew Daniel was leaning over me, saying something in a soft voice.

'. . . a bit cold?' was all I made out. I followed his line of vision down to my breasts and saw that my nipples were erect and protruding through my light woollen top. Knowing he was looking at them made them harden still further.

I glanced about us. Daniel had steered us into the bank, and we were parked up beneath the overhanging branches of a willow tree. I gazed up at him, pulled my top up over my head, then reached round to free my breasts from my bra, kicking my shoes off at the same time. He laid his palms on my boobs but didn't take his eyes from mine. Then he swept his hands down over my belly to my skirt and pants. Lifting up my bum, he pulled them both down until I was naked before him, or almost – all that remained on me were my hold-up stockings, the kind that stay up without the need for suspenders. With one finger he traced the slim neat line of my pubic hair.

I stood up now, and indicated that he should lie down. When he did, I yanked at his trouser flies, then reached inside and closed my hand around his meaty responsive cock. He shut his eyes, rested his head back against the bottom of the boat, lips opening and closing almost imperceptibly as if he were muttering something to himself, or perhaps even praying. Maybe for him, just as there had been for me that morning, there was something almost religious about our fucking.

Pulling his cock out through his zipper, I took it into my mouth, rolled it around for a while then began jabbing at the base of his glans with my tongue while giving his scrotum a good firm squeeze with one hand. He went crazy, twitching and shuddering and letting out a strange low groan from the back of his throat. Beneath him, the boat rocked precariously with his movement, and with my free hand I grabbed instinctively for the side. We both began laughing, and suddenly I felt like a character in a Benny Hill sketch. What the hell were we doing here anyway, when a more than comfortable bed beckoned back at Daniel's suite?

'What can I do to turn you on?' said Daniel quietly, as if reading my mind, knowing that the mood had got lost a little. 'What's your favourite fantasy?'

I squirmed a little, suddenly shy in spite of the things we'd been doing to each other's bodies over the past twenty-four hours or so. Sometimes it's harder to talk about sex than it is to just get on with it. And I was fearful of revealing too much of myself to Daniel emotionally when we had known each other for such a short space of time.

Sensing my reticence, he smiled encouragingly. 'How about this?' he said, and reaching over he placed one hand on either side of my thigh and drew one of my stockings down over my leg and foot. Holding one end in each hand, he pulled the nylon taut in front of him, looking at me questioningly but, I thought, with tenderness. I knew he didn't want to hurt me. All he wanted was for me to experience new ways of being happy.

I lay back again, rolled over onto my belly and crossed my wrists behind me, looking over my shoulder as he bound me with the wispy stocking – tightly, but not worryingly so. I trusted him implicitly. If, at that moment, he'd have told me he was going to throw me overboard but insisted that I shouldn't worry because he would rescue me, I'd have gone along with him. Focused though I was on what was about to happen to me now, on what and how I was going to feel, his own pleasure was very much in my mind too. Whatever it took to turn this man on, I would do.

My hands were bound now, and I lay there, naked save for the stocking on my leg and at my wrists, tingling with anticipation. It was exquisite torture for me not to be able to bring my hands to my cunt or my tits, to attend to the itch in my groin or the fizz of my nipples. I imagined him leaving me there all night, burning to be touched, with no hope of satisfaction. Would I be mad by morning? Could a person lose their mind this way?

Happily, Dan was still there, and after a few minutes of letting me stew in my own juices, he prised the cheeks of my backside apart and brought his face to me. Licking my sphincter like a dog, he made sure I was amply lubed. Two fingers were pushed into my arse in an exploratory mission, then three. Over my shoulder I watched him wank himself to maximum stiffness, then, at a point where he deemed both of us ready, he brought the bulb of his cock to my entrance. He let it rest there for a few minutes, and I felt the silky polished skin of his head as it snuffled against my hole like some small burrowing creature. Impatient, I had the overwhelming urge to stretch my arms back behind me so I could hold his hips in place with my hands and force myself back onto him, impale myself. Only I couldn't because of the damned stocking.

'Oh God, *please* – just fuck me,' I heard myself moan, and I was shocked by the ferocity of my desire. 'Please Dan, I can't take this.'

Acquiescing at last, he drove into me, slowly but powerfully, one hand clamped on my breast beneath me. My pussy ground against the wood of the boat as we moved back and forth, but not uncomfortably – in fact, the way my clit rubbed against its damp surface, the friction that was generated, soon had me on the verge of climax. I managed to stave it off until I felt Dan was nearing his, and then I closed my eyes and gave myself over to a darkness deeper than night.

We'd fucked ourselves raw, and back at the hotel we wanted nothing more than to share a bath, a plate of pasta and a bed. The doors to the dome room opened invitingly onto the circular table where we had had such an extraordinary encounter the previous night, but even that wasn't enough to lure us in. Propped up against a mountain of squidgy pillows, we lay together, me between Daniel's legs with my back against his chest. He was in his bathrobe, though it wasn't fastened; I was naked, and could feel his balls nestled against the crack of my bum, the soft hairs of his chest against my back. I felt safe, protected. We found a double bill of old Hitchcock movies on some cable channel and watched them before ordering up more hot chocolate. As I abandoned myself to asleep, I imagined I could still feel the rocking motions of the boat as we laying holding each other, our orgasms subsiding, lulling me.

4

The following night I stayed at home, recuperating from my two days of excess with Daniel over an Indian takeaway, a bottle of Kingfisher beer and a rental DVD of *Alfie* – the original with Michael Caine, not the inferior remake with Jude Law. Daniel had been in meetings all morning but I was scheduled to show him some of the key locations of the film the next day, including 22 St Stephen's Gardens near Notting Hill, site of Alfie's grimy bedsit. Needless to say, I was really looking forward to seeing him again.

It wasn't to be. The morning after, while I was still in bed, my phone rang.

'Ally, I'm sorry about this,' Daniel began, and as I heard him exhale a mouthful of cigarette smoke I imagined his soft, hot breath against my neck as our naked bodies slid against one another. The thought made me swoon back against my pillow. I sat bolt upright again when I heard what he had to say next.

'I've been called back to LA at short notice,' he explained. 'There are some major post-production problems on a movie I'm involved with. But keep all your notes, yes? We'll do the tours some other time, when I next come to town. Your research wasn't in vain. And I'll still pay for the time I booked, obviously.'

I opened my mouth but the words didn't come, and I was suddenly made brutally aware of how exposed my emotions had left me. I wasn't at all sure, from the way Daniel was speaking, that our affair, or whatever you wanted to call it, had touched him on the same level. I determined to hide my disappointment.

'No problem,' I said coolly. 'These things happen. It's no big deal.'

There was a pause on the other end of the line, then Daniel said quietly, 'Well thanks for everything, Ally. I have to dash for the airport now, but I'll be in touch.'

'Bon voyage.'

It was hard, when he'd gone, getting back into the swing of things. After the fascinating tours and conversations we'd had about them, and Daniel's charisma and the amazing nights we'd spent together, my normal guide work and everyday routines seemed impossibly humdrum. Normally so perky and full of interest in life and the latest happenings in London, I found it difficult even to get out of bed in the morning, never mind leave the flat. For a while I just wasn't myself; it was as if I'd found a reason for living and then lost it rightaway. That might sound overdramatic, but my feeling of 'coming home', of having found the missing piece in my life, was so strong, it was truly gutting to have had it snatched away from me.

After an initial few weeks of waiting for a phone call or an email, of trying to persuade myself that he wasn't a bastard or a user, that he'd felt the same way as me, I began to face reality – that I would never see him again, despite what he'd said. He was a busy man with a jetset existence and by the following week had probably forgotten our little encounter, was probably humping some Hollywood bimbo. So I gritted my teeth and resolved to just get on with my life and ride out the sense of deflation; I'd wear a false smile in public and then come home and wallow over the gin bottle. I'd get over it eventually. I had to. I also told myself to forget about any kind of emotional involvement with my clients in the future: from now on, things were to be kept on a purely professional level.

I kept my promise to myself, mostly. A lot of my customers were older American couples – all pink rinses and silly camera lenses – so temptation didn't even arise. Or I was quite often hired by American parents to take their wayward teenagers off their hands for a couple of days. I saw a lot of the Natural History Museum and the Science Museum then, but also a lot of the Trocadero games arcade and Hamley's toy shop, and I ate a lot of burgers in the Hard Rock Café. But the money was good, and I was kept so busy I gradually found myself spending less time thinking about Daniel. Or was it the exhaustion that made me numb?

There were times, I won't deny it, when I thought, *To hell with it all*, and sat down and composed a cheery email asking him how his film was going and when he thought he might be in London next. Or when I brought up his number on the screen of my phone and let my thumb linger over the green 'Call' button. Mostly I'd been drinking when I did this. But I was never drunk enough to go through with it, to send the message or dial his number. My dreaded pride wouldn't let me chase after him.

A couple of months after meeting him, I took a booking from an Australian pilot called Kip Marsh, who wanted, he said, a straightforward day's tour of the main sights – St Paul's Cathedral, the Tower of London, the Houses of Parliament. We met, and though my stomach didn't flip over the way it did when I thought about Daniel, I found myself attracted by his brawny physique and his pleasant, regular features arranged above an impressively square jaw. He didn't have the conversational sparkle of Dan, but he was pleasant enough. We spent an enjoyable day seeing many of the historical sights, and then I went home, settled down in front of a classic movie – *What Ever Happened to Baby Jane?* with Bette Davis and Joan Crawford – and didn't think much about him again.

Not long before midnight, when I was already in bed with a herbal tea and a gossip mag – my weapons against the insomnia that had beset me since Daniel went away – my mobile rang and I was surprised to hear Kip's voice on the other end of the line.

'Sorry to disturb you so late,' he said, 'but I really wanted to find a way of thanking you for today. I was talking to the concierge at my hotel and he was telling me you can book a capsule on the London Eye to yourself, so I thought I'd treat you. Are you free for lunch tomorrow?'

As it happened, I was, and though I'd been on the Eye countless times with different clients, I'd never experienced the luxury of a private ride. The idea was seductive – normally twenty or more people occupied a pod, and at busy times you sometimes had to fight for a bit of the view.

We met at the giant wheel at noon the following day, and I was delighted to find that Kip had ordered us a bottle of champagne to take with us on our 'flight'. I was equally struck by the fact that he was already in his pilot's uniform: he explained that after our lunch he was catching a cab directly to the airport.

'I'm Kip, come fly with me,' he couldn't resist saying as we boarded, and for a change I was in good enough spirits to repay him with a bright smile.

We began to ascend, at a pace almost imperceptible, and watched as the vista grew gradually more spectacular as we gained height. When we were about quarter of the way up, Kip turned and cracked open the bottle of Laurent Perrier. I listened to the satisfying fizz of the golden liquid as he poured just one glass for me, reminding me that he was to fly later that day. I should have realised then that he had an ulterior motive.

'Cheers,' I said, and looked back out over London. We were almost at the top now, and could see, as well as Buckingham Palace and Tower Bridge in the foreground, the distant landmarks of Windsor Castle, Alexandra Palace and the new Wembley Stadium arch. I pointed them out to Kip as he passed me a chocolate and refilled my glass.

'Here's to awesome views,' he said, and his eyes held mine. It was then that I finally realised – naïve little me – that he wasn't just there for the sights. I smiled nervously.

'I like you a lot, Alicia,' he said, frowning a little as if he, too, had suddenly been beset by unexpected nerves. Placing my glass on the wooden seat in the centre of the pod, he put a hand on either side of my waist. I didn't pull away; I'd been lonely since Daniel, and I longed for the feel of a warm, pliant body against mine, for the adrenalin rush of desire. I didn't want just anybody's body, mind; it helped that Kip was such a fine physical specimen.

By now his hand had slipped inside my flimsy blouse, inside my balcony-cup bra, and I felt the tips of his fingers, sure but gentle on my puckering nipples. I glanced around, concerned that we could be seen by people in other pods, but because we were about two-thirds of the way round, we couldn't be seen by anyone from above or below, while people in the capsules opposite were too far away, with their view obscured in any case by what I took to be the support struts or mechanism by which the wheel rotated. Our invisibility couldn't last long though.

'*Quick*,' I urged, but Kip appeared not to hear me as he fell to his knees before me and slipped my skirt up and my knickers down. Keeping one hand on my hip to steady both him and me, he began to explore my pussy with two fingers of the other, running his fingers all over my lips before encircling my hole.

'We don't have much time,' I panted, shooting anxious glances toward the neighbouring pods to see if we were overlooked. Kip turned his head from side to side, but I guessed from the expression on his face – utterly lascivious – that he might actually be hoping that someone could see us. The thought gave me an odd little thrill. Unfortunately for Kip, though, those people who were now coming within our orbit of vision were directing their attention firmly at the views of London unfolding beneath them.

Inflamed, desperate now for a man inside me again, I pulled down his boxer shorts and lapped at his cock, giving it little nips with my teeth that, to judge by his groans, seemed to drive him crazy.

We were almost right around now, and time was of the essence. From our position I calculated that we had roughly seven minutes. I wasn't sure what the staff would do if we were caught *in flagrante delicto*, but I wasn't keen to find out, especially given that I was bound to be coming back here with future clients. Stepping back, I lowered myself to the central bench of the pod and presented myself to Kip, splaying myself for him with my fingers. He smiled, sank once more to his knees and plunged himself into me with a yell of pleasure. Bringing my knees up almost to my chest, affording him even greater depth within me, I reached around myself with one hand and kneaded his silken balls in my palms. With the other I wiggled my clit convulsively. An irresistible tempo built up between us, inside us, and I lay off my clit in my struggle to stave off an orgasm that I knew would bring his on, all the while conscious that if we didn't finish soon we would be providing a hell of a floor show for everyone stationed at the landing stage.

On the point of saying words to that effect, I noticed that Kip's eyes were raised to the right. Excitement flickered in them like fire. We were very near to the ground by now. I followed his gaze and saw a man standing above us in the pod that followed ours, palms pressed against the glass carapace as he stared down at us. I repressed a cry, but it was too late: the stranger's presence and the look on Kip's face had unleashed my climax.

Fuck you, Daniel, I remember thinking as I gave myself over to its ravaging might. It reminded me of being caught in a rip tide on a beach in south India a few years before: there was the same sense of losing control, of struggling against a greater force than me as wave after wave sucked me under.

I was so preoccupied with my own orgasm that I felt strangely detached from Kip's rapture as he pulled out of me, stood above me, and, prick in fist, let a froth of sperm rain down on me. We were just in time: the pod was about to land, and we had scant moments in which to pull together our clothes and neaten our ruffled hair.

As we walked away from the Eye and the river, a rather uncomfortable silence insinuated itself between us. There certainly wasn't that cosy sense of companionship that I had felt with Daniel in the hotel, after our passionate fuck on the old boardroom table, or the morning after our second night together, when he had rolled over and just slipped inside me as if he belonged there. And as I saw Kip into a black cab and wished him a safe flight, I found myself suddenly missing the American with renewed force, just when I had started to think I was getting over him.

5

Three dry martinis and a couple of hours' maudlin reminiscing at Claridge's Bar and the alcohol has started to dilute the pain again and I'm ready to brave my dinner with Paco Manchega. He wanted to go somewhere discreet, unsurprisingly given the pararazzi's interest in him, so Fenella and I discussed the various options and finally agreed on the Krug Room, a private dining space at the Dorchester Hotel. It's obviously not the kind of place a lowly tour guide gets to experience more than once in a blue moon, and I'm almost as excited about seeing it as I am about meeting Paco.

It's a short walk from Claridge's to Park Lane, through the sedate streets of Mayfair and across Grosvenor Square in front of the imposing bulk of the American Embassy. I live not so far north of here, in a snug top-floor flat near Marylebone Station, with a view over surrounding rooftops from its wide balcony. It's a good area, too, but somewhat scruffier than Mayfair. I'm constantly thinking about moving, developing crushes on places I've gone to check out for my work – from Little Venice to Docklands. But property inertia always gets to me in the end. It's easier just to stay put.

I'm outside the Dorchester now, looking up at its glittering facade. The trees in front are covered in fairylights year round, as if it's Christmas all the time. I guess it is, in a way, for the people rich enough to stay here. I remember coming down to London with my family when I was a child, or rather passing through

London on the way to the airport, before the M25 was built. We'd drive down Park Lane, and I'd press my nose up against the window, positively tingling with the longing to be grown up and able to participate in all this glamour. The Dorchester, I already knew, was where Taylor and Burton had lived together and subsequently spent their honeymoon – or one of them. Vivien Leigh had come here with Laurence Olivier, and everyone from Marlene Dietrich to Brigitte Bardot, from Duke Ellington to The Beatles, had made it their London base at some point.

And here I am now, partaking of some of that glitz, and still I feel like an awestruck kid looking in on life from the outside. I swallow back my stagefright and walk towards it. A uniformed doorman welcomes me and directs me to the subterreanean Krug Room, which – as I am shortly to discover – is actually located within the master kitchens, though sealed off from all the steam and fumes and bustle by a glass wall. There, an immaculate receptionist takes my jacket and leads me through to the private room, explaining that Signor and Signora Manchega are already waiting for me.

I look at her askance, then decide she must be mistaken. Paco Manchega is, I know from the gossip mags I've become addicted to, a resolute bachelor – in fact, something of a playboy. In the last year alone, I recall him being linked with two supermodels and a Brazilian diva. Just two months or so ago, I saw a picture of him on the arm of Lauren Slater, star of the latest Tarantino offering. No, he's certainly not married: the receptionist has got it wrong somehow.

She opens the door of the room and my breath catches in my throat as I look over at Paco Manchega, sitting smoking a cigar at a glass oval table in the centre of the room. He's as relaxed as you could be without being flat-out unconscious, one arm draped over the back of his red leather chair. A slim-fit green shirt unbuttoned at the neck – to my untrained eye it looks like a Thomas Pink – reveals a chunky silver necklace. His hair is shoulder-length – he's had it cut, I think, since the last photo I saw of him.

'Alicia,' he says with a genuine-looking smile, gesturing me into the room without getting to his feet. He draws out the 'i': *Aleeeecia*. 'How nice to meet you. Do come in. And please –' he waves his free hand across the table '– meet my wife, Carlotta.'

I step forwards, and in the part of the room hitherto obscured by the open door, I see a girl who can't be long out of her teens looking at me from the chair opposite Paco's. Her complexion, like his, is a rich Mediterranean olive-brown, but her mid-length hair is bottle-blonde and she has startling blue eyes. She looks more like a Russian mafia chick than a Spaniard.

'Delighted to meet you,' I say, composing myself, stepping forward to shake first Carlotta's hand, then Paco's. When the formalities are done, Paco wags his hand at the chair next to Carlotta's and invites me to take a seat.

'What would you like to drink?' he says, and it is all I can do to look him in the face now those smouldering brown eyes are trained on me. I remember, at the same moment, that I'm half-cut from the cocktails I knocked back at Claridge's, and remind myself that I'm working and need to be on the ball.

'I'll just have a mineral water to start with,' I say to the waiter who has appeared, soundlessly, at my side. He nods, hands me a menu and explains that the chef is personally on hand for us should we wish to discuss the philosophy and preparation of the food. I suppress a chuckle as he disappears, closing the door behind him.

I imagine Jean-Paul Sartre here with Albert Camus, discussing the existential implications of omelettes as they lay into the red wine.

'So,' I say, turning to Paco, knowing that I ought to leave him to get the conversational ball rolling but suddenly feeling nervousness bubble up in me like fizzy wine, exacerbating the tongue-loosening effects of the martinis. 'Welcome to London. Is this your first trip?'

I immediately want to take back my words, rewind time like Superman does to save Lois Lane, come in again and say something sensible. *Of course* this is not his first visit to London: he's an international dance superstar, for God's sake. I know for a fact he did a season at Sadler's Wells just a couple of years back.

But Paco is all smiles and good cheer. 'Oh no,' he says. 'I have been here many, many times. I just *love* this city. But I've never really had time to see much of it, I've always been so busy. And Carlotta –' he smiles over at his wife '– this is Carlotta's first time here. So when an acquaintance mentioned your tours, I thought I would treat her.'

I'm mentally riffling through my client list, avid to know who recommended me, but I can't bring myself to ask. I wouldn't hesitate with asking a regular customer, but with a celebrity it seems like an intrusion. I resolve to pluck up the courage when I've spent a little more time with Paco, or try to worm it out of Carlotta sometime. It would be interesting to know who rates me highly enough to recommend me to a superstar.

The waiter returns to convey the chef's recommendations and before long we're enjoying a starter of lobster, langoustines and scallops in an anis-infused saffron nage. Carlotta, I notice, eats hers almost wolfishly, and I'm relieved. If she was one of those faddy picky women who shuffle their food around the plate in the hope that no one notices they're not eating any of it, I'd be worried about looking like a glutton next to her. But no, she tucks in heartily, and I am pleased to have met another woman of appetite. She's slim, mind, as her clingy strapless red dress testifies.

It's Paco, surprisingly, who really only toys with his meal. It rapidly becomes clear, as the starter is cleared away and a main course of veal fillet with foie gras ravioli is set down before us, that he loves the sound of his own voice, regaling us with tales of his globetrotting and the big names he regularly rubs shoulders with – Baryshnikov, Bono, Damien Hirst. Carlotta pays me virtually no heed during all of this: her eyes are riveted to her husband, though she must have heard all these stories countless times. Or maybe not, if they had such a whirlwind romance.

As our desserts arrive, I finally get a space in which to broach the subject that has been bugging me all night. Turning towards Carlotta, keen to hear the facts from her rather than Paco, I say:

'So Carlotta, how long have you and Paco been married?'

Carlotta turns her electrifying gaze on me, pausing for a minute as if weighing me up. 'A month,' she says then, and smiles a little coyly. 'Just one month.' She looks back at Paco, adulation in her eyes. Without moving them from his, she spoons some of the unctuous chocolate soufflé with black pepper sauce into her mouth.

'Well, congratulations,' I say. She hasn't looked back at me. 'Where did you meet?'

Paco wades back in before his new bride can continue. 'Carlotta's an actress,' he says. 'We met at a party thrown by my agent. We kept the wedding very hush hush. We want to be left alone.'

'Have I seen any of your films?' I ask Carlotta.

'She's not been in any yet,' says Paco, smiling encouragingly over at her, as one would, it strikes me, a child. 'She's only just really started out. But it's only a matter of time. She's incredibly talented.' He winks at her. 'As well as beautiful.'

I'm starting to feel a bit queasy now, in the presence of all this mutual adoration, and as our coffees arrive I finally turn talk to business, which is after all what we're here for – to formulate a sightseeing itinerary. I open my virgin Smythson notebook, which I picked up on Sloane Street just before my beauty treatments at Harvey Nichols. Specially chosen to impress a client of Paco's calibre, its thick, luscious, creamy pages are bound by a cover of the best black leather. It shrieks professionalism and good taste.

'So,' I say, pen poised. 'What would you like to see while you're in town?'

Paco leans back, resuming his relaxed pose of earlier, and runs his fingers through his luxuriant locks before lighting another slender cigar.

'Well,' he says thoughtfully. 'There are lots of places I should have visited by now, and which I'd like to. But realistically speaking, I am not going to have a great deal of time. It's really Carlotta I'm concerned about. I want her to have a good time while I'm stuck in all my boring meetings and rehearsals and shows.'

I hope my face doesn't show my feelings as I hear these words. I was all fired up for my celebrity client, envisaging incognito trips to Somerset House and the British Museum with Paco disguised behind Gucci shades, diving in and out of taxis in a bid to shake off the press. Instead I find I'm little more than a glorified babysitter to his *ingénue* wife. To a nobody.

I turn to her a little tetchily. 'And what would *you* like to see, Carlotta?'

She's about to open her mouth when Paco, surprise surprise, answers for her.

'Carlotta likes shopping,' he says, smiling at her indulgently, as you would a spoilt child. 'And she likes art, modern art especially.' His eyes flit to me. 'She used to be an artists' model in Madrid,' he says proudly, raising his chin a little, then looking back at his wife. 'My little nymph has posed for some of the most talented Spanish artists of our generation, haven't you, angel?'

Carlotta nods, tracing her finger around the rim of her wine glass. She's looking at neither of us now, and I sense a little tension in the air that wasn't there before. I jot down a few words in my notebook, more for show than for anything else, then slap it closed and slip it into my bag.

'Well, it's getting late,' I say, 'and I suppose that Carlotta and I can discuss itineraries between ourselves, since you are not going to be involved.'

'Sure,' Paco nods. 'I have a lunch appointment tomorrow followed by a meeting at one of the venues, so perhaps you could go out for lunch together and take it from there. Is that OK, darling?' he says to Carlotta, almost as an afterthought.

'Of course.' She smiles up at him, her dark mood dissipated.

'Great,' I say, and after making arrangements to meet in the lobby of her hotel the next day, I leave for home.

6

The next morning my mobile rings as I am getting out of the bath after a lie-in and a long, leisurely breakfast. I've reconciled myself to two weeks of trawling designer clothes shops and making vapid art gallery chat with Paco's petulant bride, and I am in fact congratulating myself on the money and wondering about booking myself a holiday when the job is over. The past few months have really knocked the wind out of my sails.

It's Paco on the line, relaying the news that Carlotta has been called to an audition in Madrid at very short notice. I feign disappointment but I am secretly pleased; they have booked up my time, and now I can extend my slobbish morning and not feel guilty about it.

Just as I am about to hang up and research the best airfares to the Caribbean, Paco speaks up again.

'Listen,' he says. 'I don't have plans for this evening, as Carlotta and I were just going to chill out in our suite. How about if you show me some of London, after all, while I'm at a loose end?'

'Sure,' I say. 'Do you have any preferences?'

'I'm easy,' he says. 'I put myself in your capable hands.'

'Great,' I say, starting to flick through the copy of *Time Out* in front of me for inspiration. 'I'll pick you up from your hotel at – say, seven?'

'Fabulous. *Que le vaya bien.*'

* * *

I'm not at all sure that Paco will enjoy *Stomp*, a West End musical inspired by street theatre. I'm worried that it will be a bit downmarket for him. But I chance it, and afterwards I'm glad that I did because he proclaims himself an enthusiast of the wordless show in which dancers move to rhythms generated by oil drums, rubbish bins and brooms. Indeed, he confesses that he may go and see it again if he has time, as some of the moves have given him inspiration for his own performances.

Although I know very little about the dance world, I manage to bluff it as we stroll from the Vaudeville Theatre on the Strand up through Covent Garden to Hakkasan, a stylish contemporary Cantonese and dim sum restaurant where I have booked us a corner table. This is the only time, it seems, I am likely to have Paco to myself, so I'm hoping he won't be recognised. The low lighting should help.

Not that he has particularly endeared himself to me so far – I found his attitude towards Carlotta at dinner last night, and his general monopolisation of the conversation, more than a little macho. But then I suppose most celebrities must be this way – self-centred, dominating, insensitive to others' feelings – from being indulged and kowtowed to the whole time. For all that, I am more impressed than I would openly admit by being in the presence of someone who's in the papers just about every day. And I'm curious to find out more about him.

I watch him as he browses the menu. He's *divine*, even more so in the flesh than in the magazines, and suddenly, from out the blue, I have a vision of him lying naked on a big hotel bed being straddled by Carlotta, her tight little pussy slotting down over his straining cock. It is all I can do not to splutter my wine all over Paco, so stunned am I by the lewd workings of my own imagination.

Paco is looking at me a bit funny now. 'Are you OK, Alicia?' he says, and I am heartened to detect what seems like real concern in his eyes. Maybe he's not such a big phoney after all.

'I'm fine,' I said, and I cringe at what his reaction would be if he'd been able to read my mind, to discover the dirty thoughts that are germinating there.

'Good.' He smiles, and looks back at the menu. 'What about if we shared a few dishes?' he proposes. 'Carlotta and I often do that, especially in this kind of restaurant.'

My reservations about his machismo notwithstanding, I'm secretly flattered by the offer, by being placed in the same situation as his wife, and readily agree to the proposal. In fact, I even go so far as to give him total responsibility for choosing what to have. Still, I don't regret it as I listen to him ordering – most of the dishes are the very ones I would have picked myself, including mango spring rolls filled with scallops and prawns. He also orders one of the best bottles on the wine list, a Sancerre. I grin, sit back and prepare to let myself be seriously pampered.

We end up drinking several bottles of the wine, and the evening turns into a long one. I am pleased to have the distraction, and also touched to sense that Paco is slightly lost without little Carlotta at his side: gone is his braggart talk of yesterday evening, and in fact most topics of conversation turn inevitably back to her, to the point where it doesn't feel cheeky of me to probe a little more.

'So you say you met her at your agent's house,' I prompt.

He nods, his eyes already far away as if he is reliving the scene in his head. 'She was talking to my best friend,' he says, his voice small now, constricted in his throat as he re-experiences that flowering of desire. 'At first I saw virtually nothing of her – she was wearing a scooped-back dress, and her hair swung short of the small of her back. But already I wanted her. I had to stop myself from going over and placing the palm of my hand on her naked brown flesh, from licking it.'

I observe him intently as he speaks, watching tiny beads of perspiration erupt on his brow while he bears witness to his lust, with no trace of self-consciousness.

'What did you do?' I almost whisper, awed to be privy to a moment of abandonment as strong as I felt with Daniel.

He looks at me, his eyes lost to the memory. 'I put the woman I was with in a taxi,' he says. 'I was a complete bastard – I told her I had a headache and was going to call my chauffeur to fetch me.' He sighs. 'Then I went back in and I got her.'

'How?'

'I told my best friend someone was looking for him in the next room.' He snorts, shakes his head. 'I lied to my best friend. Can you believe it?'

I nod. 'You really wanted her,' I say.

'My God, yes. Alicia, I think I might just have died right there and then if I couldn't have her. And I hadn't even seen her face by then.'

'But you did now.'

'Yes, my friend left – looking a bit pissed-off, I must say. But Carlotta told me later he stood no chance with her, so I didn't feel too guilty. And he forgave me in the end, when he saw how we are together.'

'What did you say to her?'

'Do you know what? I don't remember. I've thought about it so many times since, and I have absolutely no idea what our first words to each other were. Isn't it

43

ridiculous? – something so important. All I know is, within twenty minutes we were fucking each others' brains out on the clifftop beyond my agent's villa. Screaming the night down.'

I look away over Paco's shoulder, at the other people sitting chatting at their tables, none of them in the slightest degree aware of how my cunt has gone up in flames at his words. Part of me can't believe he is telling me all this, although I know I have goaded him on. I want more, and yet I don't know if I can handle it. The only thing I'm at all sure of is that I am going to have the mother of all wanks when I get home tonight.

Prolonging the agony, Paco orders us a couple of Chinese plum brandies while he waits for our bill to be brought over. I'm half-considering sneaking off to the loo to pleasure myself while he settles up, when he leans in towards me and says:

'Since Carlotta's not back until tomorrow evening and you don't need to get up for work, why don't you come back to my hotel? I'll order up a nightcap and you can bounce some ideas off me about things to do with Carlotta. She gets easily bored, poor thing. What she really needs is a good friend in life. Other than me, of course.'

I look at him. I'm a bit pissed, he's a bit pissed. More than a bit, in fact. In the light of his last statement and what he's just told me about his first time with Carlotta, I don't think he's going to make a move on me. But do I trust myself? Horny as I am right now, how am I going to stop myself jumping on him and making a complete fool of myself? No, far better to just hop in a cab and get the hell out of here, to my own bed and the friction of my own fingers on my yearning clit, or better still the pulsing of the big pink vibrator that's currently nestling in my bedside drawer, ready for moments like this.

But as these thoughts spin through my brain, already we're outside on the pavement and Paco is flagging down a cab. We're inside before I can say another word, and within minutes we're racing along Goodge Street and then Mortimer Street, just off which the driver swings us into the forecourt of Paco's hotel and a waiting doorman helps us out.

Once up the front steps and inside the hotel, Paco ushers me into a lift and we ascend to the Infinity Suite, which I happen to know is just about the most expensive in London. I've been itching to know what it is like since Fenella mentioned that he was booked in here.

He passes his card through the swipe and pushes the door open for me, revealing a dramatic vestibule with walls sheathed in sumptuous aubergine silk. At the end of it, an abstract sculpture made from optical glass seems both to reflect the light and capture it within itself. I'd thought I'd seen some swank in London, but this place is in its own league.

We walk down the hallway towards the drawing room, where a strange fluffy modern chandlier twinkles above a dining table, beside two huge armchairs swathed in purplish velvet and a gently curving cream sofa. I plump myself down in one of the former, marvelling at its softness, and gaze around me.

'Some suite,' I say.

'Isn't it just?' smiles Paco. 'I'll get us those drinks.' He presses a button on the phone and within minutes a butler appears to take care of our needs.

'I used to stay in the Hempel in Bayswater,' he says, 'but last time I decided that whole Eastern minimalist vibe is getting rather tired. And the area is a bit of a

45

dump. This suits my mood perfectly – a grand old hotel but contemporary decor, and about as central as you can get. Shall I show you around?'

I nod, unceasingly curious about London's most exclusive nooks and crannies, and keen not to waste any opportunity my job grants me to have a peek at them.

As we are about to set forth, the butler reappears with a tray bearing two brandy glasses and a whole decanter full of the rich amber liquid. Setting it down on the enormous square coffee table, beside a ceramic bowl filled – rather pointlessly, I think to myself – with outsized ceramic eggs, he pours us two generous measures and, bowing slightly, slips away, leaving us alone again.

Paco hands me a glass then gestures towards a door. 'The master bedroom,' he declares. I walk in ahead of him and am confronted by a massive mahoghany four-poster bed dressed in velvet of the deepest burgundy and black and white toile de Jouy. Paco points out to me the separate dressing rooms, then we go back through the entrance hall and he shows me the 'guest bedroom' with its two queen-size beds clad in eau-de-Nil fabrics, followed by the small pantry kitchen from which the butler operates. All in all, I'm pretty impressed, and I say so.

'Well, that's not all,' says Paco with a smile. 'I've saved the best until last. Come this way.'

I follow him, and he leads the way back through the master bedroom and into its ensuite bathroom, in the middle of which stands a huge, deep bath. Paco steps forward and presses a button, and the bath begins to project colours, running through a spectrum from red to white.

'Chromatherapy,' explains Paco. 'You hit the button

to stop it on the colour that best suits your mood, or the mood that you would like to be in – red is stimulating, indigo is sedating, green is harmonising and so on. Your eyes and your skin absorb the colour, apparently, and you get happy, or sleepy, or whatever you want to be.'

'Why don't you try it?' he says, leaning forwards to start the bath filling. 'It also has a hydrotherapy option, basically lots of fizzy bubbles. Please, be my guest. I'll get my man to bring up an extra bathrobe.'

I umm and err, sipping at my cognac. I'd be an absolute fool to pass up on an opportunity like this, but I feel so cheeky taking him up on the offer. My mind turns to young Carlotta: Paco may be offering his bath in all innocence, but how would it look if she were to walk in on the scene? Wouldn't she freak out?

'*Go on,*' urges Paco. 'You only live once. Look, I know it's late and you're thinking about all the hassle of drying your hair, getting dressed, going back out into the cold. But I'll give you some money for a taxi door to door, or better still, why don't you stay in the spare room?'

That decides it for me. Carlotta's not here and isn't coming back tonight, and I'm not one to turn my nose up at a bit of unadulterated luxury without a damn good reason.

'Thanks, Paco,' I say, and he smiles.

'Just shout if you need something,' he says. 'I'm going to make a few calls. I'll have the butler leave the robe on the bed.'

He takes my empty glass and exits the room, leaving me standing there looking around in wonder at the walls covered in indigo, purple and brown gilt and glass tiles, at the flatscreen TV set into the mirror above the two vanity units, and lastly back at the bath. I shrug off my blouse, unzip my skirt and step out of it, then peel off my underwear. I step up to one of the mirrors. They're the expensive distressed silver-leaf glass-panelled kind that, combined with sensitive lighting, make your skin look young and soft and peachy. I touch my breasts with both hands, look down at my flat stomach and freshly waxed bush. I know I look great. I like to take care of myself. Not for anybody else, but for the pleasure of feeling toned and clean and smooth. Even, or especially, when I'm feeling a little low. I masturbate a lot, probably more than the average girl, but my body is a source of great pleasure to me, and nobody knows what I like better than I do, though Daniel seemed to be getting the hang of things pretty quickly.

Daniel's face in my mind, I slide one finger between my fanny lips, rub my clitoris a little; I'm wet and need no further lubrication. I look back at the bath, just in time to see it begin to overflow. I sprint over to turn it off, but water continues to slide over the edge.

I panic, sling a towel around me and run out of the bathroom in search of Paco. I find him lying on the sofa watching a flatscreen TV that has materialised from behind a screen in the drawing room, talking into a cordless phone. Worried that he's speaking to Carlotta and not wanting her to hear my voice, I gesture wildly at him.

'I'll call you back in a minute,' he says and kills the line.

'What's wrong?' he says. 'There a giant spider in there or something? The butler creep in on you? You women...'

'It's not that,' I squeal. 'Paco, the bloody bath's overflowing. I don't know how to switch it off. The whole place is going to be flooded and you'll be...'

I stop. Paco is laughing hard, his hand on my forearm.

'What is it?' I say testily.

'Alicia, it's *supposed* to do that,' he says. 'Sorry, I should have said – it's also an infinity-edge pool, which means that it's set to overflow the whole time.'

I stare at him. 'Right,' I say at last. 'Silly of me not to realise.'

He rubs my arm where he still holds it. 'Go back and have a proper look,' he says. 'You'll see that the water is actually going into a recirculating channel. Now just get back in there and enjoy it while it's still hot.'

I trot off, wondering why I'm feeling so stupid. How could I have guessed? I didn't know such a thing exists, although if I hadn't lost my head I would have noticed that the overflow wasn't going onto the floor. I tut under my breath, shake my head. Boys and their toys, I think. Gadgets and gizmos. Whatever's wrong with a good old soak in a normal bath?

Still, I slide in, allowing the bubbles to caress my skin, trying to decide on the right colour for me. I finally opt for white; I don't know what it means, but I guess it has something to do with purity, and pure thoughts are what I most need if I'm going to spend a night in this seductive suite within a few steps of one of the world's sexiest men.

Immediately I'm in, the air jets beneath the surface of the water begin to work their magic, loosening my muscles, and the sound of the water cascading from the rim of the bath is strangely soothing. I lean my head back and start to drift away, a little sleepy now from the cognac. Then Carlotta pops into my mind again: I imagine her face if she walked in here and saw me languishing naked in their extraordinary bath. From there it's only a small step to me imagining her in here herself, as she undoubtedly has been, all fleshy and pink from the force of the jets, scrubbing up after a

49

wild session with Paco on that huge bed in there. She's got the colour set to red: relaxation is not on her mind. The minute she's out of the bath she'll be back in the bedroom, rousing him from a post-coital doze, clambering onto him like a pantheress, insatiable.

So much for being purified. I twist my hips a little, so that my pussy is in front of one of the air jets, and feel the tiny champagne-like bubbles whirling around my lips, the pressure prising them open slightly. With my fingers I rub at the bead of my clitoris, excitement mounting to the point where I *have* to satisfy myself now. I don't care where I am: it's an imperative. I roll back but find that this bath's too deep and its edges are too wide to assume my normal position for bathtime wanks: legs looped over the edges. Nor can I turn over and do it on my knees: it's too slippery. After trying out a few angles, I give up and climb out.

I lie down on the bath mat and assume the missionary position. It may sound staid, but it's my favourite both for fucking and for masturbating. I'm willing to try anything, and generally have, but I've never found anything that affords me as much pleasure. I think it's partly to do with how wide I can open my legs: my cunt positively gapes, and that arouses me no end. There must be something of the exhibitionist in me. And then, when I'm with a man, it allows the most powerful combination of vaginal and clitoral stimulation, virtually guaranteeing an orgasm – in me, at least.

I'm going at it hell for leather now, finger-fucking myself with four digits of one hand, while the thumb of it works at my clit. With the other hand I'm palpating my breasts. Then a little extra something is required down below, and I bring my second hand to my pussy and vibrate my clitoris wildly with the heel of my hand. I'm exploding now, rocking and bucking on the bathmat, trying hard not to cry out as stars dance behind my closed eyes.

The climax is still ripping through me when I hear a voice and open my eyes just in time to see Paco's head appear in the doorway. In his hand he's holding up my cognac glass: I guess he's come to offer me a refill and I didn't hear him tap at the door.

We're looking into each other's eyes, unembarrassed. I'm surprised I'm not mortified, but Paco's gaze is so frank, so curious, that I don't feel at all ashamed of myself. It's natural, after all; everybody does it, even – or perhaps especially – in the four-thousand-pound-a-night suites of international superstars. Who can blame me?

Paco clearly doesn't. Nor does he do what I expect him to do and back slowly out of the room and close the door behind him. No, he's still there, still looking at me – not at my sopping cunt, mind, or my breasts, but into my eyes as before. I sit up, smile at him.

'That was beautiful,' he says. 'Really fucking beautiful. I wish I'd come in a little earlier.'

I raise my eyebrows, emboldened. 'I could do it again,' I say. 'If you wanted.'

His face lights up. 'You bet,' he breathes, and he steps into the room and scoops me up in his arms, carries me through into his bedroom like a new bride. Through his trousers I can feel the head of his dick pressing into my hip, urgent for me.

'Do you need a rest?' he says. 'You were really going for it in there? I've never seen anything like it.'

'I'm fine,' I say. I don't tell him I can keep coming and coming like a train, with the right partner. Or by myself.

He sets me down and I look around, assessing the room. There are two richly upholstered sage-green and red chairs either side of an oval silver chest of drawers, and I pull one over to the bed, lower myself onto it. He sits down on the bed and I place one foot on either side of him, knees slightly bent. I'm on full display, giving this virtual stranger the most intimate of views, and I'm loving it. I'm loving the look on his face as he watches me bring my hand to myself and spark myself off again. The numbness succeeding my first orgasm has faded, and I'm electric again.

I start with my arsehole, licking my fingers and then running them around the tender rosebud of my rim. I often do this in front of the mirror at home: it gives me a big kick. Next I part my lips and hole with my hands, wide as they will go. I stay like that for a few moments, letting Paco enjoy the scene. I can tell by the play of his hands on the top of his thighs that he's fighting the urge to get his dick out and start going at himself. There's nothing, in many ways, that I'd like better than to see his undoubtedly beautiful member spring forth from his Calvin Kleins and come to life in his hands, especially for me. But I also want to prolong this: he'll come really quickly, I think, and then I will too and it will all be over. I'll retrieve my clothes from the bathroom, get dressed and take a taxi home. Carlotta will be back tomorrow, and I'll hardly see anything of Mr Bigshot Dancer. That's if he doesn't dispense with my touristic services after this little adventure. There's a boundary, and we've overstepped it.

I was right: his hand moves to his fly, and I have to reach out and stop him from releasing himself.

'Not yet,' I say. 'Wait.' I turn over on the chair, so that I'm kneeling now, and he gets a whole new angle on my arse and cunt. I can feel myself drizzling down my inner thighs as I push my fingers inside me and fish for my core. I don't know who's moaning more now, Paco or me. I put my head down, close my eyes. I imagine he's taking himself out now, but I'm too far gone to protest any more.

And then all of a sudden he's upon me, between my thighs, pulling my hands away and parting me with his cock, pushing into me. I haven't set eyes on his prick yet, but I can feel its superb girth as he arches in and out of me, punctuated by the bounce of his balls against my arse. Rightaway – with a little help from my own fingers on my clit – I'm soaring, gasping, carried away by an orgasm that seems to lift me up into the air.

Its contractions are still rippling deliciously through me when Paco pulls out with a yell and sprays my back with his come, then collapses onto me. We both slide from the chair and hold each other close on the floor.

I don't know how much time passes before Paco picks me up in his arms again and carries me through to the guestroom, where he pulls back the sheets on one of the beds and lays me down, wiping my back first with a tissue.

'Do you need anything?' he smiles down at me. Part of me wants to pull him back down to me, tell him to fuck me again, so hard that I'm begging for mercy. But I'm aware that the moment is gone, that something exploded between us that shouldn't have, and that we each need to be alone now, to think about the implications and where we go from here.

Do I tell him, for instance, that I am going to have to stop working for him and Carlotta? That I can't be her escort after what's happened tonight? Or can we salvage something out of the situation – act, in essence, as if it never happened? I'm not sure, for my part, that's possible. We may not have fallen in love, but something extraordinary has taken place. Everything has changed.

7

I wake up not knowing where I am, and then I look around me and remember, and an ache starts up in my pussy and I have to have a long lazy wank. I'm not thinking about Paco, specifically, as I do it. A whole host of people run through my mind, from Eric, to whom I lost my virginity during a stay with my French pen-friend, via Arvind, to whom I was briefly engaged at university, to Daniel – of course – and Paco himself. Life has not been uneventful for me, from an erotic point of view. I've never been one to deny my lusts, even when it's got me into trouble.

I'm still not sure who blabbed about me, but I can't imagine it was Daniel. God knows it hurts that he hasn't been in touch, but when we were together he was so gentlemanly towards me, so solicitous to my needs and desires, that I can't imagine he would gloat or gossip about what happened between us. Although I ought to face the fact that he may not be the man he seemed, or that I wanted him to be.

No, I'm more included to think it must have been Kip, boasting to mates back in Sydney about his little adventure on the London Eye. Somehow word got round, as it usually does, with the net result that I lost my Blue Badge.

Not that I'm too bothered: business is brisk, and I'm enjoying myself. Enjoying myself a little too much, some might say. Perhaps they're right: Daniel and Kip were all well and good – harmless flings, if only, in the case of the former, I'd had the good sense to just enjoy it for what it was. But Paco has an adoring new wife to contend with, a wife who I am tasked with taking care of for the next two weeks, after being taken doggy-style by her husband right there in their bedroom. It's a complication I didn't expect, and certainly didn't need.

I get up and wander through into the lovely drawing room. The curtains are open and there's a wonderful view right onto the church opposite, which I happen to know is John Nash's All Souls. From where I stand I see mainly its pale-faced clock, but when I step up to the window I can look up at its famously slender spire, on which the architect was depicted impaled in one 1820s press cartoon. As a phallic image, it's woefully inadequate to convey the majesty of the member I felt deep inside me last night yet never even clapped eyes on. Knowing that I'm unlikely to get the chance again, I creep into Paco's room – the door is slightly ajar – and tiptoe up to his bed. The curtains are drawn around it; I tweak one corner and peep inside.

He is sleeping, but the reading light inside remains on, and he is spotlit in all his glory. His cock, indeed, is a thing of beauty, a smooth olive-brown baton coiled in a nest of frothy black hair. My hand reaches involuntarily towards it, but Paco stirs and I retract it as if electrocuted. I head for the bathroom to get my clothes.

I am washed and dressed and ready to leave when Paco saunters out of the bedroom with a cheery 'Good morning!'

We smile at one another; one of those smiles behind which a thousand secrets lurk.

'Sleep well?' he asks.

'Very well,' I say. 'That bed is dreamy.'

'And there's nothing like a good fuck to send you off, is there?' he adds.

I look at him. I'm surprised he has brought the subject up, but then we are adults, and pretending that nothing happened would be a silly game. He is right to call a spade a spade, a fuck a fuck.

'I enjoyed myself,' I say, feeling brave. 'Though I must admit it did take me by surprise.'

'Me too,' he admits, looking away from me, out of the window. Some new emotion flits across his features; I wonder if he's having misgivings. But if he is, he manages to brush them aside pretty rapidly, for the next minute he's saying, 'How about I call down and order us a limo for the morning and you show me the sights in style?'

I agree without hesitation; this sounds like fun, and I haven't had much fun lately. And a few minutes later we're in the lift and on our way down to a waiting car.

We head down through Soho; I'm at a bit of a loss as to an itinerary, preoccupied by thoughts of what – if anything – is going to happen now. I was expecting to be headed home by this point, not in the back of a stretch limo with Paco and a mini-bar full of goodies.

Paco is looking out of the window, watching the procession of Soho streets.

'I've heard such a lot about this place,' he says, 'but never had chance to explore it.'

'It's lost its bohemian edge,' I say, 'now the media offices and designer hotels and expensive restaurants have moved in. There are still some classic haunts – like Ronnie Scott's jazz club – but they're gradually being ousted. Raymond's Revue Bar, for instance, which used to be the most famous strip club in London, has been replaced by a cult gay cabaret. It's great here if you're queer – you can come and cruise to your heart's content on Old Compton Street. But there are more interesting places to discover in London.'

'Like where?' We are spilling out of the southwestern edge of Soho now, into the bottom of Regent Street and the traffic hell of Piccadilly Circus. As we grind to a halt, I wave my hand up towards the statue to our right.

'Eros,' I say, launching into tour guide mode. 'One of London's most famous landmarks. Only the winged figure is not really the pagan god of love – it's an angel of Christian charity, built as a memorial to a philanthropist called Lord Shaftesbury in 1893.'

Paco nods politely, but I can tell he's not really up for the guidebook spiel.

'Look, is there something particular you want to look at?' I say, suddenly not at all sure what the point of this little jaunt was.

Paco doesn't answer at once, instead reaching into the mini-bar and pulling out a bottle of champagne and a couple of crystal flutes. It's a little early, I think, but I'm not the kind of girl who sneers at a glass of bubbly any time of the day or night.

'What you were just saying,' he replies at last. 'About more interesting areas. Take me there.'

I reflect for a minute, then lean forward and tap on the glass partition separating us from the uniformed chauffeur. 'The City, please,' I say when he draws it back. 'St Mary Axe.' The driver nods, closes it again, and I sit back and enjoy my champagne.

We're parked at the bottom of a circular, glass-clad tower rising up through forty storeys to a gently pointed tip.

'That is the biggest dick I have ever seen.' Paco is laughing, looking away from the Swiss RE Tower only to slip another strawberry into my mouth.

'Then you won't be surprised to hear it's also nick-named the "erotic gherkin", and the "towering innu-endo". You'll notice,' I add mischievously, 'that it's uncircumcised.'

Paco grins at me. 'You're a mine of weird and won-derful information,' he says. 'You're worth every penny.'

I look at him. 'Then I'll still be working for you?' I say. The question's been simmering away in my mind ever since we left the hotel.

He nods, eyebrows raised a little. 'Why not?' he says.

'But what about Carlotta?'

'What about her?'

'I'm just – I don't know if I'm comfortable after what's happened between us. You said you want me to be her friend, but I've betrayed that friendship before it's even begun.'

Paco leans toward me, brushes a stray hair from my face, then plants an almost chaste little kiss on my nose.

'I never imagined I would cheat on Carlotta,' he said. 'She is a woman in a million, and I never want to risk losing her. But I know you are discreet, Alicia. I trust you.'

I nod. 'I would never say –'

'I know that,' he interrupts, placing a finger against my lips. 'I can see that you are a sensitive woman, that you will have picked up on how vulnerable Carlotta really is. She is so young, Alicia. Don't forget that. She has seen a lot of life, but in many ways I think she is still one of life's innocents. What is happening between us is to do with you and me alone. It mustn't touch her.'

Even as he's talking, I'm telling myself I should get out of this now, that something important is at stake here. This is not going to be a casual fling, and at least one person is going to get hurt. But his hands are on me now, his eyes are burning into mine, and I feel like I'm melting into the seat, I want him so much. And before I know it I'm hoisting my skirt up over my hips, pulling down my flimsy knickers and proffering him my pussy, glistening with the juices he has called forth in me.

He responds by unbuttoning my blouse, pushing my bra up and plunging his face into my breasts. He hasn't shaved yet today, and his stubble chafes at my skin. That turns me on even more. I reach down and fumble with his belt buckle, then slip down his trousers. I feel his cock leap out, find me with the efficiency of a heat-seeking missile. I'm crushed up against the door, the handle in the small of my back. The pain only adds to my excitement, as does the shadowy presence of the chauffeur in the front seat. He's eating a sandwich, gazing out of the window; even if he turned round he'd be unable to see us through the mirrored glass. But he must have some idea what's going on in the back here, and the thought that he knows drives me crazier still.

For a moment, before driving himself into me, Paco hesitates, back arched, eyes closed. I reach up my hand and run my fingers the length of his taut throat, around the angular sweep of his jawbone. I wonder, looking up at him, what he's thinking of now, what he's feeling, lost there in his private moment of elation. I'm almost certain it's not me; is it Carlotta, or would the thought of his wife only puncture the euphoria? Is he thinking of anything at all beyond the immediate sensation of his cock edging into me, parting me so slowly that I feel almost delirious with need and longing?

I become aware that my nails are digging into the flesh of his upper back; I slide my hands down his back and clutch the flesh of his buttocks, squeezing them towards me in an effort to fill myself with him. His slow advance has been delicious, but I have to have him now, all of him, inside me. The feel of my manicured talons on his arse cheeks must excite him, for suddenly he's plunged into me, not thrusting but just pushing, pushing, to the point where I'm worried that the limo door might not be locked and that I might be forced out onto the pavement. I'm soaring like a bird now, being lifted higher and higher, already sensing the approach of one almighty orgasm, like the preshock of an earthquake.

I inch my bum backwards, over the leather seat; there's not much room to manoeuvre but it's just enough for me to set myself in motion, to start sliding myself up and down his pole, which is well lubricated by now. He's still trying to hold off, I can tell, but he hasn't got a hope in hell now; within moments we're working in synch. I ride him beautifully as he saws in and out of me, matching his movements, keeping my pussy walls tight around him.

As the first moans start escaping from his throat, I too start to wail, half afraid I'm going to go out of my mind with it all. I feel that I'm on a precipice, that there's an edge beyond which madness lies. But something inside me knows that this madness, should it be provoked, is the price to pay for this pleasure, this pleasure that comes liberally dosed with a kind of sublime pain.

He hits the spot, all of a sudden, and I'm thrashing in his arms almost as if I'm trying to fight him off, bright lights flashing behind my closed eyelids like fireworks. He comes too, pulling himself out of me while my orgasm is still rippling through me, whimpering something in Spanish. Then we lie in a crumpled heap on the back seat, clothes strewn around us, the rich, salty smell of his semen around us.

After a minute he splashes me down with champagne, where he's come on my tits, and then leans forwards to lap it off.

'Where next?' he smiles.

We drive around the City for a while, happy, for a time at least, to be aimless. We look at fragments of Roman walls, at old churches, at modern skyscrapers, sometimes accompanied by a little running commentary by me. Paco, for his part, talks a little of his native Madrid and tells me I should go there sometime. He also speaks lovingly of Chicago, where he lived for five years during his training.

On the way back into central London, I have the driver stop by Liverpool Street Station, and we walk through into the plaza behind it, where office workers are sitting eating packed lunches or takeaway sushi in the sunshine. I point out the sculptures dotted around the place.

'An open-air art gallery,' I say. 'Free to everyone. And you can not only look but touch. Neat, huh?'

We stroll around Exchange Square for a few minutes, looking at the various pieces. Paco confesses that he's not wildly into art, that he's much more at ease with music, which he claims is in his blood. But he is much taken by a voluptuous reclining figure on the east side of the plaza, hips swathed in fabric but otherwise naked: the *Broadgate Venus*.

'I don't like skinny woman,' he muses as he admires the figure. 'Slim, yes, but a few curves are essential.'

I remind him that he's been photographed on the arms of some of the world's most emaciated women.

'Ah yes,' he smiles. 'My supermodel phase. But you'll notice it didn't last long. I was just making a name for myself. My agent encouraged me, said it would get my name about. And he was right. But it wasn't a whole lot of fun. I prefer women who love life, and that includes good wine, good food and making love. Making love spontaneously,' he adds, 'not because of some cocaine buzz.'

He pauses, looks at me thoughtfully. 'Like I said,' he continues, 'the last thing on my mind was being unfaithful to Carlotta. But when I came in and saw you on the bathroom floor, when I saw how you sent yourself into some kind of delirium, I knew I had to have you.' He looks deadly serious as he speaks. 'You are, in many ways, very similar to Carlotta. Carlotta is an extraordinarily passionate woman.'

We fuck again, on the way back to his hotel, this time with me astride him, riding his lithe brown hips. The subject of what we are going to do when Carlotta is back – whether this is to be an ongoing thing – isn't broached, and when he drops me off on my street on his way to the airport to fetch her in the very same limo in which we have been screwing like fury, I have no idea what is going to happen next.

At home I listen to my phone messages as I shower: there are two from potential new clients, enquiring about availability later in the year, and one from my best mate.

'Ally,' I hear her say through the jets of water that are pummelling my shoulders. 'It's Jess. I am, needless to say, absolutely creaming my pants to find out how it went with that gorgeous hunk of a flamenco dancer. So call me back the very second you get this. Love ya. Bye.'

I climb out of the shower, dry myself with a towel

and slip on my silk kimono. Part of me is dying to talk to Jess, to tell her what's been going on in my life. She was there for me when I was on my big downer about Daniel, and I even told her about the incident with Kip; in fact, we had a good laugh about it over a bottle of plonk or three at Gordon's Wine Bar one girly night. She's the first person I turn to when I need an ear, or a shoulder.

Yet I can't bring myself to pick up the phone and dial her number. I'm not ashamed, as such, but I am confused, and I'm thinking she might confuse me still more. Or rather, I'm thinking that she will raise blue murder when she hears what's happened, will demand that I put an end to it straightaway.

She's right, of course, but I don't want to hear what's right. I want to feel Paco's hands on me again, feel his dick parting me like a ripe fruit, surging into me. Just one more time, I say to myself. I'll just do it one more time, and then I'll stop. And in a couple of weeks he'll be gone and I'll forget the whole thing. It will have been no more than a strange but beautiful dream.

8

It's midday, and I'm standing in the lobby of Paco's hotel, waiting for Carlotta to come down. My hands are shaking a little, and I've half a mind to leave a message that I'm in the bar and go and calm myself with a few stiff vodkas, when she appears. Her hair is freshly washed and she has on a leaf-green halter-neck dress and gold stilettos with straps that wind around her shapely ankles like those of ballet shoes. Yet she looks morose. I know the reason for that: Paco told me on the phone that she didn't get the part she was auditioning for.

He called last night, his business-like tone indicating that he was with her. He would be in rehearsals all the following day, he said, but would like me to take her out for the afternoon, to cheer her up after her 'bad luck'. It was strange to be talking to each other in such a detached formal way after the night and day we'd just spent together, and I felt my first pang of jealousy towards Carlotta, for being the one who would get to share his bed that night. For being the one who shared his bed at all, I reminded myself, since he had not conferred that privilege on me the previous night despite having just fucked me on the chair right next to it.

I tried not to give myself over to the luxury of self-pity: I'd known the score, I told myself, when I offered to bring myself off in front of him a second time, and I couldn't complain now. To ward off the return of the blues that it had taken me months to dispel, I made a hot chocolate and busied myself preparing some tours arranged for the weeks after Paco and Carlotta's departure. There was life, I reminded myself, after him.

Just as I was getting into bed, my phone beeped. I checked the screen: number withheld. I clicked on the message icon and read the text:

ENJOY TOMORROW. WILL BE THINKING OF YOU. SEE YOU SOON, AND THANKS FOR A GREAT DAY. P X.

Unable to resist a smile, I lay back, let my unbelted kimono fall open and, clutching my pussy with one hand, tapped a message back with the other.

THINKING OF YOU TOO. SEE YOU WHEN? A X.

Now, fifteen hours later, he still hasn't replied. Carlotta's standing in front of me, blue eyes looking washed out and more than a little jaded with life. I'm shocked to find how easy it is to face up to her, now she's here, given what I've done. She looks so young, so unworldly – in spite of the glamour-puss get-up – as if she inhabits a planet where people don't go behind each other's backs, don't keep secrets from one another.

'How about a little retail therapy?' I say with a cheery smile. 'Paco said you love shopping.'

She shrugs, lights a cigarette. I think of a sulky schoolgirl, the sixth-form rebel, the one always caught behind the bike shed with the boys. There's something so intrinsically naughty about Carlotta, somehow co-existing with that unworldly air. Or maybe not. Maybe what Paco told me about their first fuck on the clifftop is giving me preconceptions. After all, what chance did this little thing have against the force of his will? Maybe she's just been caught up in the wake of this human whirlwind. I wonder if she's got any idea what she's taken on.

'I was sorry to hear about the audition,' I say in the taxi on the way to Selfridges. 'It must be difficult.'

'What difficult?' She's staring out of the window, but there's suddenly a combative look in those eyes.

I hesitate, but it's too late, and she's onto me, turning in her seat and fixing with me her penetrating blue glare.

'It must be difficult to be failure when Paco so big success, no?'

I look out of the window in turn; there's nothing to be said to that. If that's the frame of mind she's in, though, I'm not standing for it, money or no money. We'll do a quick tour of the designer floor and then I'll drop her back at the hotel and she can wallow in self-pity to her heart's content. I'm a tour guide, not a nanny to a moody child.

We've pulled up at the side of Selfridges, and I lead Carlotta through the high-street clothes department with its throbbing rock soundtrack, and through the beauty hall and perfumery, to the lifts. On the second floor we get out and begin to make our way through the designer clothes concessions.

I may not be wealthy but I pride myself on having a bit of an eye for labels, and on sussing out what people might like, and when I lead Carlotta straight to Versace, I sense her thawing a bit. She's in her element here, and has soon amassed a pile of outfits to take through into the changing room. I sit down in a leather chair by the till to wait for her. Twenty minutes later she's out and grabbing more clothes off the rails. It's going to be a long afternoon.

An hour later, her bank account a few thousand pounds lighter, Carlotta asks where the lingerie department is, and we take the escalator up to the next floor. She's definitely cheered up; in fact, she's positively bubbling now, all thoughts of her stillborn career erased from her mind by the adrenalin rush of spending someone else's money. Her enthusiasm is contagious, and soon I'm joining her in flipping through the rails, secretly marvelling at the prices some people are prepared to pay for a transparent sliver of fabric with which to barely cover their Hollywoods.

'What you think?' she calls over to me at one point, holding up a baby-pink bra and matching knickers in wispy fabric. They look like candy floss. I nod.

'Paco will love it,' she says. I smile, nod again, hoping my cheeks aren't reddening. I know what your husband likes, I hear a voice in my head say. I know more than you think I do, anyway.

She comes closer to me, lowers her voice. Suddenly we are conspirators, something I wasn't prepared for.

'He love it,' she says, looking into my eyes, 'when he see my pussy right through my underwear. When he see my nipples. Bizarre, no? I think that strange at first. I think it will be sexier if he can't see me to start with. It funny,' she smiles, 'the different things turn men on.'

I turn my head away, flustered; pretend to rifle through the racks in search of my size. I'm thinking back, in spite of myself, to what I was wearing yesterday, in the limo. It was my favourite Calvin Klein black bra and pants, plain, transparent. His favourite sort, without me even knowing.

'What *you* like?' she says, leaning into me. Suddenly we are mates, it seems.

I grab something, anything, off the rail. 'I don't know much about lingerie,' I lie. 'I'm a bit of a Marks and Spencer traditionalist, I'm afraid. Give me a cheapo multipack any day.'

Carlotta looks at me curiously. 'Really?' she says. 'You no think you worth more than that?'

As a matter of fact, I do, but I want more than anything in the world for this conversation to end and for us to get the hell out of here. I turn away, pretend to be inspecting a bra in ebony and nude lace.

Carlotta pays for a few items at the till and then asks if we can go back to the clothes section and find out if they stock any Moschino. On the way back down the escalator she places her hand lightly on my arm.

'I sorry if you think I being rude about the lingerie,' she says. 'It's just I cannot imagine not wearing best I can buy.' She looks away from me, surveying the scene below – a treasure trove of friths and froths just waiting for her to plunder.

'I know I rich,' she adds. 'But you can make best of yourself even with no money. I know – remember I was a starving artists' model once.'

Starving model my arse, I feel like saying. She doesn't look like she's known a moment's deprivation in her life. I also feel like telling her that I do take very good care of myself, as her husband will testify – I have regular Brazilians, facials and manicures, and my underwear drawer at home is positively overflowing with everything from Rigby & Peller to Agent Provocateur. With something to suit every mood and fantasy. She's preaching to the converted.

She finally changes the subject, twigging on, I suppose, to my lack of enthusiasm for the current topic of conversation. But no sooner has she started asking about other department stores she's heard about and would like me to take her to when she's spotted a hip new design concession and is making a beeline for it, cooing and cawing. And for another hour she's lost among the racks; I catch just the occasional glimpse of her and then she's gone again and I hear only the odd birdlike squawk to indicate she's still there in the shop at all.

It's actually very peaceful, just sitting there watching

all the ladies-who-have-lunched saunter in and calmly spend thousands of pounds on a single skimpy garment without so much as batting a false eyelash. It doesn't inspire envy in me, much as I enjoy dressing well and looking good; I value my independence far too much, and part of the attraction of treating myself to a new pair of slinky Joseph trousers or some Lejaby underwear is knowing that I have worked my butt off for it, have saved up and – often – denied myself other things in order to have it.

No, I think, looking at Carlotta strolling back over to me, arms heaped with yet more clothes to try on (we've had the bags of clothes she bought earlier sent to the hotel in a taxi, otherwise we'd have been too laden down to shop anymore): not for me the role of trophy wife, with nothing to do in life except nibble salad leaves before spending the day flexing my husband's plastic. I'd go out of my mind before a week was through. I'm lucky, I think, to have found a job that gives me a real buzz; the considerable perks are the icing on an already pretty tasty cake.

I smile up at Carlotta from my comfortable leather armchair. I'm having a relaxing afternoon; she can take all the time she likes. She's brandishing a scrap of reflective lilac material at me that, on closer inspection, reveals itself to be a strapless dress with crisscross lacing on the back and a deep slit at the back of the already breathtakingly short skirt. It's deeply horrible, but I smile and nod encouragingly.

'Very chic,' I say, trying not to sound a note of irony. Carlotta's taste can only be described as Eurotrash, yet that doesn't stop her from looking fabulous. In fact there's something incredibly sexy about a woman who has the confidence in her body to wear such risqué things.

'Not for me,' she grins. 'I thinking of you. Come with me and try it.'

And before I can say another word, she's marching off to the changing rooms, remarkably steady, I notice, on those spindly stiletto heels.

Inside the changing room, she flings open the curtain to one booth and steps inside, then beckons me to follow her.

'Plenty room for two,' she says. 'And I need your advice on this dress, on which colour suit me best.' She pauses, musing. 'Unless I buy many,' she adds, and flashes me a coy smile.

She starts undressing, unwinding the straps from her ankles and kicking her shoes off, then turning her back to me.

'Untie strap will you? I always get Paco to do. He not mind, of course. He not need reason to undress me. That man an animal.'

I frown, glad that she can't see my face, trying to concentrate on loosening the knot of her halterneck. It finally gives way, and the straps fall forwards over her shapely shoulders. Like this, without her heels, she's tiny – a good few inches shorter than me – and again I am reminded of a beautiful wilful child.

As the dress falls and settles around her hips, she waves her arm up towards the clasp of her strapless shiny black bra.

'You undo this too?' she asks over her shoulder. 'Or you will see through dress.' I fumble with the fastening, thinking of Paco's hands on this very spot. I imagine him pressing himself across the back of her thighs as he unleashes her breasts, his cock already straining for her through his trousers. I'm surprised to find that the thought makes me moist.

'You have boyfriend, Alicia?' says Carlotta as her bra

falls to the floor. She turns to reach up for one of the outfits she's hung on the hook next to the full-length mirror. I can't help but look at her breasts as they lift and separate with the movement of her body, and I'm awestruck. They're neither too big nor too small, and jaunty without having the poke-you-in-the-eye audacity of augmented breasts. Her large nipples are the same colour as her skin: a lovely olive tinged with honey-gold.

She turns to me, pushing down the rest of her dress to reveal a thong that matches the bra I have just helped her out of. Her buttocks are superbly rounded, almost heart-shaped.

'Well?' she smiles. 'You have?'

I'm lost, have no idea what she is asking me. I'm feeling more than a little distracted by all the flesh that's suddenly on display.

'A boyfriend?' she reminds me. 'Or is it a big secret?'

'Oh no,' I laugh nervously. 'My life's not interesting enough to have secrets.' I look down at the floor, where Carlotta's shoes and underwear are scattered around our feet. 'There was someone,' I say, trying to keep regret from my voice. 'Someone I liked. But nothing came of it.'

'Ah well,' she says, shimmying into a tight little white dress with a sequin-studded hem and neck detailing. 'You very pretty girl. There will be someone new for you. Here –' she hands me the dress she picked out for me '– try this.'

I hold it up against me on the hanger. It's totally not me, but I suppose I ought to humour her now I'm here. She seems to be warming to me after our frosty start, opening up to me, and Paco *is* paying me to entertain her, after all. There's no point in getting all upset again about Daniel, about what could have been.

I pull my black jersey top up over my head, then undo my boot-cut trousers and slide them down. I don't look at Carlotta. God knows I'm no prude, but I feel a bit shy.

'Oh!' I hear her exclaim. She's pulled the white dress up over her head and is standing topless looking at me. 'So you lying when you say you don't like nice lingerie,' she says.

I shrug, as if I hadn't been aware I was wearing an expensive set of lacy Aubade panties and bra.

She's looking me up and down now, quite openly, but I turn to take my dress off its hanger and pretend not to notice. I still feel a little self-conscious, but in some secret part of myself I'm also enjoying the attention more than I would have expected. Carlotta is clearly impressed by what she sees, and that makes me feel good about myself. Not that I had any doubts about my body, but it's always gratifying when someone else is appreciative of it. Especially when that someone has a hot little body of their own.

Pretending to fuss with the zip on my dress, I angle my head so that I can see into the mirror out of the corner of my eye. Carlotta is still looking at me, at my long slim legs, at my arse, at the curve of my waist and the swell of my breasts. There's a funny little smile on her lips, and I'm dying to ask her what she's thinking. If only she knew, I think, of what her husband did with this body just the day before. A vision comes into my head of me, bent over the back of the chair, cheeks high as Paco crushes himself into me from behind.

I lean forwards, step into the dress and start to wiggle it up over my hips. When it's up and over my chest, I fumble for the straps at the back but can't reach them.

'Here,' says Carlotta, and I feel her fingers brushing

my back as she pulls the lacing tight and secures it at the top. She steps away from me, places her hands on my bare shoulders and spins me around.

'*Perfecto*,' she says, looking me up and down again. '*Fantástico!*'

The dress fits like a second skin, and when I turn to check myself out in the mirror I am surprised to find that it actually looks pretty great. It's still not me, taste-wise, but there's no denying that it really brings out the natural hourglass of my figure. I turn around and look over my shoulder, and I'm shocked to see how high the slit goes up, revealing a hefty portion of buttock.

'It's pretty special,' I confess, 'but a bit daring for me, I think.'

'No!' snorts Carlotta. 'You got a beautiful body. Why hide it?' She waves her hand at my classically cut top, at my trousers. 'You too safe.'

I start to peel off the dress. I'm not going to argue with her about taste: like I said, she may wear trashy clothes, but she looks a million dollars. Each to their own. It's what you're most comfortable with, isn't it, and Carlotta is obviously happy with a much greater degree of display than I am.

I've pulled on my clothes and am bending over to slip on my shoes when I happen to glance in the mirror again. Carlotta seems to have abandoned the idea of trying on the rest of the clothes she picked out and is getting dressed again herself, leaning forwards to manoeuvre her breasts into her bra and fastening it with both hands, then stepping into her dress and knotting the halter at her nape. Funny how she's able to do that just fine, when she claimed she couldn't even undo it herself.

She appears to be lost in thought. I look down at my

shoes again, then glance unthinkingly back and I'm shocked – and strangely aroused – to see her rubbing furtively at her pussy through the fabric of her dress.

I can't take my eyes off her. She, meanwhile, closes her own eyes, and tilts her head back a little, lips slightly parted. I'd give anything in the world to know what she's seeing behind those closed eyelids.

As if suddenly realising where she is, she opens her eyes and lets go of her pussy. I look away quickly, feeling like a voyeur, though it was she, after all, who invited me in here.

'Meet you out there,' I say, pulling back the curtain and stepping out.

She's right behind me, following me back onto the shopfloor, face flushed. I'm surprised, I think, that she didn't stay in there. She's obviously got something on her mind and may as well have taken the opportunity to give herself a bit of relief after I'd gone.

'I'll just go hang this up,' I say, gesturing towards a far rail of hangers.

'Oh no no no,' she replies quickly. 'Come with me.' And already she's steaming towards the cash desk and handing over the white dress she's chosen. 'Here,' she says, turning back to me and taking the lilac number from my hands. 'A present from me.'

'Carlotta, I couldn't,' I say, horrified.

'To thank you, for fun afternoon,' she says, gazing into my eyes. 'You cheer me up,' she adds, winking.

'But –'

She lays a finger against my lips. 'Shhh,' she whispers. '*Please*. It make me happy.'

There's nothing I can say, I reason, that will change her mind – even if I tell her I will never have occasion to wear it, that it will hang in my wardrobe for a few months or years and then, one day, when I'm having a big clearout, be bagged up and taken to the charity shop along with all my other castoffs. Or rather, I think, as I see the four-digit number that flashes up on the till display, be auctioned on eBay, with the proceeds put towards my holiday fund. Suddenly the Caribbean is looking increasingly likely.

Shouldering our trademark yellow Selfridges bags, we head back toward the lift. Carlotta has linked her arm through mine and is chatting merrily in her sing-song Spanish accent when she is interrupted by a call. She digs in her Gucci bag, flips open her mobile.

'*Hola?*'

There follows a volley of Spanish, and I don't understand a word of the conversation. When she ends the call, she tells me that Paco has finished his rehearsal earlier than expected and has suggested meeting her for a drink. He was at the Royal Albert Hall, she tells me, and is heading this way in a taxi. She's to call him back with a good place to meet, once she's asked me.

My blood runs cold. I wasn't prepared for this, and I'm not sure how I'm going to handle being with the two of them at the same time. In my mind, I run through various excuses, but I'm beset by a feeling of futility. Carlotta, I have seen, is a girl who likes to get her own way. She won't let me off that easily, and I don't want to ring alarm bells in her head by ducking out with no good reason.

After a quick ponder, I suggest we stay in Selfridges and get Paco to come and meet us in the food hall, where there's a good champagne and oyster bar. Carlotta is enthusiastic: she just *loves* oysters, she says, ostentatiously licking her lips, reaching for her mobile again and calling her husband.

Half an hour later, we're still waiting for Paco, who's

got stuck in traffic at Knightsbridge. We're well into our second glass of champagne and I, at least, am feeling a little bit tipsy, not having eaten since breakfast. We've ordered a dozen oysters to keep us going, and soon a gleaming platter of the raw crustacea is set in front of us, garnished with wedges of lemon.

Carlotta picks one up, cups the pearlescent grey shell in the palm of her small hand and brings it up to her lips. From behind her regular white teeth the tip of her tongue darts out, teases at the shellfish. She's looking right at me as she does so, and unless I am pissed already, I discern a funny expression in her eyes. She's toying with me, I tell myself, and again I think of her playing with herself in the changing room. Is it possible, I ask myself, that it was me she was thinking of as she rubbed at her pussy? She had, after all, just been watching me in the mirror.

She's running her tongue over the flesh of the oyster now, then yanking it free from the shell with her teeth and slurping it up. I can't tear my eyes away from her. What the hell's she playing at, I think. Or is she just hamming it up? Sometimes actresses – even, or perhaps especially, unsuccessful ones – don't know when to turn it off.

I pick up an oyster myself, inhale its salty ocean tang, then close my eyes and tip it into my mouth. I wince involuntarily as it slithers whole down the back of my throat; I like oysters, but they do make me a little squeamish. When I open my eyes, Carlotta is still looking at me, her eyes twinkling. Mischief is on her mind, I'm sure of it, but I don't know her well enough to know in what form it's going to manifest itself.

She leans forwards to ask the waiter to bring us more champagne, wobbling slightly on her high stool. Then she turns to face me.

'I have idea,' she says.

Here it is, I think: whatever's been brewing in her mind for the last half-hour. I take a deep breath.

'Go put dress on,' she says, and though she's not exactly ordering me, her voice brooks no dissent. 'Paco,' she adds with a smile, 'will love. He love it when I wear such a thing.'

She hops from her seat and passes me up my bag. 'I wait here while you go to bathroom.' She glances around her. 'But just one thing,' she continues in a low voice.

'What's that?'

'Don't tell Paco it me who buy it for you. Or him buy it – it his credit card!' She smirks. 'Our little secret.'

When I get back to the oyster bar, Paco and Carlotta are sitting on adjacent stools, all over each other. They barely even register my return and, as I'm sitting back down and reaching for the fresh glass of champagne that's appeared in place of my old one, I can see their hands on each others' thighs – his creeping under the hem of her dress to the shadowy realm between her legs, hers right next to the bulge in his trousers, where his cock is no doubt throbbing for her. She's leaning in towards him, face nuzzling his shoulder, eyes all wide and adoring. His hand is on the back of her head, stroking her glossy yellow hair. Then he lifts his magnificent brown eyes and looks straight into mine, and my belly does a somersault.

'Hi Alicia,' he says, and Carlotta lifts her head and looks at me too. All the mischief has gone from her eyes – in fact, she looks a little glazed and sleepy – and I tell myself I must have imagined the whole thing. How could I have flattered myself to think that she was flirting with me, when she so obviously worships her husband? It was clearly him she was thinking of when she had her crafty grope in the changing cubicle. One look at her now tells me there's nothing on her mind beyond getting him back to their hotel and sliding between the sheets with him.

Carlotta doesn't even mention the dress. Neither, in fact, does Paco, though I look, I know it, so utterly unlike myself, especially with half my bum hanging out. I already got some pretty strange looks on my way back from the loos. After a few minutes of watching them melt into each other on their stools, I'm feeling like a bit of a spare part. I look at my watch and sigh.

'I'll make a move, then,' I say. 'Call me later, Carlotta, about what time you want me to pick you up tomorrow.'

Carlotta is standing up now. 'OK,' she says, leaning in to kiss me on the cheek. 'And thanks again, Alicia. I have a great time.'

She turns back to Paco and says something in Spanish before walking away; I guess she's gone to the toilets, since she's left all her bags. I wait until I'm sure she's gone and then turn back to Paco, smile uncertainly.

'Thanks,' he says simply.

'For what?'

'You know –' His eyes blaze into mine. 'I know it's not easy.'

I shrug, cast my eyes around the food hall at all the people shopping for their supper. Why do other people's lives always seem so cosy and uncomplicated when your own is in turmoil? And why does turmoil suddenly seem to be my *modus operandi*?

'Can I see you again?' I say finally. 'Alone, I mean.'

Paco sighs, runs his hands through his hair. 'It's difficult,' he says. His eyes are on the door through which Carlotta will reappear sometime soon. 'It's just crazy right now, my schedule.'

'Fine,' I say, feeling like an idiot. I take my handbag from the stool where I had placed it.

'Alicia,' he hisses, grabbing my wrist as I start to walk away. 'I don't want you to think I don't want to see you. It's just – difficult right now. I hardly even see Carlotta, and if I take any more time away from her she'll get suspicious. But I'll find a way. I *do* want to see you again. I keep thinking about you all the time.'

'OK,' I say, heart a little lighter. He's staring back at the doorway. 'I'll go now,' I say, equally anxious that Carlotta doesn't see us still together.

He tightens his grip on my wrist, then lets go. 'I'll call you as soon as I can find a way,' he says.

And then I'm gone, across the food hall and out into the rain, feeling more than a little ridiculous in my tarty dress, looking for a taxi. I can't face a sweaty, overcrowded rush-hour bus, can't face walking home alone through the grey streets, seeing all the lovers getting together after work, holding hands, linking arms, heading for bright bars and restaurants full of the tinkle of carefree laughter.

9

I need a girly night out, I say to myself back at my flat. I've had a shower, poured a large vodka and tonic, and talked some sense into myself since my moment of despair on the street outside Selfridges. There are two messages from Jess, who's beginning to sound cross, and even a little worried, now. I'm not surprised: I've been blanking her calls on my mobile all afternoon. She knows something's up.

I don't divulge much on the phone, just that a couple of things have happened that I need to talk to her about. Happily, she's free this evening, and we agree to meet in an hour and a half at Julie's Wine Bar not far from where she lives in Holland Park. There's a restaurant there if we decide to eat, but on past experience we'll be having a liquid supper.

I sit down at my dressing table and plug in my hair drier. Sometimes, I think, I don't deserve a friend like Jess. She's always been there for me, and I hate to think of what would happen if she wasn't. Not that I'm an emotional disaster zone, though the last few months might suggest otherwise. Far from it, in fact. I'm pretty low-maintenance as friends go. But everyone gets themselves into a little pickle now and again. Everyone needs someone to hold their hand through the bumpy bits.

Good old Jess – she didn't even tell me, when I was obsessing about Daniel, to get a grip on myself. She never once said: look, Ally, you had the shag of your life and you really like the guy, but it was basically a one-night stand and nothing more and you have to get over it. He's out of your league.

No, she totally understands that however brief our encounter, I'd found, in Daniel, someone I just knew I could make a life with. Someone who made me laugh, who turned me on, who treated me – at least it seemed that way at the time – with respect. Someone who stayed remarkably down-to-earth when all the glamour could have turned him into the world's biggest arsehole.

Jess just held my hand, and called me up, and sat drinking vodka with me when I didn't feel like going out, watching reruns of *NYPD Blue*. She'd even turned up on my doorstep one night with a pair of Eurostar tickets, and we'd spent a weekend in Paris looking at art, and wandering along the Seine, and drinking cheap red wine and talking about everything and nothing. Our hopes for the future. Our careers. Which rock stars we'd like to fuck. The best positions for orgasms (she prefers it doggy-style, with manual stimulation of the clitoris – whether by herself or her partner, doesn't matter).

I've never had lesbian inclinations, but sometimes, when I hang out with Jess, I think she's so damn perfect that I don't know why I don't just tustle her into bed and fuck the living daylights out of her. Ever since our first term at uni together, when we were neighbours in our hall of residence, we've been the best of buddies. And she is gorgeous to boot. But we both like dicks, and that's that.

One night on that visit to Paris, when we got back to our room in the early hours, drunk on booze and talk, I'd seriously considered – for one mad, lonely moment – just going for it anyway, to see what it was like, to see if it could work. But I knew she didn't want me, as I didn't *really* want her, and that we risked losing our friendship through one pissed experiment. And so after she'd gone to sleep I settled for a woozy wank, lying in front of the silently flickering TV, thinking about Daniel Lubowski in the dome room.

Afterwards, my hands still sticky with my juices, I'd sneaked out of the room and – in direct defiance of all Jess's advice to just stop thinking about him and get on with my life – dialled his number from my mobile. This time I actually went through with it, rather than just thinking about it, rather than calling up his number on my screen and then bottling out. My heart was in my throat, and I don't know what I would have said if he'd picked up, but the call clicked through to his answerphone anyway, and I hung up. I never told Jess I did that, but nor did I try calling Daniel again after that weekend, though I still thought about him when I wanked.

Jess is already sitting at a table when I arrive, sipping a glass of Chardonnay and making puppy eyes at the new barman, who's pretending not to notice, although you can tell from his body language that he's secretly rather enjoying the attention.

She nods over at him as I sit down opposite her. 'Might take him home tonight,' she mutters. 'Could do with a damn good shag.'

Jess split up with her banker-wanker boyfriend a year ago and has been happily single ever since, although she's not averse to a bit of rough and tumble when the mood takes her.

'Could do worse,' I say, looking over appraisingly at the object of her desire. He's polishing glasses now, affecting to look out of the window as his honed pecs flex and then slacken with the movement of his arms.

'So anyway, how are you?' says Jess, leaning towards

me over the table. 'You've been a pain in the arse to get hold of. Mr Primadonna Ballerina been keeping you on your toes?'

She stops when she sees my face, my averted eyes.

'You haven't? Ally, tell me you haven't.'

I open my mouth to speak, but I can't. I can hardly believe it all myself. I feel like I'm in some weird dream. I'm fucking Paco Manchega, I say to myself, and it sounds completely unreal. Maybe I just imagined the whole thing.

Jess is right in my face now, hers all flushed and excited. Then she leans back, tries to look stern. 'Hang on,' she says. 'Why are you looking so damn miserable if you're copping off with one of the world's great love gods? And why, more to the point, didn't you ring me the minute this happened?'

I slump down in my seat, wishing I wasn't here, that I'd just stayed at home and drunk myself into a stupor. Jess is going to go ballistic when she hears what I have to say, and I don't know if I can handle it.

'I'll get you a drink,' she says, relenting, tuned in now to my despondency and figuring it needs the softly-softly approach.

'So hit me with it,' she says with a coaxing smile when she sits down again, placing a large glass of Cabernet Sauvignon on the table in front of me. 'What's the story?'

'He's married,' I say bluntly, and I watch as her face falls.

'Bloody hell, Ally, when did that happen?'

'A month ago. Her name's Carlotta. She's trying to be an actress.' I look out of the window. 'She's nice, actually,' I add. 'In fact she's making a lot of effort to be my friend. It's her that I'm showing round while Paco struts his stuff, actually.'

Jess leans forward to extract a cigarette from her pack, offering me one at the same time. I take it, and for a few moments we smoke in silence.

'So what happened?' she asks at last, and I recount the whole tale for her, from my wank in the bath via our illicit doings in the stretch limo to his parting words at the oyster bar. As I'm talking, she alternates between anger and laughter, but when I've done she's deeply serious.

'You have *got* to stop, Ally,' she says, wagging a finger at me. 'I don't know what this guy thinks he's playing at, but you're on a crash course with disaster, no doubt about it. You don't need me to tell you...'

'I don't,' I interrupt. 'I knew exactly what you were going to say, and I would say exactly the same thing if it were you in my place: *get the hell out.*' I feel in my pocket for some notes to go buy another round. 'But admit it – you'd have done the same thing if the chance presented itself.'

Jess looks at me through narrowed eyes. 'That is *not* the point,' she says, mock-sternly this time, and we laugh together. A weight lifts off my shoulders: this is what I came here for, I tell myself – to be reminded that problems are sometimes only as serious as we want to make them. I've been silly, but I have time to get out before anyone is hurt.

Of course, now we've got the moral reprobation out of the way, Jess is desperate to know all the nitty gritty of my night and day with Paco – everything from the colour and maké of his briefs to the size of his dick and how many times I came. She can't help herself, asking more and more questions, and as I answer them I notice her head turning more and more frequently to look at the guy behind the bar. I sneak him a glance, and I realise with a secret thrill that he's listening in on our conversation now. He's got a odd little smirk on his lips, and he keeps looking up and catching Jess's eye. Both of them, it's clear, are getting all in a froth at my descriptions of what Paco and I got up to, and after a few minutes I decide to leave them to it.

Jess and I have a giant hug as I wait for my taxi. 'Just remember what I said,' she admonishes. 'Leave well enough alone, girl. This one's too hot to handle.'

'Message received loud and clear,' I say. I shoot a look at the barman, who's already undressing Jess with his eyes while she's preoccupied with me. Jess lives only five minutes away, but I seriously doubt they're going to make it back to her place before getting down and dirty.

'Have a lovely night,' I say to her, and then a thought occurs to me. 'Listen,' I whisper. 'I don't know exactly what lover boy over there heard, but I don't want it getting around about Paco, for obvious reasons. Will you try to sound out what he did and didn't hear? And if he thinks he knows who we were talking about, make sure you get it straight that it wasn't Manchega, OK?'

'Don't worry,' says Jess, ushering me out of the door. 'You can count on me. Now just get the hell out of here. *Some* of us haven't had a decent fuck in months, you know.'

On my way home in the taxi, I turn my mobile back on and there's a message from Carlotta. There's langour in her voice, as if she's drunk, or has just made love. She tells me she's been thinking and has decided she'd like to go see some art tomorrow. She says she doesn't mind where, but then Paco's voice can be heard in the background:

'The Tate Modern. Tell her to take you there, angel.'

'The Tate Modern,' reiterates Carlotta. She's strangely pliant with Paco, I think, for a woman who seems to know her own mind so well the rest of the time. 'I expect you midday again. Thanks Alicia.'

I climb out of the taxi outside my flat, suddenly incredibly weary from all the emotions and complications of the last few days. But it's all over now – I've promised Jess and I've promised myself. I'll get a good night's sleep and tomorrow will be fresh and bright as a blank canvas.

10

It's past noon, and the meter on my taxi is ticking over as I wait for Carlotta outside the hotel. I called up quarter of an hour ago to let her know I was waiting, but there's no sign of her. Still, at the rates Paco's paying me, I could sit here all day, letting the fare go through the roof. I sit back and watch the world go by. It's a balmy summer's day and there's a lot of flesh on display by the office workers and students strolling out of Fitzrovia and down towards Oxford Street – lots of midriff T-shirts and short skirts and little denim shorts.

Suddenly Carlotta's there, sliding into the back beside me. She's somewhat toned down today, in a short-sleeved baby-pink cashmere top and flared black linen skirt that comes down almost as far as her knees. She's still in heels, of course, and her hair is loose as yesterday.

'Sorry,' she says, clearly not really meaning it, and not offering any explanation. A sickly caramel smell floats in with her.

'What's that perfume?' I say.

'Angel,' she says. 'Thierry Mugler. You like?'

I don't have any choice but to say yes, though I'm not into perfume or aftershave at all – I much prefer the human body *au naturel*, within reason.

'Paco take me to Liberty's on the way home last night,' she explains. 'The beauty hall is *amazing*. He buy incredible massage oil with sandalwood and – what it called? – patchouli and geranium in it. I dripping in it when he finish with me.'

I don't respond, don't even look at her. I don't want to know, I think sulkily.

But she's obviously in the mood for sharing, and there's nothing I can do to stop her without being rude. Or without changing the subject. Nothing comes to mind, however, and afterwards I wonder whether this is probably because, deep down, I *did* want to hear all about it.

She's reclining against the seat of the taxi, legs crossed, tapping her foot against the floor as she talks. I suspect she notices that the taxi driver, overhearing a few words, gradually turns down his radio and is now listening in. Afterwards, I think, he'll probably have to try to find a quiet sidestreet where he can wrist himself off.

'Paco always wonderful lover,' says Carlotta. 'But last night he on fire. I so tired, so tired.'

She senses me look at her and raises her eyebrows meaningfully. 'We get home,' she says, 'and he pull off my clothes and take me right there, on the floor in the hallway. He like a man possessed. We leave our clothes there and he carry me into bedroom and lay me down and massage me for hours. And then just as I falling asleep, he turn me over edge of the bed and start fucking me so hard from behind, I not sure if I can take it.'

She closes her eyes, swoons back. Her hand is between her legs now, and I look at her with dread, afraid she's going to start openly masturbating right here in the cab.

'I keep coming and coming and coming,' she says. 'And still he not stop.' She opens her eyes, grabs my hand besides hers. 'Until you have a man like Paco,' she says, looking at me, 'you don't know what sex is.' She blinks, affords me a pitying little smile. 'I know I very lucky woman,' she says.

I want to tell her to shut up now, but I'm fascinated, too, by what I am seeing through this unexpected window onto her and Paco's sex life. And, most peculiarly, there's a damp bloom in my knickers where I'm getting more than a little turned on. I can't stop thinking about how it felt when Paco mounted me on the chair, drove himself into me like – as Carlotta describes it – a thing possessed. I *have* to have him again. Just one more time. And then I'll keep my promise to Jess.

'So I hardly get any sleep all night long,' says Carlotta.

Now I come to think of it, she does look a little peaky, a little less fresh than yesterday.

'He just not leave me alone,' she goes on. 'It is exhausting ... and beautiful. He is extraordinary lover. I hope you experience man like him one day, Alicia.'

I'm biting my tongue as we pull up behind the Tate Modern, where I hand the driver his fare and a large tip. On our way inside, I try to take my mind off the subject by telling Carlotta about how the building was converted from an old power station and explaining that the artworks are arranged thematically rather than, as in most galleries, chronologically. She says that sounds interesting and that she's looking forward to the visit.

It's at this point that I realise I have absolutely no idea where to begin, and I ask her what kind of art she likes and what she would like to see.

She looks a little sheepish for a minute, and then she replies: 'You think I have just one thing in my head,' she says, 'but I like to see some nudes.'

I nod a little too earnestly. 'We can do that,' I say,

pointing towards the escalator. On the fifth floor, I remember, are the Nude/Action/Body galleries. There should be plenty there to tickle her fancy.

We come out in front of Rodin's *The Kiss*, on the threshold of the galleries, and stand to admire it. Carlotta studies it from several angles, says she doesn't know a great deal about Rodin or sculpture in general but loves the way the bodies appear to be melting into each other, that that's what she feels when she's kissing Paco – that they are becoming one.

She wonders aloud if I have ever felt like that and I think for a minute and I say, 'Yes, just once.' I don't tell her any more than that, but not because it's Paco I'm thinking about – his lovemaking was far too vigorous and carnal for that, for me at least. No, I'm thinking about Daniel and the morning after our second night together, when I lay awake in the dawn light, just looking at his face as he slept, and then he stirred and turned to me and, as he held my face between my hands and kissed me, his cock slipped into me without any need for lubrication, and I came with the sheer joy of it, and felt, yes, like I was melting into him.

And then half an hour later he was gone from my life for good.

I look up at the sculpture and I feel like crying, but Carlotta is moving away into the first room, pointing excitedly at a work that she's obviously familiar with and is happy to have discovered here. I follow her across the room and look at the plaque: *Reclining Nude*.

'Picasso paint this just weeks before he ninety,' she tells me, and I realise that she's no art amateur after all.

She steps closer to it. 'Imagine, such old man.' She laughs. 'Even when ninety he can't – how you say? –

keep it in pants.' She leans into me a little – more, I think, to make me feel like her confidante than because she really doesn't want anyone else to hear. I've already learnt from the taxi ride that she doesn't mind who knows about her bedroom antics.

'When I artists' model,' she says, 'I sometimes fantasise I am posing for Picasso. Not that I don't pose for talented men. But they not *him*, you know. And I love to have posed for Picasso, to have been his mistress, to fuck him, even if he treat his muses like shit.' She gestures back at the canvas in front of us. 'Even as old, old man, I think that would be amazing. He a genius, but more than that, he had big thirst for the world, for painting, for women, right to the end. To be immortalised in painting by him – that really something.'

We stroll through the galleries, stopping to look at pieces that catch our eye, and I listen to Carlotta talk passionately about art and realise that there's much more to her than I'd given her credit for. It's no bimbo, after all, who can knowledgeably discuss nude photography, from Man Ray to Helmut Newton, who can debate whether Surrealism was a sexist movement or not. I'm hanging onto her every word, spellbound both by what she's saying and the ardour on her face as she talks about a subject that is obviously very close to her heart. I'm not surprised when, at one point in the conversation, she lets slip that she has aspirations to be an artist herself, even if her acting career pans out.

One of the last works we see before we head off for afternoon tea is an amazing 'soft sculpture' by Dorothea Tanning, *Nue couchée*. Carlotta is overjoyed to finally see it in the flesh, as it were: she says she's been a fan of the artist for a long time.

'She still working now,' she says. 'She start to work

with Surrealists in 1930s and become famous with topless self-portrait in 1942. She still live creative life.' She lets out a barely audible sigh.

Nue couchée is a remarkable work – a 3D female nude made up of cotton, cardboard, wool and table tennis balls, covered in pink crêpe. As an artwork, it's incredibly tactile – especially where the rounded protusions of the balls suggest a string of vertebrae and at the swell of the almost outrageously voluptuous hips – and Carlotta can't resist reaching down for a squeeze when she's made sure the guard isn't looking our way.

'There was once,' she says, 'an exhibition in gallery in New York, and this sculpture was placed on a low table – plinth, you call it? – and protect by Perspex. Tanning say it remind her of a scene in a adult fairy tale from Victorian time, when hero goes into a cave and finds block of alabaster in which he see beautiful sculpted woman. He bring her to life by singing to her, but it turns out she an evil spirit who nearly lure him to his death.'

She rises from where she was crouching beside the piece. 'Just look at it,' she whispers reverently. She turns her head to me and then back. 'Only a woman truly know a woman's body,' she says, and there's wistfulness in her voice.

I can't help but risk a glance at her face. She's still looking down at the piece, but her thoughts are clearly elsewhere. Whoever she's thinking of, it's not Paco, no matter what he did to her last night, how many times he made her come.

A rumble from her belly breaks the spell, and we laugh and agree that it's time to refuel. We descend to Level Two, where the lunchtime crowds have thinned out and we can look out over the Thames and see the shiny Millennium Bridge stretching over to St Paul's

Cathedral like a silver spinal cord. We order chocolate muffins and lattes, and I confess to Carlotta that I forgot that Paco had told me she'd been an artists' model.

'I was young then,' she says, with a half-smile of nostalgia. 'I start when I was seventeen and go on for about two years. It was wonderful, most times, but I very naïve. I am ... taken advantage of, in many ways.'

'Do you regret it?'

'Not at all. But artists are – let say, egomaniac. Everything revolve around them and their work. In the end, you just a piece of flesh.' She sighs. 'You never get away from that.'

'Sounds like you had some hairy moments,' I say.

She chuckles throatily. 'You can say,' she says, taking a nibble from a muffin. She stares out across the river. 'I not say names,' she says, 'but there is one time, I am posing for a quite famous artist in his sixties. He painting giant canvas of me, going up to ceiling of his studio, so he has to use ladder. It take forever, because he climb up, and look back, and find something not right and come back down and change me. I am just dying of boredom after few days. And I am cold, and hungry, and just smoking until I hoarse.'

She picks up her cup, blows on her latte. 'After about two weeks, he up his ladder and happy painting, for once, and because I say he must bring in electric heater for me, I'm all warm and I don't know it but I'm falling asleep. Then I wake up, and he standing on ladder with trousers around knees, staring down at me like he dreaming. He got his cock in his hand and he going at himself like madman.'

I've just taken a bite of my muffin, and I'm trying not to splutter it all over Carlotta. 'What did you do?' I croak.

'I lie there, shocked. I not know what *to* do.' She lets

out a guffaw. 'And then,' she goes on, tears of mirth springing into her eyes, 'there is a noise outside, and at the same time we know it must be midday and his wife is bringing our lunch. My famous friend start wobbling on ladder and falls down, with his ass out.'

'His wife saw?'

'Oh yes. She see. And that the last time,' she smirks, 'I model for *him*, and the work is never finish.' She looks thoughtful. 'Shame,' she adds almost ruefully. 'It could have been something.'

'So it wasn't all glamour and starlight?' I say.

'Not at all,' she replies. 'It boring, most of time.' She smiles. 'There are good parties,' she says, 'and I learn a lot about craft of painting. But . . .'

'Why did you do it?'

'Well, there the money, which I use to pay for my own art lessons. And then I maybe, I not know – maybe I think of myself like Anaïs Nin, or Françoise Gilot – she also a painter when she meet Picasso. But I not know, then, about other side of coin. Like Victorine Meurent, who model for Manet's *Olympia*. She said to be his mistress, and die a drunk on streets of Montmartre, where she performing with a monkey to get money. This after having some of her own paintings displayed in a Salon that reject Manet a few years before! Then there Louise Weber, a – how you say? – laundry maid who become a Moulin Rouge dancer and who is in one of Toulouse-Lautrec's most famous paintings. They call her *la goulue* or 'greedy girl' because she always take other people's drinks, and she get too fat to dance can-can and gets sack.'

'Is that why you stopped?' I say.

She laughs. 'Maybe I would have end up a fat drunk,' she says. 'But no. I stop because I meet Paco, and he not want me to show my body to other men any more.'

'Didn't you put your foot down? He doesn't *own* you, you know, just because he married you.'

Her brow creases. 'I not have time anyway,' she says, a little defensively, I feel. 'We travel all time, I not commit myself to any project. And then –' she doesn't look convinced by what she says next '– then I decide I'd like to try acting.'

I gaze at her. I can't imagine Carlotta would cut the mustard as an actress: she's too upfront, too open, I suspect, to playact. Her feelings seem to be written all over her face, inscribed in every movement of her lovely body. Most likely it's Paco who suggested she become an actress, as a diversion, knowing full well nothing would come of it.

'Anyway,' she says, 'I not miss it at all. It was like being a doll. A life-size doll, like one of Alma Mahler.'

I look at her questioningly. 'What was that?' I say.

'You not know story of Oskar Kokoschka's doll?'

I shake my head.

'Well, when he come back from First World War, the artist Kokoschka find his mistress, Alma – she was earlier wife of Gustav Mahler and later of Bauhaus architect Walter Gröpius – has left him because their passion for each other too tiring. His revenge is to get made a life-size doll of her, with it own special clothes and underwear by best Parisian houses. Some people say Kokoschka even took doll to opera, although he say that was a wild tale by his maid. So everyone say he must be fucking it too; I suppose that what he want them to think. He draw about thirty portraits of it, and several paintings. That how he exorcise Alma. Then he behead her – the doll, I mean – at a champagne party in his garden.' She giggles. 'I think she a better model than me. At least she never fall asleep on him.'

I'm looking at Carlotta with barely disguised admiration; I could listen to her talk like this all afternoon. The late-afternoon sunlight is filtering in through the large windows, dappling her young, flawless skin. I'm no painter, but I can imagine the way those artists felt as she arrayed herself before them, how they must have had to struggle with themselves to look and not touch. Carlotta has a body that was just made for touching. But she also has a mind, I've discovered this afternoon, that's possibly even more stimulating. Perhaps these two weeks are going to be more interesting than I thought.

In the taxi home, we talk about going to some more galleries over the next few days, but as we near her hotel I sense Carlotta's mood suddenly slumping. I don't think I'm being presumptuous to consider that a friend-ship has begun to blossom between us, so I ask her if anything is wrong, and she tells me she's feeling a little lost at the thought of spending the evening alone. Paco, she tells me, has a business dinner.

She's staring out of the window, her finger tracing vague patterns on the glass, and again I sense the loneliness of being a kept woman in a strange city. It's greater, surely, than that of the single girl: I may not have much, but I do have my work, and my flat, and I have Jess. No Carlotta, I may covet your husband, but I don't covet your life.

'I suppose you have plans . . .' she murmurs, without turning to me.

I hesitate. I have a host of calls to catch up on: with most of my clients American, I deal with a lot of the telephone conversations in the evenings. But I feel sorry for Carlotta, and I tell myself there's no harm in going in for a drink. Just the one.

We sit in the hotel's Russian-themed bar, at the bar itself, swinging our legs and smoking Carlotta's French cigarettes and enjoying the looks the businessmen at the surrounding tables are giving us. It's a buzz, I think to myself, to know that we could just walk over there and spark up a conversation and in ten minutes be up in one of their rooms, being royally fucked. What would Paco think to that?

He thinks Carlotta belongs to him, and so does she. I wonder if she realises her power, the overwhelming aura of sexuality that encircles her like a radioactive glow. She could have anyone she pleases, and Paco would just have to live with that or lose her. What right does he have to forbid her from doing anything that she likes?

It must be the drink, or drinks – for one has inevitably turned into several. Or maybe it's Carlotta's own frankness of earlier today. Whichever, I find myself telling her about the image I've just had of us up there, in one of these men's rooms, kneeling side by side on a four-poster as we are each taken from behind.

She chases a piece of ice around her mouth with her tongue, looks at me without surprise. '*Interesting*,' she says. 'But I never imagine myself with other man. Not now. Why dream when you have lover like Paco?'

She waves at the barman and signs her room tab, then stands up. 'Come up,' she says, and when she sees me demur, adds, '*Go on*. Just for one more.'

I follow her. She's no good at being alone, that's clear, and if I insist on going home I won't get anything done, I'll feel so bad about leaving her here, pissed and aimless. Not that it's my responsibility – I've fulfilled my duties for the day. But I sense that she really does need a friend, tonight at least, and I'm willing to play the part.

It's the first time I've been in the suite since the night with Paco, and despite all the booze I feel a little bit odd stepping in here again, and seeing, through the open door, the bedside chair on which I displayed myself to him. My imprint is here, invisible to Carlotta's eyes: the ghost of me haunts the place unbeknown to her. Some friend, huh?

The mood has shifted a little, become a little more mellow: Carlotta's put on an Ella Fitzgerald CD and kicked off her shoes, and is perusing a stack of books on the huge coffee table.

'Here it is,' she says at last. She leans towards me over the sofa, and I breathe in her scent, glad that the sickly perfume has faded now and it's just her I can smell.

She opens a large glossy art tome and flips through a few pages. 'Victorine Meurent', she says, stopping on a pictured labelled *La Gare Saint-Lazare*, Eduoard Manet, 1874. 'The one who drank herself to death. He pick her up in street,' she says. 'And one day, when she leave his studio, she just disappear. She turn up again six years later: she'd been to America. You can see her in many of his works – this the last one she pose for.'

She's looking at me intently; a sweet, hopeful expression has suddenly blossomed on her lovely face. 'She remind me a little of you,' she says at last. 'I was – I hoping you pose for me.'

'Now?' I'm shocked, and flattered, and confused at once. This is the last thing I was expecting. 'What would I have to do?' I say.

She laughs, a little bitterly it seems to me. 'Oh, just lie like lump of meat,' she says. She turns a few pages, taps a glossy reproduction with one manicured, cerise fingernail.

'*Olympia*,' she says. 'The one I tell you about. I take Paco to see it in the Louvre only few weeks ago. It's hard to imagine it can cause such a scandal.'

I inspect the painting; it's vaguely familiar, but I don't know anything about it. The young model is reclining on her bed. She's naked but for a black ribbon at her slender throat, a chunky gold bracelet, a single slipper and a big pink flower behind one ear. One hand covers her sex. Her black maid is tending a large bouquet of flowers towards her, and by her feet is a rather spiky-looking black cat. It find it far from shocking, and I say so.

'She a prostitute,' says Carlotta, 'in the painting. And in those days you not paint portraits of prostitutes, even high-class ones like this. If you do, you certainly not paint them looking at viewer the way Victorine is, so direct. It was insult to bourgeoisie.'

I nod. 'I can see that it must have been,' I say. Indeed, the model's gaze is one of astounding frankness, combined with boredom. You want me? it seems to say. Then hand over your money and stop all this flowers nonsense. Let's not pretend this is something other than a transaction.

'This the one,' says Carlotta, 'that I like to do.'

I look at her, startled. I wasn't expecting to have to strip off, had no idea that she had a nude in mind. I should have guessed, given her interest in them, but my brain cells are a little pickled from all the vodka and I'm a bit slow on the uptake tonight.

'I go find my sketchbook,' she says, patting the sofa. 'You make youself comfortable. Here is just right.'

I sit in the silence, horribly self-conscious. This is something so new for me, I don't know what's expected of me. Can it really be as easy as just lying here while Carlotta traces my contours, reproduces my features, brings me to life on a piece of paper? Will I be able to bear her sustained scrutiny, the lingering of her eyes on parts of me that relatively few people get to see?

But already she's coming back in, and not wanting to seem a killjoy I stand up and begin to undress. Naked, I lower myself to the sofa and lie back, glancing down at the book on the coffee table to make sure I've got the right position. I adjust myself slightly, look at Carlotta for approval.

'Here,' she says, bending down towards me, sliding a black scarf around my neck and tying it loosely. 'It the best I have.' Then she puts her hands on my shoulders, twists them slightly towards her.

'I think,' she says, turning back and reaching for her notebook and pencil, 'it all in the face. Try to think what she thinking – the prostitute, not Victorine. You looking at someone you despise, but you got to have sex with them and pretend you like it. You know you better than them even though they look down on you, but you need their money.' She pauses. 'I don't know, maybe Victorine thinking same thing. Manet must be bastard if she have to run away to America to get away from him.'

While she's musing, I try to relax, to zone out, to melt into the pose. To think of nothing but the role, although I keep getting mixed up: am I Victorine, or am I the whore? Where did one begin and the other end?

Carlotta grows quiet now, reflective, becoming absorbed fully by her task. Every so often she reaches over and adjusts me just a touch, but it's almost as if she's not seeing me anymore. At least that's how it seems for a while. I feel warm and weightless, and decide that this modelling business is really not so bad after all. But then I'm in a five-star hotel and not some freezing artist's garret.

After a time, Carlotta goes and places her sketchbook down on one of the armchairs where I cannot see what she has drawn and comes back to park herself on the coffee table in front of me. She's holding the bowl of olives she had the butler bring up with our drinks, and she's offering one to me with her fingers. She brings it to my mouth and I suck it in and bite down into it. Then she takes one herself, dabs at it with her tongue.

'It's funny,' she says. 'I not think how much you look like Victorine until I talk about her in café, then I cannot get it out of my mind.'

She passes me a vodka martini from the tray the butler placed on the coffee table, and we clink glasses and sip at them. Behind her glass, her eyes are drinking me in, and I'm surprised to find myself holding her stare. Perhaps I've been infected by the whore in the picture. All my shyness and self-consciousness are gone.

'You have lovely body,' says Carlotta, breaking the silence that has insinuated itself between us, running her eyes up and down me, lingering for a moment on my pruned bush. 'You take care of yourself. I like that.'

I want to repay the compliment, but before I can speak she's walking back to the armchair, taking up her notebook again.

'Back to work,' she says, at my side again.

I resume the pose, but after a few minutes of Carlotta sketching and clicking her tongue against the roof of her mouth, it's clear there's something wrong, and soon she is on her knees in front of me, remoulding me with her hands.

'No like this – like *this*,' she says, frowning, teasing my arm back a little, straightening a leg, tweaking my foot. 'Hmmm, it a bit more ... here like so ... that right, twist it just a little.'

I'm putty beneath her hands, all floppy now from the heat of the room and the last cocktail. I'm worried I'm not going to be able to hold the pose at all anymore, that I'm just turning to liquid beneath Carlotta's hands.

I look at her, helplessly, afraid I'm going to ruin it for her.

But she's stopped now, perhaps drawing the same conclusion, and she's just looking at me, right at me – not at my body anymore, but at my face, into my eyes, searchingly, and her hand has stopped on my hip, and I feel its weight there, feel her fingertips pressing into my flesh, and I realise I *am* turning to liquid, that my pussy is suddenly all wet, and I think, oh my God, what is happening here?

Carlotta jumps up, electrified, and looks towards the door in panic.

'Paco,' she whispers, and I'm up like a cat too, fumbling around for my clothes where I draped them over the arm of the sofa, heart thudding like a jackhammer. Carlotta, meanwhile, is sprinting into the master bedroom with her sketchpad. I follow her and through the doorway I see her yank open the middle drawer of the silver chest and push it inside.

Somehow, before Paco's made it through the vestibule, we're both back on the sofa, fully dressed, breathing calmly, the empty glasses on the table in front of us by the bowl of olives.

'Angel!' exclaims Carlotta as he comes in. 'I not expecting you so soon. I just having last drink with Alicia. We have *such* a lovely day.'

I can't bring myself to look at Paco: the situation is really so absurd, I'm afraid I'm going to burst out laughing and then won't be able to stop until it becomes a kind of very painful hysteria.

'Evening, lovely ladies,' I hear him say. 'What a nice surprise to see you, Alicia,' he says, and I wonder how he can be so blasé. Perhaps, like us, he's had more than his fair share of booze tonight.

'Come sit and tell us all about your evening,' says

Carlotta, patting the space between us on the sofa. 'You go somewhere wonderful?'

'Nobu,' says Paco, stifling a yawn. Before he's reached us, I'm up from the sofa and looking around for my bag, trying hard to hide how drunk I am. I can barely look at either of them as I plead exhaustion and say goodnight, especially as they're already entwined on the sofa, hands all over each other. Within seconds of me leaving, I'd stake a year's pay on it, they'll be screwing each other's brains out on the sofa on which I lay naked just a few minutes ago, juicing up as Carlotta's hand lingered at my hip.

I walk home: it's not so far, and I'm hoping the cool night air will sober me up, put things in perspective. I've never had a lesbian experience, and wouldn't know one if it hit me in the face. Carlotta was just trying to ease me into the right position, and in my vodka haze I mistook it for something else. Having said that, I remind myself, there was that comment by the Tanning sculpture, about only a woman being able to know a woman's body. Was that Carlotta's way of telling me that she's dabbled, that she dabbles?

But what about me? I've never wanted a woman in my life, not even my lovely Jess, and there I was frothing up when she happened to rest her hand on my hip. Was that the alcohol speaking too?

I reach my apartment building, trudge up the three flights of stairs, wanting nothing more than to curl up in a ball but certain that sleep will elude me. Besides, I note from looking at my watch, it's not even nine o'clock yet. I unlock my door, go in, and while the kettle's boiling, log on and read through my emails. There's a number of work-related ones that need attending to immediately, and I make myself a cafetière of coffee and before long have managed to put the whole Paco and Carlotta thing out of mind, for a while at least.

At eleven, just as I'm thinking of turning in, my mobile beeps and I see there's a message – Jess, I say to myself, finally touching base after her night of passion with the barhunk. But it's not from Jess, it's from Paco.

MEET ME TOMORROW PM, it says simply.

I text right back. CARLOTTA?

GET RID OF HER, comes the reply.

I swear under my breath. What the hell am I going to tell her? We have plans – the National Gallery, then the Zandra Rhodes Fashion Museum in Bermondsey. What does he expect me to tell her?

I think of Jess, of what she would say. Tell him where to stick it, or words to that effect. He might be paying you, but he doesn't own you. Another version, in a way, of what I told Carlotta earlier today.

And I promised her too, Jess, that I'd put a stop to it all, that I wouldn't sleep with Paco again. That, however, was before the taxi ride with Carlotta, when I realised, as she boasted to me of his prowess, that I wouldn't be happy without one last mindblowing fuck with him.

Think, think, I'm saying to myself under my breath, and then I have it and I'm reaching for the phone and calling Carlotta's hotel, where I ask to be put through to the spa and book her a two-hour aromatherapy massage for two o'clock tomorrow.

Pleased with my brainwave, I run myself a lavender-infused bath and climb in, wondering how tomorrow afternoon is going to pan out. In my mind's eye I sort through my underwear drawer, trying to decide what I should wear. What was it Carlotta said Paco likes best: stuff you can see right through? There's my black Calvin Kleins, but I was wearing those last time. How about the tan ones? They're pretty sexy. And on top my floaty black Ghost dress with the low ruched cleavage – feminine but classy. There's no point in trying to make myself into Carlotta: she's one in a million.

I'm just soaping my tits when I hear the phone ring, but I know the answering machine's still on so I let it click through. I'm barely even listening when something about the voice catches my attention and I'm leaping out of the bath and skidding all over the polished floorboards with my wet feet in a desperate bid to pick up before the caller hangs up. But I'm too late: I pick the handset up just in time to hear the line go dead.

'Fuck,' I almost scream, hitting the replay bottom. And there it is, that West Coast drawl I've heard so often in my dreams over the last five months, that lazy, laidback, unspeakably sexy, honeyed drawl. I listen to it once, and then I sit down on the sofa and I listen again, feeling all shivery and heated up at the same time.

'Alicia,' he begins. I know it off by heart by now. 'It's Dan, Dan Lubowski. You probably don't even remember me.'

Oh yes I do, Daniel. Oh yes I do.

'You did me a tour, a while back, in April, I think it was. A movie tour. And I'm passing through town tomorrow and I wondered if we could meet up? If you could do me another? Here's a number you can reach me on.'

I finally come to my senses, after listening to the message five times, and scribble the number down on a piece of paper. Then I go into the kitchen and pour myself a large glass of red wine.

Back in the living room, I switch off the light and sit in the semi-darkness, my heart galloping away inside me. I'd come to think I'd never hear his voice again, never mind him calling me to arrange another meeting. I feel like a schoolgirl on the verge of her first date – prey to a kind of delicious terror. I should be angry, but somehow the mere sound of his voice has magicked away all the pain and confusion and all I want is to see him again as soon as possible.

I take a hefty swig of wine, put the glass down on the floor and start punching in the number, screwing up my eyes in the dim light cast by the streetlamp beyond my window. It's a long one, I think, but the code's not American. A female voice answers almost immediately, heavily accented, and when I ask for Mr Lubowski she says she will put me through. The phone rings a few times. He's gone out, I think. I left it too long.

Then he answers, and I'm struggling to speak, my throat constricted. 'It's – it's Alicia,' I finally manage to say. 'I just got your message.'

'Alicia,' he says softly, and I feel a warm glow spread right through me. 'How *are* you?

'Fine. Fine.' I'm struggling to find something to say.

'That's great. I've often – often wondered.'

Then why haven't you bloody well called? I want to shout, but I don't. We had a fuck, a couple of fucks, he owed me nothing, owes me nothing. We talked vaguely of other tours but nothing was fixed. He paid me handsomely. Why *would* he have called?

'How's business?' he says. 'What's been going on with you?'

He sounds genuinely interested, and before I know it I'm chatting away to him, the ice broken, the anger dissipated, telling him about my summer and about some of the nutty American clients I had, the teens full of attitude and the camera-toting clichés. He's laughing, and asking more questions, and I remember why I fell for him for quickly, so hard. Then I ask him how he has been, and he starts telling me about a film that he's been involved with that required several months of shooting in the wilds of Alaska, and that was beset by numerous post-production problems that ate up most of his summer. I decide, not knowing whether I really believe it or not, that's nevertheless reason enough to forgive him.

I take a sip of wine, put my glass back down. I'm listening to him, trying to picture his face again, and all of a sudden I get that image of him with his head thrown back on the old boardroom table, gasping as I shoot one buttery finger up his arsehole and he sheds his load.

Wedging the handset between my ear and my shoulder, I pull open my towel and start fingering my pussy. I do it slowly at first, but just the sound of his voice is sending me out of control, and soon I'm lying back on the sofa rubbing frantically at my clit. It's not long, inevitably, before I'm biting down on my knuckles to suppress my moans as I come, savagely, almost painfully, thinking of nothing but his beautiful cock inside me, of his mouth on mine.

There's a silence on the other end. 'Alicia, you OK?' says Daniel after a minute.

'Uh huh. I was just – just reaching for a cigarette and nearly dropped the phone.'

'Well, listen, I'd best let you get to bed,' he says. 'It's late, and you're a working girl. The reason I rang so late,' he adds, 'is that I'm in Paris now but I'm in London for lunch tomorrow and I wondered if you could could maybe squeeze me in for a tour in the afternoon, before I fly out?'

I grit my teeth. Why does it have to be tomorrow, I

think, when already I'm running between Paco and Carlotta like a fucking lunatic?

'It was just on the off chance,' he says in response to my hesitation. 'I guessed you'd probably be booked up.'

'No, hang on a sec!' My mind is racing, trying to work out how I'm going to do this. I *have* to see him, yet at the same time I know I mustn't seem desperate. In any case, the imperious Paco is not going to let me off lightly; my only option there would be to pretend that I'm ill and cancel my morning outing with Carlotta too. But I'm just too professional to pull a stunt like that. It's just not me.

'OK,' I say calmly, as if I'm flicking through my diary. 'I have morning and afternoon tours, but I'd love to meet you in-between.'

'No can do,' says Daniel. 'I've got a lunch, remember.'

'Oh yes. OK, how about two o'clock? Will you be out by then? We can meet for a quick drink before I start my afternoon tour.'

We agree to meet at Mash on Great Portland Street, which gives me just enough time to drop Carlotta off for her massage and run a couple of blocks to him. I'll tell Paco I can't make it until three – in fact, I'll deliver him an outright lie and tell him that Carlotta is having just an hour's massage from three. That gives me an hour with Daniel. It's not enough, but it's the best I can do. Whatever is going to happen in that hour is in the hands of fate.

11

Of course I hardly sleep, and the face that greets me in the mirror is not the one I want Daniel to be gazing at this afternoon. But there's not much I can do about that now, beyond smear some MAC Studiofix concealer under my eyes, be a little more inventive with my makeup than usual, and pick up a raw apple, carrot and beetroot juice on my way to a late breakfast with Carlotta in the club lounge of her hotel. There, some strong coffee and fresh berries perk me up a bit more.

Carlotta herself is looking all pink-cheeked and radiant, and I wonder if she's just had a bath or been in the steam room, or whether it's a post-coital flush. The thought, for the first time, doesn't bother me. I'm impatient for this morning to be through. What Carlotta's husband has been doing to her is the last thing on my mind.

I tell her, to get it out of the way, that I've got an urgent, unexpected meeting with my accountant that afternoon and have booked her in at the spa. She's fine about it, says that one can never have too many massages, although she also takes the opportunity to point out that she's never met anyone who can do it like Paco. I don't feel much like talking about Paco, but in any case she changes the subject, and instead begins complimenting me on what a great model I was last night.

'So natural,' she says, folding her lips around a raspberry. 'I can't believe you never do it before.'

I suddenly realise I didn't see the result, in the pandemonium that followed Paco's impromptu return, and ask her if I can have a look at it sometime.

She looks at me, all big-eyed and apologetic. 'I not want to, Alicia,' she says, 'but I have to destroy it. I worried Paco might find it.'

I study her face, wondering what she's afraid of – Paco knowing that she was drawing me naked, or him knowing that she was drawing at all? Did he stifle more than her career as a model? Did he stifle her artistic dreams too? Or is it that Carlotta has, as I am starting to suspect, certain inclinations that she doesn't want Paco to know about? Suddenly I realise how much there is that I don't know about this couple who have drawn me into their orbit, entangled me in their lives.

After breakfast we head for the National Gallery. This time we make our way round fairly randomly, although Carlotta gravitates towards nudes again. Her favourite, by far, is Renoir's *A Nymph by a Stream*, which, she tells me, reminds her a little of Victorine Meurent, and, by extension, of me. The theme, she tells me knowledgably – the association of the female body with the primal forces of nature, here represented by the water and the mossy bank and grasses on which the wide-eyed model lies – is a traditional one in French art.

The one I find most fascinating, on the other hand – or perhaps the most compellingly uncomfortable – is Bronzino's *An Allegory with Venus and Cupid*. The erotic but erudite subject matter, we read on the plaque, endeared it to François I of France, who once owned it. Its foreground is dominated by Cupid kissing Venus, a hand on one of her breasts, but the painting is haunted by other faces half-hidden in the shadows around the main figures, contorted faces representing other facets of love – Fraud, Jealousy, Despair, Folly and Oblivion.

I'm aware that Carlotta is watching me as I examine it, and I sense that I have awakened her curiosity. 'It not so happy view of love,' she says at last. 'You think love like that?'

'I don't think so,' I say, not at all offended by her probing, and marvelling at how perceptive she can be. 'Deep down,' I tell her, 'I'm as romantic as they come.' I think of Daniel, of my hopes for this afternoon. 'I'd like to believe in happily-ever-after,' I say.

Carlotta smiles. 'I sure you get it,' she says. She gives my arm a little squeeze. 'You deserve it. You so lovely.'

Over coffee afterwards I listen to her talking animatedly about two male nudes we've seen on our journey through the galleries. The first was an *académie*, which, as Carlotta explains, means an anonymous life study made as part of the curriculum of a classical art training in early-nineteenth-century France. It was a naked man seen from behind, and as she looked at it Carlotta had compared it aloud to Paco's lithe, athletic dancer's body. I'd had the same thought but not been able to voice it, for obvious reasons.

We agree on another thing, and that is that Gustave Caillebotte's *Man at his Bath* is, in some ways, even sexier. The guy in it is pale and a good deal stockier, lacking Paco's grace, but the sense of domestic intimacy, of a glimpse into a private moment, makes it a turn on.

'It like Dégas' bathers,' says Carlotta, tonguing the froth on her cappuccino. 'It make us all into voyeurs; that the point. But a domestic male nude like that is rare, even shocking, at time.'

We discuss the shock value of art for a while, how we've become deadened to it, for better or worse, but I find myself more and more distracted now, and am constantly shooting glances under the table at my watch, counting down the minutes until I see Daniel. Finally, at twenty to two, anxious not to be a second late for my big date, I bundle us into a taxi and head back to Langham Place, where I deposit Carlotta at the spa and set out on foot for Mash.

I'm a little early, which is fine, because it gives me the opportunity to refresh my makeup in the loos and have a quick brandy to dampen my nerves. Then I pop a mint in my mouth, order a mineral water and place myself on one of the retro-futuristic chairs in a pose that, I hope, looks both alluring and effortlessly casual.

Half an hour later I'm still sitting there, only now I'm on my third brandy and I'm deflating rapidly, slumped in my seat. Every few minutes I look idiotically at the display screen of my mobile, though I would hear it if it rang or beeped a message. Thirty minutes is not so late in London, where everyone's always getting stuck in traffic or in a tube tunnel, but time is ticking away – I have to be with Paco in another half-hour, and there's no way I can fake illness now Carlotta's seen me and knows I'm fine.

At ten to three I give up on my dreams of Daniel Lubowski. He wasn't interested enough to call me after those two nights together, and he's not interested enough to keep our date. Something better came up, no doubt. I pay for my drinks, push open the heavy glass doors and head back to Langham Place, the bitter taste of the brandy still on my lips.

12

There's more booze at the hotel, in the Infinity Suite, where Paco awaits me. He's actually on the phone when I tap on his door, but he waves me towards two flutes of champagne set on a little silver tray on the coffee table, and I take one gratefully. I stand in the window, look back at him on the sofa, one leg crossed over the other, his ankle swinging jauntily. Seemingly unthinkingly, he starts fiddling with the remote control as he rattles away in Spanish, and the flatscreen TV flickers into life to show him, Paco, strutting his stuff.

I watch, mesmerised. For all I know about him from the gossip rags, I've never actually seen Paco dance, and it's true what I've read of him: he's fiery, expressive, thrilling. He positively burns, in this most passionate of dance forms, with sensuality.

Paco finishes his call, and for a moment we remain in silence, watching the rest of the performance.

Like I said, I'm no dance expert, but the combination of fleet footwork, graceful arm and hand movements, and – most of all – the surprising vibrancy of his naked upper body, which has an almost sculptural quality to it, are dazzling. The long flowing locks he had back then add to the full-bodied drama of the spectacle.

'What do you think about?' I say at last, flicking my eyes from the image on the screen to Paco in person and back again, unsure which is the most compelling, unable to believe that I'm here with him. That I was *summoned* by him. 'What do you think about when you're dancing?'

'Nothing,' he says without hesitation, looking back at me. 'You don't have room in your head for anything that's not your body, or the music. When you're dancing flamenco, you use every part of your body, and co-ordinating your hands, arms, feet, legs and upper body is pretty demanding.' His eyes roam beyond me, fix on something out of the window.

'I don't know,' he continues musingly, 'whether that's not part of the attraction for me. You can leave everything else behind you, in the dressing room. You go into another world – a dark, mysterious, almost operatic world with a language all of its own. Where there's only the music and the beat of your blood in your veins. It's pretty intense.'

'So it's an escape, of kinds?' I hesitate. 'Like sex?' I add shyly.

'Definitely, although when I started out I was too young to understand that aspect of it.'

'How old were you?'

'Just nine. I lived in Seville then, and my parents took me to visit my cousin in Madrid. He was a well-known flamenco dancer, and it was he who inspired me to begin. A few years later I started training in classical ballet and that held my attention for a few years. That's when I went to the States, to train in Chicago with one of the greats for several years. But it was to flamenco that I returned after my apprenticeship. I had turned into an American boy, but I became Spanish again.'

I'm looking at the screen again, fascinated by the sinuous contortions of his bare chest as he moves. 'How much of it is made up as you go along?' I ask.

'Improvisation is considered essential,' he replies.

'There are certain rules and constraints, but they are not as many or as rigid as in ballet. In fact, a flamenco piece will never be performed exactly the same way twice. That's the whole point, in a way – its very essence is passion. Its movement is supposed to be a reflection of life itself. So depth of expression is crucial.' He pauses, then goes on. 'Many people think flamenco is lighthearted. An entertainment while you're eating your paella. But *cante jondo* – the "profound song" – is the music of the persecuted poor, who developed it out of need and hardship, to convey the pain of life.'

'Then it's not about sex at all?'

He laughs. 'It's sensual – that can't be denied. But more than anything, it's spiritual. At its best it's as powerful as a religious experience. Probably because of what it started out as.'

'Which is what?'

'Well, opinions differ, but it probably had its seed in ancient and sacred Hindu dances, which were influenced by Greek, Roman, Egyptian, Arab and Jewish cultures as Gypsy peoples passed through various countries. Finally they came to Andalucian Spain, and flamenco was born of the meeting of the two cultures.' Abruptly he stands up, flicks off the set with the remote, with a dismissive 'Anyway, enough of all that.'

I'm still standing in the window and I don't shift as he comes over to me. Putting his hands on my waist, he looks into my eyes. 'I'm glad you came,' he says.

I want not to succumb, but I'm weary and tipsy and more than a little heartsore, and so I bring my own hands to those hips I've just seen moving so fluidly, and then I just find myself falling into him. And he takes me in his arms as he did when he lifted me from the bathroom floor a couple of nights ago and carries me over into the guest room, where he lays me out on the bed with the flourish of a bullfighter with his cape. This is a man who knows the value of drama.

There's the same sense of urgency as the first time we fucked, but I don't know if that's us or the fear of Carlotta returning early from the spa, or just my sense of despair at having been stood up by Daniel, making me give myself so ardently to Paco in solace. It's funny to think of it: this international sex-god and shagger of supermodels being used as some kind of consolation prize by a humble tour guide, but that's how it is, this time at least. Everything I told myself about having to have him just one last time, and it turns out not to be about him at all.

Still, I enjoy it, the feel of this hotblood's hands on me, sure, expert, pulling up my breasts to his mouth. The rhythmic thrust of him, the way his cock fills me, his hips snaking from side to side, sending wave after wave of delicious friction through me. He takes control, as if he's at the helm of a ship, steering me, directing the pace. It's as if I'm not really involved, in some ways; as if he wants nothing more of me than for me to hold on and enjoy the ride. And pretty soon I'm coming, coming hard, biting down onto his shoulder and then falling back as the contractions subside, watching him pull back and direct his jet of come all over my belly with a satisfied yelp.

There's no lingering afterwards, no post-coital cigarette or chit chat. I'm washing and dressing hurriedly, checking my watch to make sure I'm not late for Carlotta, and he's all businesslike too, taking a call that comes through on his mobile even as he's wrapping a towel around his waist and heading for the shower. He looks over as he's about to disappear, waves and mouths 'See you later', and that's that. Paco and I are through. I still haven't told him that, but something tells me the news won't break his heart.

Five minutes later I'm standing in front of Carlotta in the spa. She's reclining on a lounger in a fluffy bathrobe, flicking through a copy of Spanish *Vogue* as she sips a cup of herbal tea. For a moment she doesn't see me, and I have time to admire her without all the warpaint, all fresh and girly. Her skin is dewy, almost edible-looking.

She looks up at me, smiles. '*Holà*, Alicia,' she says.

'How was your massage?' I ask.

'Wonderful, thanks,' she purrs. 'How your meeting?'

I shrug. '*Comme çi, comme ça.*'

'Boring, no? Poor you. Well, I not in a hurry to leave this place now. Paco's busy all afternoon, he say. So why you not come and have swim with me? The pool is empty last time I look.'

'I'd love to, but I don't have anything to wear.'

'That not a problem,' she says, rising slowly and walking over to the reception, languid as a cat. She looks at the receptionist behind the desk.

'You please send up to my room for bikini?' she says. 'My maid know where they are. Tell her the gold one is good. And my friend need to sign in as guest.'

That done, we're off down the stairs, where a little pool glitters invitingly beneath muted lighting in a former bank vault. Like Carlotta said, it's deserted, as is the big Jacuzzi tub set on a little mezzanine overlooking it. Carlotta points out the changing rooms, and we head inside, choose a pair of lockers and strip off.

You must be wondering how I'm feeling at this moment, what thoughts are running through my mind. After all, I've just come downstairs from Carlotta's suite and a rampant fuck with her husband. Well, perhaps my brain can't cope with the enormity and complexity of it all, but I'm not feeling as terrible as you might think. A bit numb and spacey, actually – maybe a combination of the booze and the orgasm. But not really *guilty*. That, I guess, will set in later, when I get home and have the leisure to look back on my day a little more soberly. I'm not looking forward to that, not at all – to my cold, dark, empty flat, and the sofa where I lay last night, pleasuring myself to the sound of Daniel's voice. I'll stay here as long as Carlotta will have me.

Carlotta's maid arrives, two teensy-weensy scraps of coppery material in her hands. Carlotta takes them and hands them to me.

'Versace,' she says, with obvious relish. 'I last wear it on beach in Rio.' She giggles. 'It very popular.'

I laugh too, a tad nervously, but less at the thought of Carlotta wowing them on some Brazilian beach than because of the strange little frisson I feel as I pull the bikini pants up over my hips and lower my pussy into the gusset that has encased her own on at least one occasion. I can't help but touch myself when I'm sure she's not looking, at the swell of my aroused clitoris.

Carlotta turns around just as I'm struggling with the tie on the back of the bikini top.

'Here,' she says, stepping up to me. 'You should ask me do that.' She fastens it dexterously, then spins me round and lets out a low whistle from between her cosmetic-white teeth. 'You are *fabulosa*,' she says.

Carlotta has somehow squeezed herself into a post-age stamp of a metallic lilac bikini with thong-style bottoms. God knows how drastic a waxing she must have had to dare to wear something like that, but I'm thinking she must have gone the whole hog: a Holly-wood. It's something I've often considered but never quite had the guts for; I'm worried I'd feel a little exposed.

Carlotta passes me a fluffy towel from the pile and we head downstairs and plunge into the pool. It's a good temperature: not too hot for lap swimming. Soon we're both doing energetic lengths. We're side by side to start with, but then Carlotta – who's a real water baby, I soon see – is outpacing me.

I settle into my own rhythm, surrender to the feel of the water on my limbs, trying to let my mind drift away, alight on nothing – not Daniel, not Paco and Carlotta, not on my empty flat. For a while, I almost succeed, and then I see that Carlotta has stopped and is waving me over to her.

She's leaning against the pool edge, kicking her legs out in front of her. 'I going up to Jacuzzi,' she says. 'Come find me when you done.'

I do another few lengths and then I go upstairs and join her where she's luxuriating in the tub.

'This is the life,' I say, clambering in.

She looks at me seriously, perhaps even appraisingly. 'I suppose you get a lot of extras in your job,' she says.

'It's not bad,' I smile. 'There are ... *opportunities*.'

'I bet there are.' She's smirking now, and I realise too late I chose the wrong word. The same expression crosses her face as when she was looking at the Caillebotte nude bather: more than a little lustful. She relaxes back against the side of the tub, letting one hand drop below the water's surface.

'Have you ever ... ?' She stops, runs her tongue over her top lip.

I frown a little, make out I don't understand, and she knows she's onto something and is at me like a terrier its prey.

'Come on, Alicia,' she chides. 'We friends now. Have

you ever been –' she pauses for the right word ' – *seduced* by a client?'

I suppose, partly, it's to stop myself feeling guilty about Paco that I start blathering on about Daniel, although there's no doubt that, like all lovesick people, I'm actually rather grateful to find someone willing to listen to me harp on about the object of my affections. I find myself telling her everything – the tour, the screening room, the dining table, the hot chocolate waiting for me on the bedside table, the boat on the Serpentine. I even confess – though it's actually a lie – that I trumped up my accountant's meeting for *him*, that I booked her in here to go off and meet him, only to be stood up. It was sort of true, in the end.

Bless her, Carlotta listens and nods and smiles sympathetically in all the right places, and I actually start to feel that yes, this woman is a friend to me. She's not even cross that I fibbed to her. In fact, she says she'd have done just the same thing under the same circumstances, that *love* – that's the word she uses – comes before everything.

I'm not even sure I am in love with Daniel. I've only met him once, really, which is not a good basis for anything. But like I said before, I felt comfortable with him. He made me laugh, he was on my wavelength, and I thought there, at last, was someone I could see myself snuggling up in bed to watch old movies with, getting old with. What a fool I was. I was just another notch on one of a thousand designer bedposts around the world.

Talking helps, and I tell Carlotta so, and she reassures me, tells me all will be well, that if it wasn't meant to be, that the right man will come along, and so on and so forth. They're platitudes, of course, but sometimes platitudes can console, can invoke an image in your mind of a universe where everything has a reason, where everything works out for the best. We all need to believe those things, once in a while.

We grow silent, each lost to our private thoughts about love and fate. I lean back and adjust my position until the jets are pummelling me. Immediately I feel myself begin to slacken and relax as the tension is worked from my muscles. I close my eyes. Perhaps I will sleep well tonight after all.

I give myself up, picturing the different areas of my body as the jets pry at them like eager fingers. My lower back, my shoulders, my hands, the soles of my feet, my inner thigh . . .

My eyes open. I look down, then up at Carlotta. Her eyes are closed too, and there's a warm sleepy smile on her face. Her arm is moving from side to side, and I'd bet a million pounds I know where her hand is.

And where her foot is for that matter. I jump up, reach for my towel, and Carlotta's beautiful eyes flutter open, hold mine fast.

'Where you going?' she says in a lazy, clotted voice. Her arm, I notice, has not stopped moving. I can't handle this.

'I'm overheating,' I say. 'I'll see you back in the changing room.'

By my locker I stand embarrassed, perplexed, wondering if I overreacted. Was that really Carlotta's foot creeping up between my legs, and even if it was, did she know where it was straying? The girl was clearly having a bit of sneaky pussy play; she probably wasn't paying too much attention to what was happening to her feet.

I sit on the bench for a while, and when Carlotta doesn't show up I decide she's probably enjoying herself too much to get out. I'll kill some time in the steam room. I've never used one but have always wondered what they're like.

Bloody hot, is what they are. I guess that goes without saying. But it's a kind of heat you would probably only experience in nature at midday in a tropical forest at the height of summer. The ferocious dry heat of a sauna seems almost bearable next to this fuzz of hot steam and floating water. Your every pore is open and your lungs feel like they're filling and it's like you're drowning and suffocating all at once.

I lie down on my towel, wriggle out of Carlotta's bikini, thinking that might make me more comfortable. It will get more bearable in a moment, I keep telling myself, and besides, all the sweating will be great for expelling the toxins from my body. But the booze must still be in my bloodstream, combining with the heat to rapidly send me into some kind of trance.

It's all I can do to open even one eye when I hear, muffled by the steam, the click of the door. I turn my head with effort, peer through the clouds, but see nothing. Something else I must have imagined. I open my eye again, not convinced, and she's there, naked, in front of me – the divine Carlotta.

The first thing I notice – I can't really miss it given that her bush is on a level with my face – is that she's got a Brazilian, like me, rather than a Hollywood. So there's a fuzzy little strip of pale hair reaching from the top of her mons down to where her lips begin. From between the latter protrudes a fat purplish clit, like a little questing tongue.

In fact, that's all I have time to notice before Carlotta's swung one leg over me where I lie and is straddling me. As I feel the pressure of her groin on mine, she falls forward, and somewhere in amongst the cloud of blonde hair that falls about my head and shoulders I feel her mouth on my neck, on my earlobe, on my own mouth. I open mine, and our tongues and teeth slurp and clash as we almost eat at other's faces.

Then she breaks away, sitting up on me, and I open my eyes and realise I can't even see her face, can't see her shoulders or her breasts through the thick steam. There's just this little rounded belly and that beautiful blonde cunt.

I'm reaching out for her but I don't have a clue where to begin. She must know that, must know I'm a novice where this is concerned. At a loss, I bunch two fingers together and slip them between her pussy lips, rub gently at that clit resembling the bud on some huge flower.

'That's it,' she encourages. 'Only harder.'

I increase the pressure at the same time as I feel her mashing herself down on my fingers, rocking back and forth. I feel a little braver, reach further between her legs and gently dab my fingers at the pink frill of her sphincter. Meeting no opposition, I slip a finger inside, while with the other hand I take her clitoris between my thumb and forefinger and give it a little tweak. She squeals, starts juddering backwards and forwards. I put another finger up her arse, start thrusting, and I'm amazed when she throws back her head and the muscles of her throat bulge and then slacken repeatedly as she gives voice to her rapture, arms folded behind her head, breasts shuddering like jellies on a plate.

Lesbianism, I'm thinking to myself as she sits panting on top of me, trying to catch her breath, is really just a matter of doing unto others as you do to yourself. Unlike with men, you have the advantage of knowing first-hand what a woman's body likes, what gets her going, which buttons to push when she's burning for an orgasm and won't take no for an answer. After all, if you don't come up with the goods, she's perfectly able to sort herself out – maybe with a little help from a vibrator in one or other orifice, though it's surprising what you can achieve with your own fingers and a little imagination.

Speaking of which – Carlotta has recovered from her shock at being brought to a juddering climax by a novice lesbian in about five seconds flat and is repaying the compliment with a two-pronger approach on my own arse and pussy from behind. She's flipped me over onto the tiled bench, and my breasts are squidging and sliding and slapping around on the wet surface as she pushes in and out, thumb in my arsehole, two fingers in my cunt. And then three, and then four. Slowly she leans down on top of me, reaches round me and cups one of my breasts in her palm, clamps the nipple between her fingers. In-between nibbling at my shoulders, she's moaning in my ear: 'Licia. Oh, 'Licia.'

We slink and slide against each other like this for a while, and then she says, more forcefully, 'Touch yourself, baby. Your clitoris.'

I bring my hand down, gently tease apart my upper lips with thumb and index finger to give my middle finger the best purchase on my little pink nub. The stimulation of my nipple, my clit, my cunt and my arsehole all at once is a rare occurrence and proves too much – my climax rips through me with the force of an explosion, leaving me heaped on the bench like a ragdoll. Meanwhile, above me, on top of me, Carlotta is so excited she's frigging herself off again, and in spite of all the moisture in the room I feel her juices leaking all over my back when she starts to buck and scream. As she does, I roll myself underneath her and ease my hand into her in time to feel her contracting around the fist I make of it.

Then suddenly she's quiet, flopped over me, my hand still inside her, feeling the pulses of her orgasm die away like a ship's beacons as it travels out into the night, bound for strange shores. Her breath is ragged, ruined, in my ear. I hold her to me, like a child in need of consolation. I think she may be crying, and I wonder if I will too.

We're subdued, afterwards, in the club lounge of the hotel, where a complimentary afternoon tea is laid on. I was all for rushing away, but Carlotta insisted we talk about what has happened between us. And she's right – if I ran home and avoided the issue, I'd spend all night worrying about facing up to her again. Far better to get it all out in the open, set out our respective stalls.

I'm expecting Carlotta to tell me it was all a big mistake, that it mustn't happen again, especially given her serious expression as she toys with her plate of fancy little cakes and fiddles with her teaspoon. And all considered, that would be the sensible thing to do. She's married, and I'm her husband's employee, for the time being. The fact that I've been fucking her husband is an extra complication she doesn't need to know about.

'Listen,' she says, avoiding my eyes for a moment, looking everywhere but at me, then suddenly fixing me with an almost pleading gaze. 'I think I need tell you this, but Paco is *not* to know what happen. He – he more vulnerable than he seem, and I think my infidelity will be a knife through his heart. I fear what he do.'

I nod dumbly, heart pounding both at the irony of what she's said and my doubts over my ability to keep myself from breaking into hysterical laughter. But then she surprises me, both by what she says and the way she says it, a little shyly, like a nervous teenager trying to summon up the guts to propose a first date.

'I want to see you again, Alicia. Not – not *just* as my chaperone. I mean as we are just now. I *want* you.'

My belly lurches, and I realise there's no chance I'd turn down the offer of re-experiencing a little of what Carlotta and I had in the steam room. If I'd known it could be that much fun with a girl before, I wouldn't have waited this long.

And then of course there's the flattery of it, of this bronze goddess actively wanting to fuck me, wanting *my* breasts, *my* pussy, *my* arse. Bestowing *hers* on me, like the most precious of gifts. A jewel box concealing rare and priceless gems, glittering beneath my touch. All those men who look at Carlotta's body in the streets, in the bars, in the galleries, as it oozes out of her clingy little dresses. And it's mine for the taking. All mine. And Paco's of course.

I'm thinking all this, and Carlotta must take my dumbstruck silence for a refusal, or at least a hesitation, for in a few moments she leans forwards and whispers, plaintively, like a lost little girl, '*Please*, 'Licia.'

I grasp her hand over the table, lean forwards. 'Of course,' I say, smiling. 'You just try keeping me away.'

At home, a handful of messages await; in among them there's one from Daniel. I tut as I hear his voice; Carlotta has more than distracted me from thoughts of that little rat and his no-show.

'I'm *so* sorry about earlier, Alicia,' he says. In the background I can hear flight numbers being called. 'My jacket went missing at lunch, and with it my cellphone with your number on, not to mention all my credit cards, passport, etc. It was a bit of a panic. Eventually they found it – a long and boring story to do with a cloakroom attendant who'd gone off duty – but when I called your cell it was just going through to messages, and I guessed you must have been with your afternoon client by then.'

Yes, I think bitterly. I was otherwise engaged. In all likelihood I was flat on my back with superstud flamenco dancer Paco Manchega between my legs. Either that, or I was in the spa with his blonde bombshell of a wife, his nubile new bride, feeling the spread of her pussy lips on the small of my back as she climaxed for the second time. So don't worry about me, Daniel. I had more than my fair share of fun. I'm in demand – maybe not by you, but that's your loss.

He's winding up his message with some trite comment about still wanting to do some more tours next time he's in town, and promising he'll take me out to dinner to make up for what happened today, but I can hardly bear to listen and I press the delete button and go on to the next message and decide, once and for all, to forgot about Daniel Lubowski. He hurt me before; he won't do it again.

It won't be hard to forget, I think – not with Carlotta Manchega in my life. It's funny, I muse, that it is her I am falling for and not Paco, given that I've always thought of myself as hetero. Given how gorgeous Paco is. But I feel somehow detached from Paco, whereas I have begun to consider Carlotta a friend, of sorts. Perhaps that's what made the sex so intense.

But soon enough, it occurs to me now, I'm going to have to face up to the fact that she and Paco are going to be heading back to Madrid. I'm hoping, given what she said over afternoon tea, that we'll stay in touch. They're bound to come back to London before long, and when they do I will want to see her. But I won't press her for now: let's see how it goes over the next week before making any plans or promises.

I decide to go to bed early: Carlotta wanted to venture east tomorrow, to see some of the small commercial art galleries such as Victoria Miro and White Cube2. After that, she'd said with a roguish twinkle, we should find somewhere *cosy*.

I pull my duvet up, think of that mass of blonde hair descending on me, of that mouth on me, of those breasts pressing down against mine and that groin – rubbing, rubbing, desperate for me. Bloody hell, I think, I fucked a woman, and not just any old woman, but this amazing creature Carlotta.

I think guiltily of Jess: she left a message too, wants to 'catch up'. I don't even know what happened with her barman yet. But I can't call her now, can't tell her that not only have I broken my promise to her but I've actually been frolicking with both Paco and his wife. She'll go mad, come round to my flat and read me the riot act (albeit wanting to hear all the titillating details about the spa, no doubt). I start to drift off, fingers caressing my pussy, thinking about Carlotta. Jess will have to wait for another time.

In the morning, I wake with the remnants of an orgasm rippling through me, and I know I've just come in my sleep. I sit up, feeling all warm and beatific. I must have been dreaming of Carlotta, I think, and then I have a moment of panic: what if the whole thing in the spa was a dream? What if I never had Carlotta, can never have Carlotta? How will I go on?

But the phone rings, and as soon as I hear Carlotta's voice, the new edge to it, I know that what happened was no dream.

'Let leave the galleries for tomorrow,' she breathes. 'Paco going out in half an hour, for all day. Come here.'

I dress rapidly, tucking my still-damp pussy into a pair of nearly-nude Lejaby knickers that I team with a matching bra. As it doesn't seem we're going to be leaving the hotel at all today and I don't need to look particularly smart, I slip on my skinniest jeans and a sleeveless black T-shirt, with a tailored black cord jacket over the top. I'm in too much of a hurry to bother with a bath or shower, especially when I know my pants will be soaked through with excitement by the time I've got to the hotel. But I take a little time over my hair, brushing it carefully before folding it up into a loose chignon. Afterwards, I feel confident adding the barest hint of mascara and Kiehl's lip balm – my complexion is glowing with health and vitality, unsurprisingly given all this strenuous activity.

Tripping down the stairs in a pair of spike-heeled black ankle boots that I've chosen in favour of the flat pumps I usually wear when working, I rush out into the street and hail a taxi, which takes me across Marylebone and to Carlotta's hotel in five minutes. Asking the driver to pull up on the opposite side of Langham Place from the hotel entrance, I climb out and stand outside the Nash church looking up at the windows of her semi-circular drawing room. I breathe in, savouring the moment, the anticipation. What pleasures await me inside? What new raptures will be mine today?

Suddenly I see Carlotta step up to one of the windows. I gasp. She's naked – at least what I can see of her, from the waist up – palms pressed up to the pane of glass, staring down at me. She brings her hands to her breasts, starts circling her nipples with the pads of her thumbs, smiling. Then she beckons me with her head.

I start running, weaving across the street between lines of oncoming traffic, then dash up the steps into the hotel and through the lobby. In the lift I stand panting, my hand on my heart, fearful that it's going to burst. Nothing I've ever experienced has made me behave like this. Is Carlotta some kind of witch? What has she done to me?

As I approach her suite, the door opens and Carlotta is standing there, framed, resplendent, blonde mane cascading down over bare shoulders. Her nipples are still all bunched up like walnuts from where she was playing with herself. There's a soft white towel around her slender waist, tumbling down to her calves.

'Come in,' she says, taking my hand and drawing me inside, kicking the door to behind us. I go to kiss her but she holds me at arm's length, both hands in mine now, just drinking me in with her eyes. 'This way,' she says at length, and we walk into the drawing room hand in hand.

Straight out she leads me over to the cream couch, where she indicates that I should sit down. As I do so, she arranges a few of the scatter cushions into a pile behind my head and gently pushes me back. Not taking her eyes from mine, she reaches down and unzips my ankle boots, slides them off my feet together with the cashmere socks I had on underneath. Taking my feet firmly in her hands, she begins to massage them, pressing into the soft flesh of my soles, up and down their length. Still looking into my eyes, she brings her face to my feet and takes my toes into her mouth one by one, making me giggle and wriggle as her tongue slides and darts between them like a little fish.

I'm rubbing at my pussy through my jeans, more than ready for her, but she's determined to string me along, I can tell by the slow deliberation of her movements as she stands up and saunters across the room. Beneath her towel her buttocks swell invitingly. I want to get up and chase her across the room, tear off the towel and push her roughly to the ground, then mount her. The only reason I don't is that I know she has something in mind and I don't want to miss out on whatever treat she's got lined up for me.

She disappears into the master bedroom, and I hear her open and shut a drawer. Then she calls back, 'Close your eyes, angel,' and I obey, offering myself up to blackness, to uncertainty. My pussy tingles.

I hear her move back across the drawing room, towards me, and I'm reminded of some big cat moving stealthily in on its prey. The thought excites me, and I squeeze my cunt again through my jeans. Even through the thick denim I can feel my wetness. I can't help but let out a moan. I am so horny I could scream.

Suddenly she's kneeling beside me; I can feel her breath on my neck, and I know that she's turned on too because it's coming fast and irregular.

'Don't open your eyes,' she whispers, her voice choked in her throat, and I feel her hands about my head. Something is being pulled across my face, and the darkness behind my eyelids becomes inkier, a deeper indigo blue.

I feel like I'm falling backwards in space, and I submit myself to the sensation, to the delicious fear of putting myself entirely in the hands of another person, of renouncing myself entirely. At this moment I am just a body, a body that wants, ardently, but that is being controlled by another body, a body being driven by a mind. I shiver with desire: I am Carlotta's plaything, and I have to trust her. I suspect she is going to take us to places neither of us has ever been before.

Her hands are behind my head now, securing the tie,

which I suspect to be the scarf I wore around my neck when posing for the drawing, in place of Victorine's slim ribbon. She does it gently but tightly, so that not a chink of light shows through when I manage to open my eyes a slit. Then she moves her hands down my body, to the lapels of my jacket, which she uses to pull me up towards her. Our mouths touch fleetingly, and I try to kiss her more fully, but she's moved her head before I can plunge my tongue into her mouth in search of hers. Her face is against the side of mine, and I can feel the slightly angular curve of her prominent cheek-bone as she jabs at the peach-fuzz lobe of my ear with her tongue, as she snacks on it with her teeth. At the same time, she's slipped my jacket off my shoulders and, pushing up my T-shirt, is rubbing my nipples through my bra, brushing their nut-hard tips with her thumbs just as she did her own in the window not fifteen minutes ago.

I've never been blindfolded before, and I'm thrilled by how much more intense everything feels when you can't see it, by how your senses are reawakened to familiar textures when you are rendered blind to them. The fluffy towel at Carlotta's hips feels ephemeral as a wisp of cloud beneath my palms, and when I yank it away from her, the skin of her buttocks reminds me of the padded little cheek of a well-nourished baby. I bring my hand round to the front of her, entwine my fingers in the scant tendrils of her bush, fine as spun sugar. They grow slick at once with the dew I can feel seeping from her core.

'Oh God, Carlotta,' I say. 'Nothing . . . has ever . . .'

'Shhh,' she says, placing a finger across my lips, then slipping it inside my mouth. I suck on it like a newborn at a teat. She's moved her other hand down to my crotch, where she pops the button flies one by one, then pushes my jeans and knickers down over my hips. I start as I feel a finger shoot up inside me, pull her closer to me. I want to engulf this woman, somehow take all of her inside me, eat her up whole. The sudden cannibalistic urge surges at me from nowhere and scares me with its wildness.

'Not yet,' she says as I try to pull her in, and she draws her finger out of my cunt. She's sitting beside me on the edge of the sofa, I can tell, but I can't know what she's looking at – my face, desperate with lust, my tits, my pussy, smouldering away for her, oozing all over the place.

'*Please*,' I murmur. 'I can't –'

She leans forwards now, strips off my T-shirt and then reaches round to unclasp my bra. When she does so, I feel her breasts graze my belly, and more juice leaks out of me. I can't help but reach down now and start working at my clit. If Carlotta tries to stop me, I may end up wrestling her off the sofa and onto the floor and taking control of this. I'm finding being at her mercy more difficult than I could have imagined.

She moves down my body, pulls my jeans over my legs and feet, then my knickers. 'Mmmm,' I hear her say, and I feel her grow still.

'What are you doing?' I ask.

'Licking your panties,' she says with a dirty little chuckle.

'Give me yours,' I say, straight out.

'What?'

'Your knickers,' I say. 'It's only fair.'

I hear her jump up, cross the room. In a moment she's back, and I feel her sliding something down over my head, over the blindfold, to the bottom half of my face. On my cheeks I feel the sheen of the material, but across my nose and mouth she's positioned the undies carefully, so that the cotton of the gusset is right against them. All at once my nostrils are filled with the scent of her, a musky, sour-honey aroma similar to that I smell or taste on my own hands when I've been wanking, or that I taste on a lover's penis when I go down on him after we've fucked. I probe it more, sniffing hard to bring more of its essence to the receptors inside my head, and I'm surprised by a sudden manly odour, the sharp salty tang of semen, mixed in with it. Carlotta must have worn these knickers after screwing Paco. I inhale deeply, as if snorting some powerful drug. The two of them at once – now that really would blow my mind.

Carlotta has grown silent, and I wonder what she's cooking up in that filthy little head of hers. 'Where are you?' I say, and I realise there's an almost plaintive note to my voice.

'I'm here,' she says, from an indeterminate point in the room. 'Come and find me.'

I sit up and am immediately disoriented, probably partly because the smell of Carlotta and Paco's melded love juices are still coursing through my brain. I reach out, find only empty air in the immediate vicinity.

'Carlotta,' I say.

'Over here, baby,' she says.

Given what I know of the room layout immediately surrounding me – namely, the large square central coffee table with its hard, sharp corners – I have no option but to slide down to the floor and start moving forwards on my hands and knees. Otherwise, I just know I'd trip over and do myself a serious injury. I giggle slightly as I envisage being tended to by ambulance men on the floor of the suite, naked and blindfolded. How fucking embarrassing would that be?

I kneel up, reach out my right hand and feel the

smooth polished surface of one of the ceramic eggs in the middle of the table. Drawing back my hand, my fingertips brush the glossy cover of one of Carlotta's art books. I inch forward on my knees, confident of my direction, if not the whereabouts of Carlotta. When I'm sure I've got beyond the table, I dare to rise to my feet. Like a ghost in a clunky old horror movie, or like Frankenstein's monster, I walk slowly forwards, arms out before me.

I run up against the rounded wooden edge of the dining table with my belly and grasp it with both hands, as if I've found a port in a storm. Fingertips graze the back of one of my hands, then fingers wrap themselves around it and coax it forwards. The pads of my own fingers meet something frilly, something with almost the texture of young, unspoilt flesh. There's a soft meatiness about it. I open my hand, allow the array of petals to tickle the underside of my palm. Then Carlotta is pushing me gently forwards over the table, and as I inhale the heady scent of fresh roses, her fingers play at my own furled little bud between my buttocks, flitting at it like a hummingbird seeking flower nectar.

Then she turns me around by the shoulders and starts steering me away into the room. I try to keep a tab on the direction we're going in, but in my intoxication I lose my bearings almost immediately. I've just convinced myself we're heading back across the drawing room towards the two deep armchairs facing the dining table when my hips bump against another jutting edge and I'm brought to a halt. At the same time I become aware that beneath my bare feet the baby-soft carpet of the drawing room has given way to cool stone, from which I deduce that we are in the hallway. I've just realised that I must be beside the table supporting the glass sculpture when Carlotta takes my hands and brings them forward to touch it.

One hand on either side, with Carlotta's hands on mine like pale shadows, I caress the sculpture from its sturdy base to its pointed tip. Carlotta's body is pressed against mine, her breasts flattening against my shoulder blades, her bush tickling the point where the ripe fruit of my arse splits. Her breath is almost scalding on my neck, on my ear, as she whispers wicked things to me.

'Feel that,' she says as our hands ascend to the tip once more. 'Feel how smooth and hard and long. Imagine it going up inside you, further than any man ever been. You feel it? You want it? You like cocks?'

'I love them,' I gasp. 'Yes, I want it.'

'You want to be filled up, full of cock?'

'Yes, *yes*.'

'But what about *this*?' she says, prising one of my hands away from the sculpture and feeding it through a slit just above the base. 'What about this hole, here, wide open for you? It turn you on?'

'Oh God, yes,' I say. 'Carlotta, you know it does. More than anything else. Let me take you.'

She spins me around again, leads me back, or so it seems to me, in the direction from which we came, into the drawing room.

I begin pleading with her, try to drag her to the ground so that we can let loose on each other. There's only so much teasing a girl can take. But she keeps leading me, guiding me round a piece of furniture, which I take to be the coffee table again. I'm proven right when she pushes me up and forwards onto one of the aubergine armchairs, with my back still to her. Keeping one palm flat against my lower back, she lifts first my left leg and then my right, so that I am kneeling on each arm of the chair.

Standing back – the more, I suppose, to appreciate the full-on view she has obtained of my arse and pussy – she reaches forwards and runs a single finger from my clit and across my slit and my perineum to my anus. I howl, beg her not to stop.

I feel her body hang a little to the right as if she is reaching for something. I seem to remember that there's an occasional table at the point where the arm-chair and the sofa meet at right angles, but it's in vain that I rack my brains to recall what's on it.

My memory is jogged by the feel of the cold, flawless glass as it rolls down over my sphincter and back across my wide slot, retracing in reverse the route taken by Carlotta's finger a moment ago. It must be the smaller of two ornamental crystal domes that grace the table. As it crushes up against my clit, my right arm shoots out involuntary and meets the larger of the balls. I run my fingers over its polished surface. It feels like a surgically enhanced breast looks – the right basic shape but too hard to be sexy, lacking the essential, delicious squidge factor of normal boobs.

My hunger overwhelms me, and I turn abruptly, ripping off the blindfold. Carlotta, taken unawares, loses her balance and hurtles backwards onto the carpet between the coffee table and the sofa, narrowly missing bashing her head on the sharp corner. She blinks up at me as I loom over her, wondering what to do first, whether to go down on her or to take my own pleasure first. Taunted ragged, I go for the selfish option, lowering myself onto her face. She welcomes me by grasping my hips and pulling me down further, so that I'm worried I might be suffocating her, not to mention drowning her in my nectar. Not that that would be a bad way to go, in the scale of things.

Still clasping my hips, she starts pushing me backwards and forwards, letting me know, I decide, that I can be active in all this, that I don't just have to sit on her face and enjoy myself while she does all the running. I respond by swinging my mound of Venus slowly back and forth, so that her tongue has the opportunity to linger on the pip of my clit for a moment before sweeping across my lips to my hole, dipping in and out before recommencing its journey. A cadence builds up, layer by layer, until pure joy is jagging through me like electricity, and I know it can't be long until I am rocked by the seismic shocks of my orgasm.

Sensing I am near, Carlotta stops her movement to focus on my clitoris with her mouth. My cunt is filled by most of one of her hands, bunched up into a fist, and as my enraptured womb begins to open and close around her, her other hand shoots down between her legs and starts grinding at her own mons. She rears up just as I'm finished, eyes squeezed closed, mouth set in a grimace that testifies to an almost unbearable pleasure. As her contractions die away, she goes floppy beneath me and lets out a long low sob.

We hold each other for an hour or more, then Carlotta gets up and leaves the room, and after a minute I hear a bath running. I climb to my feet, look out of the window in wonder, barely able to conceive that beyond it, in the heart of London, people are going about their everyday lives – shopping, sitting in meetings, lunching with friends – as if the world is the same as it's ever been. Whereas for me, in here, in this fairytale suite with this raunchy Spaniard, everything has changed. Life will never be the same again.

* * *

In the bath I sit between Carlotta's legs and allow myself to float away as she reaches around me and soaps the tender crevices of my cunt, as she takes two good handfuls of breast and gently washes them. With my sleek wet hair back against her chest, I listen to her heart beating, feel it reverberate through the bones of my skull as if it's an echo of my own pulse. Sooner or later, I think, we would fall into synch. And if we lived together, our menstrual cycles would too.

When we've climbed out and towelled each other off, I go to retrieve my clothes from the drawing room. Carlotta dresses in her bedroom, then comes to tell me that I ought to leave, since Paco could be back at any moment. I remind her that he is paying for my time, all day every day for the next two weeks. It's still reasonably early, and if we caught a cab we would have a good run at those galleries she wanted to see.

She confesses that she's exhausted, that the morning's romps have worn her out and that she'd prefer to stay in the hotel and have a little siesta, followed by a swim if Paco isn't back by then.

'You take afternoon for you,' she smiles. 'We do cultural things tomorrow, yes? Here –' She reaches for her snakeskin bag, rustles in it and passes me over a note. It's a fifty. I blush.

'Carlotta, I ca –'

'Take it,' she says, pinning me with her fathomless blue stare.

'But –'

'Buy something special, from me. Why you not go back to Selfridges and buy some lingerie to model for me tomorrow? Something that really get me going.'

We look at each other and giggle. 'OK,' I concur. 'I'll see what I can find.'

Dressed at last and having run Carlotta's hairbrush

through my lust-tangled locks, I head out into the sunlight.

By the time I've reached the street I've done the dirty on Carlotta by pocketing the fifty pounds, mentally adding it to my holiday fund. I'll wear something choice from my undies drawer tomorrow, pretend it's new. What she doesn't know won't hurt her.

I walk home slowly, stopping to do some grocery shopping on Marylebone High Street en route. As I'm filling my basket, I surprise myself by hesitating by the magazine racks, sneaking sly glances up at the top-shelf offerings as I pretend to flick through a copy of *Cosmo*. A line of busty blondes, brunettes and redheads, of Essex girls, Asian babes and black beauties, leer down at me, or smile coyly. Boobs are thrust out awkwardly; their poses look unnatural and highly uncomfortable. I feel a bit dizzy. This is the first time I've felt any interest in this kind of thing. I reach up and grab a mag more or less at random, shove it in among the salad leaves and pasta parcels and eco-friendly dishwasher tablets. On my way to the tills I slip in a few extra and rather unnecessary items in a pathetic attempt to hide it, knowing full well that what goes in must come out.

At the till, I avoid the cashier's eyes when he greets me and look resolutely away when he rings in my grocery items, pretending to be absorbed by a poster on the wall. As the groceries slide to the bottom of the conveyor belt, I pull two plastic bags from a roll and start packing them in. The wank mag comes down nearly last because I'd pushed it to the bottom of the basket. It's face up. I lurch over the belt in an ungainly fashion, grab it and crush it down the side of one of the bags. I'm still avoiding the cashier's eyes as I hand over my credit card and he asks me to punch in my PIN.

I'm home in ten minutes, lying in my bed with a glass of rosé and a tub of Ben & Jerry's on the window-sill beside me, flicking through the mag. A procession of faces simper out at me: look at what I've got, they say. But I see nothing special among the roll call of tits and pussies and arseholes. Nothing that lights my fire. Perhaps, I think, I don't like women after all. Perhaps I only like Carlotta.

And then I turn the page and the fire between my legs is reignited as I take in a blonde vision not unlike Carlottta – real boobs, cute little pussy, blazing blue eyes in a tanned face below peroxide hair. There's the same mixture of tacky wantonness and a weird kind of innocence, the suggestion of secret depths. As on the other pages, this girl's pose borders on the gynaecological – she's prying herself apart with her fingers, cunt agape for the camera. There's no mystery, no eroticism. But there's something in her eyes, as there is in Carlotta's, that sucks you in, almost against your better judgement. Something that promises pleasures you've scarcely even allowed yourself to dream of. It's as if something is beckoning me into a life that goes far beyond the one I imagined, or even hoped, for myself – a life darker, more uncertain, frightening even, but a life richer and worth every risk, every doubt, every moment of anguish.

I sit up, take a swig of the ice-cold rosé and a spoonful of the ice cream, then lie down and slip my hand down the front of my jeans, staring back at the woman as I slide one finger through my moistness and into my pussy. My hand movements get more frantic the longer I gaze into her blue eyes with their curled black lashes. As I climax, however, I close my eyes and it's Carlotta that I see in my mind, smiling that cheeky, flirty smile that makes me melt every time.

I sleep like a parched man drinks at a desert oasis, hard and long, greedily, and I wake late. Feeling fresher than I have in years, I chop myself some fruit and sit out on my balcony, still naked from bed. There's no one visible in the windows of the pub onto which these apartments back, but even if someone could see, I'm not sure I would be bothered, I'm so shorn of all cares. I bite into a slice of pineapple, chew slowly, savouring its slightly sticky sweetness. Then I close my eyes and let the stark sunlight beat down on my lids, flooding my brain with an apricot glow.

I barely register the door of the adjacent balcony open, or only in retrospect, when I hear the voice.

'Morning over there,' it says in a broad Scottish accent, and my eyes pop open.

'Hello Eduardo,' I reply, more than a little wearily, looking over at my neighbour. The idle son of Italian immigrants who made their fortune in ice-cream parlours in Edinburgh, he spends most of his time sunning himself out here, rowing volubly with his girlfriends, or scoping out local talent from a seat on the terrace of the Moroccan bar downstairs.

He's leaning on the railings of his balcony, smiling wolfishly, dressed only in his boxer shorts, hair still mussed from sleep. 'How're you doing?' he says, eyes straying down to get his fill of whatever he can see of me through my own railings.

'Good,' I nod. 'Just having a peaceful breakfast.'

'Fancy sharing?'

I shake my head, incredulous that he can be so slow in taking a hint. Either that, or he just doesn't give up easily. Whatever, I already know that he's an out and out chancer. The whole time I've lived here, he's not let up trying to get into my knickers – when I'm wearing any, that is. It's not that he's at all bad-looking, though his bandy legs let him down a bit. Ordinarily I wouldn't turn my nose up. But I guess he doesn't realise quite how much I can hear through the wall that separates our flats, doesn't realise that I know how he talks to his women just minutes after making them wail and claw at his back in their abandon. Just the feel of the hands of such a man on me would give me the creeps.

I smile falsely, then shift my chair around slightly, so that my back is almost turned to him, precluding any further conversational gambits. There was a time, early on, when he could have had me, before I learnt what he's really like, but he blew it. I had just moved in and was having trouble picking up a decent TV signal. I'd seen Eduardo out on his balcony and called over to see if he'd had similar problems and could offer any advice. He'd come right round, promising to sort things out.

It was a Sunday in late spring, unseasonably hot, and he was wearing just his shorts and some sandals. His southern Italian roots mean he is dark-skinned by nature, but a tan was turning him a deep mahogany brown, and his skin shone with sun oil. As he bent down to fiddle with the tangle of wires and cables behind my television set and I watched the sinews in his back and arms move up and down, my chest rose and fell with yearning. I would fuck him before he was out the door, I told myself.

He turned back to me. 'Gonna have to climb up on the roof,' he said, rising to his feet. 'I'll go get some tools.'

I didn't answer, just looked him hard in the face. 'No hurry,' I said after a moment. 'How about a drink? I made some fresh lemonade this morning.'

'Mmmm, thanks. That sounds great.'

'Sit down,' I said, gesturing towards the squashy blue

sofa I'd just had delivered from Heal's that morning. It had cost me a full two months' wages, but suddenly I couldn't wait to sully it. I was on cloud nine – a place of my own at last, some chic new furniture and, to top it all, a handsome neighbour keen to help me settle in. Surely it didn't get any better than this?

I brought in a tray bearing two tall glasses of the cloudy liquid, clinking with ice cubes, and set it down on the wooden floorboards in front of the sofa, then reached over to the stereo beside it, flipped open the CD tray and inserted my favourite disc of the time – the eponymous album by Lamb, featuring the sublime 'Gorecki'. Langorous and hypnotic, it was perfect for a lazy summer Sunday spent entertaining a potential new lover.

I turned to Eduardo, held my glass up. 'Here's to new beginnings,' I said, and we smiled at each other for a beat, perhaps two, more than was strictly necessary. I saw my opening, leant forward, and that's when the noise of the drill flared up outside, rending the quiet that settles over the surrounding streets when the office workers are away.

I'm not a confrontational person, and would have either ignored it or turned up the stereo to try to mask it. But Eduardo was up and across the room like a streak of lightning, striding out onto my balcony and grabbing the tip of a rail between each hand as he swung his head from side to side in an attempt to pinpoint the source of the noise.

'Hey you,' he bellowed when he caught sight of the culprit on a nearby rooftop. 'You know what fucking day it is? Do you think you can make a bit more noise, mate? We can't fucking hear you over here.'

In response to some reply from the man, I saw him brandish his fist in his direction. 'You motherfucking cunt,' he hollered. 'You wanna go down to the street and sort this out? I'll have you, motherfucker.'

My libido died a death. There's nothing unsexier than a display of machismo. Sure, it was a Sunday and there were people who wanted to kick back and take it easy, but London is a 24-hour, seven-day-a-week city, and if some bloke wants to hop out on his roof and do a spot of DIY, what are you going to do about it? Eduardo, I had quickly learnt, was an uncouth, foul-mouthed bully.

I brought him out his lemonade, told him I didn't think he was going about things the right way, and then tried to close my ears to the further torrent of abuse that he unleashed at the DIYer, as a reaction, it seemed, against my criticism. He was probably disturbing more people than the drill was now. I looked at my watch, pretended a lunch engagement.

'Shame,' he said, turning back to me, leaning in for the kiss of which he had cheated himself and that, unbeknown to him, would never be offered again. If he hadn't lost his cool, hadn't revealed his true nature, we would probably have been banging away on my lovely new sofa by now, sliding off it onto the freshly polished floorboards, making them creak beneath our interlocked limbs, the slam of our hips as he drove into me. Still, better I knew then, I've always thought, than got involved with him and had to endure the complication of continuing to live next door to him *after* finding out he's a pig. And there were countless nights when I was provided with ample confirmation of this early impression by shouts and screams in the early hours.

He's got the message, is sitting in his favourite chair, face turned up to the sun like a heliotrope. I throw him a glance, then turn away and am just reaching for a wedge of melon and thinking that I really need to have a shower and get ready to go and meet Carlotta when my mobile goes. I run indoors, pick it up, standing nude in the window. It's Carlotta's voice I hear on the other end.

'... lie-in ...' she's saying '... really tired ... meet a little later?'

I try to focus, pull myself together. 'You're not feeling well?' I say eventually.

'I'm fine, 'Licia. I just feeling a little bit lazy. So I thought we can have late lunch and go to Hoxton this afternoon?'

'Sure,' I say. 'I'll call The Zetter now, and see you at, say, two o'clock?'

'Fine,' she says, 'I go my own way, you no need to fetch me. See you later.'

She hangs up, a little abruptly for my liking, but I reason that Paco may have come in and made her feel self-conscious. Not that there's any reason we shouldn't be talking to each other, of course, but perhaps she's worried she can't keep her nascent affection for me out of her voice. I snigger, am tempted to call her back and remind her that if she wants to be an actress, she needs all the practice she can get in faking it.

And then I think, more seriously, about Paco, and make up my mind to get that little problem out of the way now, make it clear to him where I stand. I dial his mobile, but it goes through to voicemail and I don't leave a message, just in case Carlotta should somehow get access to it. I'll catch him later, I think.

It's lunchtime, and I'm watching Carlotta pile into a plate of pasta with asparagus, egg and parmagiano.

'I so hungry,' she explains through a mouthful. 'Mmmm, you try this.' She winds me a forkful, passes it over and feeds me. 'Divine, no?'

I pick at my own food, a clam and chilli risotto. I'm feeling a little odd, a little wrong-footed. Carlotta got here late, after already having put the kibosh on our morning together. It's hardly the behaviour of someone who wants me as badly as she told me she did yesterday. And now all she can think about is food and how ravenous she is. When I asked her, on arriving, what she'd actually been doing all morning, she noticeably changed the subject, started rambling on about some inane conversation she'd had with her cab driver about pole-dancing, of all things.

Now, as she polishes off her pasta, I decide to push it.

'So,' I say, fingering the stem of my wine glass. 'How come you were so tired this morning?'

She shrugs, smiles knowingly. 'Busy girl,' she says, and her little nose wrinkles winsomely. Under the table I feel her leg brush against mine, then a naked foot insinuate itself between my knees and start inching its way between my legs. My pussy melts, my whole body melts. I force myself to sit up straight, clamp my thighs together before her foot reaches my knickers, although inside I'm screaming out for her to pull them aside and give me a damn good toe-ing.

'How was your evening?' I say, fixing my face into what, I hope, resembles a sweet, mildly interested smile. 'What did you do?'

'I read,' says Carlotta, and her face is just as bland. 'Look at art books.'

I want to ask her if she thought of me at all, want to ask her what time Paco came home and what they did together, but the words are stuck in my throat, almost choking me.

'But you said you were tired,' I persist. There's a slight whininess, a need, insinuating itself into my voice. The need to know. The green-eyed monster has struck.

She sighs, pats at her mouth with her napkin and then lays it down, smoothing it out. Then she leans in towards me over the table.

'He come back later,' she says huskily. 'He been in rehearsals, was still sweaty. We order room service and he go for shower.' She raises her hand to her throat, keeps staring into my eyes. I'm like a rabbit in her headlights.

'I follow him in,' she says. 'And I watch him, for a while. He like that guy in the painting – the *académie*. So fit and slim, so perfect. He running his hands up and down, massaging the gel into his skin. And then he see me watching him, and he turn to me and he start soaping his cock, his big beautiful cock.' She closes her eyes for a minute, shifts a little on her chair.

'He lean with one arm against shower door,' she resumes after a moment, 'and with the other hand he masturbating, and I just standing, watching, wanting him inside me. But I can't move, can't take my eyes off this beautiful thing, my husband. And he comes – comes all over the shower door. And then he open the door and he pull me in, and after I sucked him for a few minutes he bend me over his arm and fuck me like a madman, from behind.'

I'm sitting on my hands now, afraid that if I free them I won't be able to keep them away from my cunt. I've been presented with the image of Carlotta, splayed for Paco in the shower, his undeniably superb cock sawing in and out of her, his long slender hands pulling open her buttocks to reveal that rosebud hole. Embellishing the story from what she's told me, I see her leaning forwards, palms against the tiles, breasts against the tiles, eyes half-closed in a swoon, the tip of her tongue between her teeth.

'After...' she says, and I'm thinking, Christ, I can't take any more of this, I really can't. Just give me a break, Carlotta.

'After, we go to bed, closed ourselves behind the curtains, make ourselves a nest, and carry on fucking for hours.' She shakes her head, tosses her blonde locks over her shoulders, smiles. 'That why I can't get up this morning,' she says. 'We need lie-in.'

I smile bravely. I'm jealous, but I don't have any right to be. I pushed Carlotta, and now I'm suffering because of what she told me. I need to back off. Paco and Carlotta fuck, like most married couples, and I can't be surprised by that. I just don't have to know the details.

Carlotta's getting up, excusing herself to go to the loo, and while she's gone I try to get my head together. I won't pry again, won't open myself up to these feelings. If I can't keep my emotions out of it, then I will have to step back.

As I'm telling myself this, a message beeps through and I open it to read a text from Paco to the effect that I am to meet him after his show tonight at the Royal Albert Hall.

FINE, I shoot back. I was going to phone him, but I may as well talk to him in person, take him to a bar and civilly explain that I can't do what we've been doing anymore.

As I'm putting my phone back in my bag, a waiter comes over and hands me a piece of paper. 'From your friend,' he says.

I crease my brow as I unfold it: has Carlotta done a runner on me, I wonder? Is it all over so quickly?

But it's quite the opposite.

'Room 411,' it says simply.

I gather up my possessions with unseemly haste, make my way out of the restaurant and back into the atrium lobby, with its red spiral staircase winding its way up to the glass roof of the former Victorian warehouse. It's raindrop sensitive, so the waiter told us, and opens and closes automatically.

Then I take the lift to the relevant floor, follow a walkway overlooking the skylit atrium, and knock on the door of Room 411.

'Come in,' I hear her call, voice like dripping honey.

I obey, and when I walk in she's already naked on the bed, in the Olympia pose but without the haughtiness. In fact, she's grinning at me, giggling a little, urging me in with a wave of the hand.

I step up to the edge of the bed, and she reaches up and tugs me down towards her, slipping off my jacket, then pulling up my top and pushing my bra over my tits and taking them in her mouth, one at a time, and sucking and nibbling and tonguing them until they're steel-hard.

I push off my skirt and knickers, push her back onto the bed and straddle her. I'm still wet from what she told me in the restaurant, and I'm sliding on her naked belly, coating her like a snail leaving its trail. Then I pull away and down, and bring my mouth to her pussy. She arches her back as I start to flick at her clit with my tongue, gently at first, then more forcefully, clutching the sides of my head with her hands as if she never wants me to stop. And I never want to stop.

A few minutes later, she brings her hands down and spreads herself further for me, as if inviting me into her, and I let myself get lost in her folds and creases for a moment, inhaling and tasting her, getting drunk on her sweet, slightly musky liquor. Then I dart my tongue inside her and it's as if she's sucking me up as she arches again, raises her hips slightly as she applies two fingertips to her clit and loses herself to her climax.

As she does so, I can't help but bring my hand down to my own sopping pussy and, with the heel of my hand, vibrate myself until I share Carlotta's paroxysm, my cries like echoes of hers.

When I wake, I don't know how long afterwards, she's waiting for me, perched regal as a Siamese at the end of the bed. She's wearing her bathrobe, but it's not done up, and her breasts are spilling forth, brown and shiny as chestnuts. With her hands she's twisting the tie of the robe around and around, and I think I know what's coming next. But is it to be me or her?

I watch with bated breath as she crawls up the bed towards me, shuffling off the robe. The lighting in the room has changed to pink, I suddenly realise – Carlotta must have been playing around with the gadgetry while I was asleep. As if all of this was orchestrated, some music is being piped in from the vicinity of the TV set – the Grace Jones' version of 'La vie en rose'.

She hands me the tie, then backs away down the bed and climbs off. Over in the corner is a Louis XV armchair that I hadn't noticed, covered with a modern fabric and co-ordinating with the flowery wallpaper art that adorns the walls and the pearlised pastel leather of the headboard of the bed. I follow Carlotta over to it, watch as she climbs aboard, holding her arms out in front of her. She's positioned in front of a huge sash window, overlooking a calm square, with the sun pouring in on her in an amber slick. Anyone strolling by who happens to look up is in for a treat.

As she waits for me, she looks over her shoulder, not directly at me, but out of the corner of her eye, surreptitiously, tauntingly, and as the chorus of the song returns she begins to hum, then sing huskily.

Quand il me prend dans ses bras,
Il me parle tout bas,
Je vois la vie en rose.

Il me dit des mots d'amour,
Des mots de tous les jours,
Et ça me fait quelque chose.

Il est entré dans mon coeur
Une part de bonheur
Dont je connais la cause.

C'est lui pour moi, moi pour lui,
Dans la vie,
Il me l'a dit, l'a juré pour la vie.

A lump appears in my throat. I step up to her, drape myself over her from behind, feeling my bush against the satin skin of her buttocks, my breasts against her slender back. I reach around her and fumble for a moment, secure her hands together then pull out the ends of the tie and wind each around an arm of the chair, knot it. When I'm done, I stand back up, waiting for her command. She seems to have some pretty definite ideas about what she wants.

'Over there,' she says, turning her head over her shoulder and jerking her chin. 'My bag.'

I go back over to the bed, open her capacious Balenciaga hobo handbag. Inside are all the accoutrements the modern girl needs for her day-to-day life – mobile, hairbrush, cigarettes, tampons, Chanel sunglasses, lipstick. And amidst them all is a pink strap-on.

'I guess this is what you meant?' I say, holding it up. The harness is basically composed of a pair of thong knickers with a ring on the front through which you insert the dildo, although at present the two are already attached. I've never seen one of these before but I guess that they're designed so you can wear the harness under your clothing like normal knickers and just whip the dildo out of your bag or pocket as required, for an impromptu shag. Ingenious.

Carlotta smiles impishly, raises her bum up a fraction in anticipation. I look at the apparatus a bit nervously, then sit down and slip it up over me. She's still looking over her shoulder, running her tongue over her lips, eyes glittering. 'Fuck me,' she mouths.

I clamber over the bed, finger her to make sure she's wet enough then mount her. Plunging in and out, I squeeze her hard, one hand on each buttock. She's threaded her own arms back between her legs and flattened one hand to squirrel it into my cunt. With the other she's massaging my clit, my lips, frenziedly. There's a slapping noise as our flesh meets and separates, meets and separates, my lower belly catching the top of her bum cleft, her cheeks ramming back against my upper thighs. A rhythm takes hold of us, and we ride on and on, moaning and wailing until we reach fever pitch, and come, once again, at the same time.

It's not a cold night, but afterwards Carlotta insists on us having the handknitted hotwater bottles filled and cuddling up in bed with some trashy TV – it happens to be reruns of *Dynasty* that we find, but we don't really mind. Our brains have turned to bubblegum with all the fucking we've been doing, our bodies are limp and sated – for the moment. It would be nice to just stay here, folded in Carlotta's arms, and then cleanse myself in the walk-in raindance shower and climb back into bed and sit reading one of the classic paperbacks that are dotted around out loud to her. Then fuck her again.

Carlotta's clearly having similar thoughts, for a few moments later she rolls over to face me from where I've been spooning her, kisses me, and suggests spending the night together.

'We can always,' she says, 'tell Paco we go out of town, to a gallery someplace, and have a long dinner and miss our last train back and decide to stay in a hotel rather than take long taxi ride. He performing until late anyway.'

She studies my face, trying to read my reaction. '*Go on,*' she hisses. 'We get in a rude movie. Something with girls. And some champagne from the machine on the landing.'

It makes me feel bad turning her down, putting a dampner on our happy day, but all of a sudden I'm feeling very jumpy about the whole Paco thing. It would be awful enough if he found out that Carlotta and I cooked up a lie in order to spend the night together. But the fact that I stood *him* up in favour of his wife would turn him homicidal.

I wish I could explain to Carlotta why I have to say no, but somehow I think that telling her I have to go and break off my affair with her husband won't go down too well. Instead, I come up with something weak and watery about meeting my best friend Jess, who I can't let down because she's been having terrible man problems.

Carlotta sulks, obviously stung by my mention of a best friend, of a life beyond her, excluding her. 'Fine,' she snaps, adding in a low voice that she obviously intends me to hear, 'I go find someone else.'

I sit down in my bra and knickers, take her hand.

Paco is not the only fiery one, I'm realising. But her reaction makes me all the more determined to stand my ground. Neither of them need think they can get away with bossing me around. I'm not their toy.

By the time I'm away from Carlotta and heading for the other side of London, it's almost time to meet Paco. I come out of the tube at Knightsbridge and walk briskly along Kensington Road and then Kensington Gore, letting the cool summer-evening air caress me. I've showered, but I can still smell Carlotta on me, on my bare shoulders, on my hands, which I sniff surreptitiously. I wonder if Paco will notice them, will disentangle them from my own womanly odours.

At the Royal Albert Hall, I weave my way through the line of waiting limos and ask a doorman to direct me backstage. When he looks suspicious, I tell him I'm one of Paco Manchega's staff, which isn't exactly a lie. At the back door, I find Paco has thought ahead, and that 'Ms Alicia Shaw' is on the list of his personal entourage to be granted admission.

I walk in, trying to look unfazed by the whole experience, by knowing that I have an assignation with this famous man who's dancing in front of an audience of thousands. My intention is to wait in his dressing room, but I get ensnared in a maze of corridors and suddenly find myself in the wings, watching the end of the performance just a few feet away from Paco himself. It's his first ever solo show, and I know that he was feeling a little apprehensive about it, especially given that over the last year he's had a bad reception from the purist flamenco press on the subject of his choreographic innovations, on his mixing of flamenco with other dance forms.

Even from where I'm standing, so close up, you can't tell he's nervous, he's so far gone into the work, so utterly absorbed by the dance. His chest is bared, and sweat is pouring down him. The audience might as well not be there, not while he's performing. He looks up and over them, and I remember what he said about flamenco having an almost mystical aspect to it. Then all of a sudden it's over, and he's bowing, brutally aware of them again, and they are going wild. I can still hear the encores ringing out as I make my way back through the labyrinth.

His dressing room, I'm surprised to find, is empty, and I sit down and start thumbing through a magazine I find to hand, to give me something to think about. A few minutes after the encores finally die away, Paco appears, flushed and triumphant, still charged with adrenalin. He's followed by a woman he introduces me to as his UK agent, Eliza Jenkins.

'Alicia's just popped in on her way home,' he says to her, giving me a look. 'She's dropping off something for Carlotta.'

Eliza nods, tells me what a roaring success the evening has been, how Paco thrilled the crowds more than ever before.

'He was on fire,' she says breathily, and I realise that she's not even been looking at me as she's been talking, that she's been gazing at Paco with undisguised adoration. I look at him, observe his body language, and quickly decide that no, he's not sleeping with her. It's all one-sided. Here's another one, I think, who's going to go home and peel off her damp little panties and give herself a good seeing-to, Paco's name on her lips.

The thought that out there, in the vast auditorium, are scores of girls and women now just aching to get home and imagine it's Paco whose fingers are teasing their clits, knocks the wind from my sails. And *I've* been fucking him, I think. What did I do to deserve this?

Eliza and I natter on for a few minutes as Paco strips off his skin-tight Dolce & Gabbana trousers – he's famed for commissioning all his costumes from them – pulls on a pair of jeans and lights a cigarette. She tells me she hears I've been showing Carlotta the sights, asks what we've been up to. I answer as shortly as I can without appearing rude, desperate to have Paco to myself. I can smell the sweat on him from his show, and it must be the pheromones or something because I actually start feeling faint.

The minute she's gone and the door is closed and locked, I turn and throw myself at Paco. You'd think I hadn't had any in years, the way I'm on him now, undoing his zip and pulling out his cock and climbing onto it as he sits in the chair, pulling my knickers aside with my fingers. You'd never believe I've come several times this afternoon, the way I'm burning for him.

One arm on his shoulder to steady me, I'm riding him as if he were a wild horse, my spine arched, shoulders thrown back, all the muscles of my cunt squeezing, locking me onto him. And then he's standing, and advancing across the room, and I'm amazed at the power of those thighs, for him to be able to hold me up *and* carry on feeding himself into me, in and out, in and out, faster and faster. Then we come to a halt, and I'm up against the wall and he's banging into me, crushing me, and we're both gasping and tearing at each other with our hands.

He binds me against him again with his arms and carries me back to the chair, swizzling it around as we sit down. I lean back again – we haven't been kissing anyway, no time for that nonsense – and this time I finger myself too, so that with the stimulation of his prick inside me and the action of my own digit, I come hyper-intensely. It's the cue for him to stop thinking of football or flamenco moves or whatever it is he thinks about to keep a lid on himself.

I take the opportunity to slide back off the chair, onto my knees, and take him in my mouth. He drives his fingers into my shoulders, jerks his hips convulsively, and I look up and find that he's watching himself in the mirror as he comes, staring into his own eyes. I nearly choke on his come with surprise. That, and the desire to laugh.

Half an hour later we're washed and dressed and having a very civilized drink in the Blue Bar at the Berkeley. We've picked a corner table, but Paco has got his shades on for good measure, not thinking what a wanker he must look. It's nearly midnight, after all. Still, needs must when you're an international superstar on the town with your bit on the side.

We're sipping dry martinis, chatting desultorily. I'm finding it hard to focus, still shocked by how I reacted to him, how much I continue to want him, after all I'd decided, after Carlotta. It seems so wrong, such a terrible muddle, but in the dressing room it felt so right. So necessary. I *had* to have him.

After an hour or so, Paco looks at his watch, sighs. 'I want to spend the night with you,' he says. 'Here, in this hotel. I wish I didn't have to go.'

I, in turn, wish that I could tell him not to rush off, that his wife, in all likelihood, is still in the room we shared at The Zetter, going down on some bit of fluff she picked up in the bar, munching on some fresh clit as she threatened to do if I left. But I can't, and I'm exhausted anyway, and in truth the only thing on my mind now is getting home and slipping into my own bed, alone, and getting a good night's sleep. Suddenly, an empty flat is just what I need.

13

The morning finds me slobbing around in my kimono, waiting for Carlotta to call. I'm certainly not going to chase her after her little fit of pique: if she wants to go out, she can contact me. In the meantime, I have a huge backlog of calls and emails to work my way though.

I sit down at my computer, log on and check my inbox. More than a hundred new messages. I groan, pour myself another cup of coffee, try to bin as many as possible without opening them and assess the rest according to priority. My eyes lock onto one about twenty down in the list: danlub@alligatorfilms.com. The subject field reads 'Sorry!!!!!Future date????'

I don't want to, but I click on it.

'Alicia, I'm sorry,' it reads. 'I was really looking forward to seeing you. Please forgive me and say you're free on the 20th, for dinner at least, but a tour if you can make it. I'll pay for your time, whatever. I'm in town for a couple of days. Dan.'

I read it over and over, wondering if there's anything between the lines, and then I get cross – as much at myself as him, and I fire tetchily back:

'Booked up. Sorry, A.'

By the time I've fetched yet another coffee, a second 'danlub' email has plopped into my mailbox. I open it:

'Will double rate if you cancel the other. D.'

I frown, start chewing at the inside of my cheek. I suppose I should be flattered, if he thinks I'm worth that, but now I'm really getting wound up.

'Not for sale to highest bidder,' I type. I pause for a second, then hit send. Immediately I do so, I'm wondering if I've done the right thing. He's apologised for the missed date, and I know, in my heart, he didn't mean it that way. All this business with Paco and Carlotta must be sending me a bit loony.

I reach for the phone, dial Jess's number. She'll be in a strop with me, for not returning her calls, but she'll relent, especially when she hears what I have to say, what has happened. And she's the only one who can talk any sense into me.

The tone goes on, then her answerphone takes over.

'Jess, it's Al,' I say urgently. 'I'm sorry. Stuff – stuff has got a bit out of control. Call me. Love you.'

My mobile's ringing as I hang up the landline. It's Carlotta, all bright and breezy, suggesting a walk on Hampstead Heath. Fresh air sounds like a good idea to me, after a succession of sweaty encounters in hotel rooms and dressing rooms, and we agree to meet at the top of Parliament Hill at four o'clock. I check my mailbox again, but Daniel has gone silent, unsurprisingly. I swear under my breath. I've well and truly blown it with him.

I see her before I get to the top of the hill: she's the only person on the heath in a pair of red stilettos. The only one wearing a semi-transparent white sundress with no bra either, I would guess. Around her, kites are colliding and getting tangled as their owners struggle to concentrate on them rather than her.

She steps forward, kisses me on one cheek, a cigarette in one hand. With the other she risks a little tweak at my nipple.

'Hello, lover,' she breathes into my ear.

'Hi,' I say shyly.

'How is your evening with your friend?' she asks, a little archly, obviously still smarting.

'Fine,' I reply. 'It was fine.'

'She is still brokenhearted?'

'She'll get over it.'

'Everybody do,' she says, exhaling a mouthful of smoke, pointing over to the south. 'Look,' she exclaims. 'You can see St Paul's. That where we were the other day – at the Tate, no?'

'It is,' I say. 'What did you do?' I probe. 'Last night?'

'Oh, I send out for that sexy movie in the end. It seem such a waste of a lovely hotel room, to go home. Our suite is so huge, you get lost in there on your own. It make you lonely. No, I felt cosy, so I stay and watch a film, and I masturbate a lot, thinking of you. Then I get a taxi home and go to bed. I hear Paco come in, feel his hand on me, but I can't.' She laughs. 'Even I have limits,' she says.

I find that hard to believe, but I'm glad she didn't fuck Paco last night. I like to think that I had him to myself, for once.

She's smiling at me in the sunlight, her hair glittering around her like a candyfloss haze, and I wonder if I should feel bad. After all, how could she be upset at Paco fooling around when she is doing exactly the same behind his back, and even with the same person?

'What are you thinking?' she says, watching me curiously, and I shrug.

'Nuthin' in my noggin,' I say, and at her raised eyebrows I knock on my head, provide a translation. 'It's all empty in there.'

She laughs, looks around her. 'Is it true, what I hear,' she says, 'that you can swim naked here? Outside, in some ponds?'

I nod. 'You want to go?' I say.

'Why not? Sounds like fun.'

I walk her to the heath ponds, explaining to her that the former brick pits are fed by natural springs, which means they get a bit of algae but are generally quite clean. It turns out to be a quiet time of the day, and we strip off and plunge in and float around for a bit, before finding a little corner where we can have a bit of a smooch. After a while, Carlotta reaches for me, starts fingering my pussy, and then I do the same to her and before long we're talking about where we can go for a proper fuck.

Carlotta's all for doing it right here, actually, but I'm a bit worried we may get into trouble. She teases me for being so circumspect, bobs her head down under the water and jabs at my fanny with her tongue, coming up laughing and blowing bubbles and crossing her eyes. I want her so badly, I'm ready to give in, just haul her out onto the bank and have her right there, without a care for who sees us. But then an old lady walks by us, skin hanging off her in baggy folds, tough-looking as a rhino's, and we get out and dress hurriedly and go in search of a private spot.

We soon find a little wooded area off a minor path and, making sure no one can see us, creep in, divest ourselves of our clothes again, and fall on top of each other, giggling and kissing and sucking and grabbing at each other. We roll around like playful kittens for a while, then things turn dirty and this time it's her reaching into her bag for the strap-on, slipping it on and ramming it into my arse until I don't know whether I'm crying because I want her to stop or because I want more. When she takes it out, she keeps it on, using it on my clit this time, until I'm actually sobbing, from the intensity, from the frustration of being on the cusp of orgasm and then having her ease off, teasing me, again. And perhaps also from love, I think as finally I do climax, clasping Carlotta's head to my chest and holding her fast against me.

Afterwards, Carlotta whips out a little digital camera from her bag.

'Look what I buy this morning,' she says, and she brings it up to her face and takes a snap. She turns the camera to show me my own image on the back screen. I'm all heavy-lidded and somnolent, the cat that got the cream.

'Souvenirs,' she says, and she takes some more, getting bossier as she goes on.

'Left, right, no left a bit more ... arch your back so your titties sticking out ... open your legs more so I see your pussy. Spread yourself for me. No, *spread* yourself, I say.'

It's a turn-on, I must admit, and I take some similar ones of her. We even take a few of us together, turning the lens on ourselves, sticking our tongues out, planting big kisses on each other's cheeks, hamming it up.

'Aren't you worried about Paco finding out?' I say as I watch her tuck the camera back into her bag.

'You no worry, I save them to CD and delete from camera,' she says. 'That's safer than prints. Then I just look at them on computer when Paco's out.' She laughs. 'Oh, I gonna masturbate so hard over you when I back in Spain,' she says. 'And I'll do a copy for you, to remember me by.'

I want to ask her what will happen then, when she goes back to Spain. What will become of us. But I so desperately don't want to mar this glorious afternoon.

So I don't say anything. And I don't say anything about maybe having fallen in love with her. That's for another time.

Over coffee and cakes on Hampstead High Street, Carlotta asks me if I can take her to a lesbian bar, since Paco is performing again that night. I tell her I'm surprised she doesn't attend his shows, and she sneers, waves her hand dismissively.

'All those ugly women getting turned on by him,' she says. 'And the gays too. *Grazie, no.* No thanks. I prefer to have him all myself when he come back.'

'So you want to go to a girls' bar?' I say.

'Yeah,' she says a little dreamily. 'To see the scene.'

'Do you go to lesbian bars in Madrid?'

She sips at her coffee, looks at me a little combatively. It looks for all the world like she's about to rebuff me with a curt 'None of your business'. But then she relaxes back into her chair, lights a cigarette and looks at me intently.

'Sometime,' she says.

The door is open for me, and I know it's now or never.

'I know you have done this before . . .' I begin.

She exhales a little puff of smoke. 'Of course,' she says.

'Often?'

'I never count,' she says with a certain aloofness. 'I just say, I take it where I find it.'

'What does that mean?'

'It mean if I see a pretty woman and she like me and I like her, I not gonna say no. You think I crazy?'

'Have you ever –' I can't say it. The word 'love' gets stuck in my throat.

'What?'

'Never mind.' I cast around for a way to skirt the subject. 'When – who was the first one?'

'Oh, Alicia, Alicia – we going back years now.'

'OK, then when was the last time, before me?'

She crosses her legs, runs her fingers through her hair. 'It was New York,' she says. 'At a gallery in the East Village. Paco was rehearsing – he *always* rehearsing – and I was alone. This girl come in – a Venezuelan, I find out later. I just have to have her.'

I stare at her, my mind racing. I happen to know that Paco and she came to London directly from New York. Given how little time they have been married, it must have been during that very trip. This must have happened only a week or two before she slept with me.

'What did you do?' I say, almost beside myself, both appalled and fascinated, knowing that what she tells me will make me suffer but obeying an ache in my groin to know more.

She breathes in and out deeply, and her breasts heave and fall. She's clearly getting excited too, at the thought of her conquest.

'I keep looking at her,' she says, 'but she don't react, don't return my stares. I *know* she know, though. That she playing with me. When she go, I follow her, and after a few blocks she turn round and she say to me, "What do you want?"'

'What did you say?'

'I come right out with it. "I want you," I say.'

'Jesus.'

'And you know what she do? She just smile and then she lead me right up to her apartment on that street and we stay in bed for the rest of the afternoon. I think I come – what? – ten, fifteen time. She do something with her tongue that –'

She stops, fishes in her suede Balenciaga bag for her

purse and flattens some notes on the table. 'Let's go,' she says, and in the space of a heartbeat we are out of the door and flagging down a taxi.

'Langham Place,' she says to the driver, 'but we in no hurry. Take your time.'

As the car pulls away from the kerb, she yanks down one of the folding seats with their back to the driver and hitches up her skirt. On her knickers I can see a blot of moisture. She pulls them to one side to reveal her tidy little cunt, all shiny and glistening in the sunlight.

'Go down on me,' she commands. 'Let me feel your mouth on me, your tongue.'

I kneel at her feet, on the taxi floor, and bring my mouth to her foaming pussy, wondering if I can satisfy her in the way the Venezuelan did, or the way Paco does. Not that she complained last time, in The Zetter, but I'm feeling a little inadequate, a little lacklustre, after her description of the girl in the gallery.

She doesn't complain though, and as she starts writhing, gripping each side of the seat to secure herself as we go round corners, I stop worrying about the other girl and about how my prowess matches up to hers and just hope that the driver doesn't slam on the brakes and ask us what the hell we're doing.

He doesn't, but after we've dropped Carlotta off at her hotel and are crossing Marylebone to reach my flat, I bury my head in a magazine, determined not to catch his eye in the mirror or to give him any chance to ask me if his ears had been playing tricks on him.

I make a few calls to find out where I can take Carlotta that's trendy but discreet, then get changed, wondering what one wears to a lesbian bar. At twenty-eight, I'm really not very worldly-wise where many things are concerned. I finally settle on some wedge heels and a black satin pencil skirt with a scooped-neck beige Joseph top. No doubt Carlotta will be wearing something rather more outré.

With five minutes to kill, I check my emails and find there's one from Daniel, apologising: the last thing he wanted, he said, was to offend me. I send one back, apologising for being oversensitive. I add that I am free on the date he asked about after all, then at the last minute before sending delete that sentence. I really don't want him to think I lied, even though I did.

And then I'm in another taxi speeding back to Carlotta's hotel, starting to feel like a bit of a human ping-pong ball.

When I knock on the door to Carlotta's suite, it's the maid who answers.

'Madame is showering,' she informs me. 'She says to order yourself a drink.' She leaves, closing the door behind her.

I step into the drawing room, stand listening to the sound of the rushing water from the bathroom for a minute, wondering whether to go and hop in with Carlotta. I'm pretty sure she's expecting me to, and I'm certain she wouldn't say no to a quick one, but left on my own for a minute I suddenly find I have an over-whelming desire to take advantage, to have a bit of a snoop.

I tiptoe into the bedroom, ears keenly attuned to what's going on in the bathroom, the door to which is half closed. Carlotta's singing something in Spanish. I imagine her hands skimming her breasts almost uncon-sciously, running down her belly and soaping the neat little folds of her pussy, the delicate little eye of her sphincter. I cast the image from my mind, try to concen-trate on what's in front of me: the silver chest of drawers. Now where did she put the picture, the one she says she's thrown away? Was it the middle drawer? I open it. It's empty. So, I find, are all the others.

I turn around, scan the room. There are two circular bedside tables, and as soon as I see them I'm consumed by curiosity. Who couldn't resist a peek, even if it's only to find a tube of KY Jelly nestling next to the Gideon's Bible?

I walk over, open Paco's – or at least the one that is most likely to be his, given that it's on the side nearest the men's dressing area. When I do so I let out a little gasp of surprise that I'm quick to stifle. But it's not the little gold handcuffs that take me unawares, nor Carlotta's strap-on, which she used on me only a few hours ago – though that does force me to confront the fact that she may have it primarily to use on Paco more than on other women. No, what stuns me most is the sight of the very picture I believed destroyed, the sketch that Carlotta did of me in the Olympia pose.

I pick it up, stare at it. Almost as disconcerting as the fact of having found it at all is what it reveals of Carlotta: she is, I see immediately, a true artist, a talent. She's combined the audacity of Victorine's pose with a real eye for my body, for my face and its nuances. The picture just *is* me, my essence. I wasn't expecting that, wasn't expecting her to be so good. Carlotta is no dilettante.

The shower goes silent, and I drop the sketch into the drawer, where I now see the infamous black scarf too. I close it and hurry back into the drawing room, staring out at the Nash steeple and chewing my lip. Part of me wants to confront Carlotta right now, ask her why she lied to me about the picture, but there's a little voice in my head that tells me I should hold off, that it would be much more fruitful if I somehow found a way to trick Paco into admitting that he knows about my modelling session.

My brain is working overtime when Carlotta appears in the doorway, stark naked, towel-drying her hair. I can't help but look her up and down, admire her. With her pubes still wet and flat against her, her large clit is more prominent than ever. Just the sight of it makes my own swell in anticipation. I walk up to her, press myself into her. She smells of milk and figs – a new shower product she bought in Liberty's, she tells me. I push my face into her neck, reach for that fat clit and tug it with my fingers. In return she slips her hand down the back of my skirt and into my knickers and rims my arsehole with her fingertip, then enters me. I cry out.

She smiles, steps back. My fingers are coated with her; I put them in my mouth. She spins away from me.

'Better go get ready,' she says.

I sit on the sofa. My mind is blown, totally blown, by this creature. I no longer know what I'm doing. My self-control just falls apart whenever I'm near her. It's like a sickness, this always wanting more, this never being sated of her. This is going to kill me.

She reappears, a vision in a gold lamé halter dress and matching heels, with a Versace denim jacket thrown over the top to make it all a little more street. Just as I feared, I feel a bit like someone's granny next to her. I'm just hoping this bar I've been recommended isn't full of short-haired dykes in dungarees. I think they'd take even less kindly to Carlotta than she would to them.

We're in the Glass Bar, a private members' club for women in one of the old porters' lodges at Euston Station, drinking large vodka and tonics. Carlotta's wondering how come I've never been with a girl before, and I'm asking her if it was that obvious. It was, she laughs, but that's not to say I'm at all bad. With a little more training, who knows . . .

She leans forwards to kiss me. 'Just joking,' she says, hand on my thigh. 'You drive me crazy.'

I confess to her that this has all been a bit of a shock to me, that I'd never seriously envisaged doing it with another woman and still can't quite believe it's happened.

'Not that I'm not happy about it,' I reassure her. 'But it's a big thing, finding out you really like doing something that had never really even crossed your mind as a possibility. It makes you wonder if you were who you thought you were.'

Carlotta laughs, rolls her eyes. 'Don't get so heavy,' she mock-scolds. 'Just enjoy yourself.'

I laugh back, but inside a trace of concern remains, niggling away inside me. If I'm not who I thought I was, who am I, and what will my life be like from now on?

After a while a couple appear at our table and ask if we'd mind if they join us. Carlotta says 'No, no', and pulls her stool over so there's room for them.

They squeeze into the narrow space, sit down. 'I'm Jacqueline,' says one, 'and this is Michiko.'

We nod and introduce ourselves, and soon we've fallen into a conversation with the pair. Jacqui, we learn, is a graphic designer from Stoke Newington, and Michiko is a waitress in a Japanese restaurant in Camden, which is where they met. They make a comic pair – Jacqui tall and lanky with bleached dreadlocks and a pretty but slightly beaky face, Michiko petite and doll-faced with cropped black hair. They hold hands, though, and are obviously very fond of each other. I sneak a look at Carlotta. What would it be like to be with her, really *be* with her?

More drinks come and the talk gets bawdier. Jacqui is telling us about a yoga teacher she once dated and the positions they used to try out, and I can see Carlotta drinking it all in, making mental notes. I'm in for an athletic time later, I think, wondering what kind of weird shapes Carlotta's going to try to twist me into. But the thought freezes in my head when I see that Jacqui has leaned forwards and has rested her hand on Carlotta's bare thigh.

She's saying something, and Carlotta's laughing, her lascivious little tongue peeking out from between her white teeth. I would even go so far as to say she's poking her boobs out a bit, as if presenting them to Jacqui.

'What the fuck . . . ?' I've started to say under my breath when Michiko, who's so far let everyone else do the talking, turns to me and says:

'My place isn't far from here, in Somers Town. Let's all go back there. I have whisky, and dope.'

Suddenly all eyes are on me, waiting for my reaction. I look at Carlotta, shake my head, and she glares at me for a moment and then looks away. She's fuming. But I won't let her bully me into this. I want her, not a gang bang with this oddball couple.

From this moment on I'm excluded, which I suppose I shouldn't be surprised about. I don't let it get to me: I sit and smoke, sip my drinks, and watch the other three giggle among themselves. I'm not even interested in what they're saying. The evening washes over me in a blur.

Later on, with the lights down low and a band providing live music, Carlotta takes the Japanese girl's hand and they move out from between the tables and start to dance together. Carlotta leads the way, one hand on the small of Michiko's back; I see them start grinding into each other, and I can imagine Carlotta's clit, all pink and throbbing for this tiny Asian girl, chafing against the lace of her knickers. She doesn't even look at me: she takes it on trust that I'm watching, that she's riling me. I wish she wasn't, but it's true.

Jacqui drifts away, strikes up a conversation with another Asian girl at the bar, and soon I see her lean in and risk a kiss. I finish my drink, think about telling Carlotta it's time to go, that she's had her fun. Her hand is on Michiko's buttocks now, pulling them up towards her. She's angling for a kiss, I can see, and the Japanese girl's lips are already parting in readiness, her eyes half-closed.

I'm climbing down from my stool when I hear a voice beside me.

'She's making a fool of you, your girlfriend,' it says, crackling from years of nicotine abuse, and I turn my head and see a woman in her late-forties flashing me a faux-sympathetic, rather wolfish smile. She's wearing a red fifties-style satin cocktail dress and a sort of furry stole, and there's a cigarette holder clamped between her yellowing teeth.

'She's not my girlfriend,' I say.

'No?'

'She's a friend's wife.'

'Some friend,' she says with a throaty laugh. She leans in towards me, and I get a blast of Chanel Cristalle. 'I saw you earlier,' she says, 'getting all cosy together. Before those minxes arrived.'

'OK,' I concur, 'so I fuck her from time to time. So what?'

'Does he know, the hubby?'

'I don't think so,' I say. I don't add that I found a certain sketch in his bedside drawer this afternoon that suggests otherwise.

'Whatever,' she says. 'She's making a fool of you with that little Japanese piece.' She nods over at them. I don't need to look to know that they are kissing.

'What you need is a real woman,' she says, leaning in further. There's stale tobacco on her breath, and garlic, and sour cheap wine. 'Come home with me,' she goes on. 'I'll show you what it's all about.'

That's it: I grab my bag and run out, jumping into the first taxi I see, cursing the day I met Carlotta, the day I accepted Paco's booking. No amount of money, none of the glamour of such a high-profile client, can make up for this kind of treatment. And all because I wouldn't go home with that lanky bitch and her girl-friend. Carlotta can go to hell.

At home I have a herbal tea and try to call Daniel's number in the States. Suddenly it seems vitally impor-tant that I talk to him above anybody else, even Jess. Suddenly no one else will do.

Of course, he's not there, and the call goes straight through to the answering machine. I hang up, call the number of the last person in the world I should be speaking to: Paco. Even as he's answering I don't really know why I'm calling him. Then I remember the drawing.

He's on his way home from the Royal Albert Hall in a taxi, I learn, and I persuade him to stop near my flat. He calls when he's on the corner of my street, and I run down and meet him at the Moroccan-themed bar there. He's still fired up, I see, from his show, his eyes bright, his skin glowing. I try to imagine how it must feel to get up in front of all those people, to hear that applause and know it's for you, but I can't. It's all worlds away from my life.

He orders a half bottle of champagne, asks what Carlotta and I have been doing. Seeing a way in, I murmur something vague about art galleries – I don't want to answer his question in case he asks Carlotta and our stories don't tie in – and then I slowly bring the subject around to Manet. Like Carlotta, I say, I'm a big fan of the French painter. It's nice that we have that in common, I add.

Paco doesn't really react, and I remember him saying he's not really into the visual arts. I carry on regardless, determined not to squander the opportunity.

'His *Olympia*, for instance,' I say. 'So shocking at the time. You know the one I mean?'

He shakes his head, looking around the room as if he's discovered a sudden interest in the decor, or one of the sweet Swedish barmaids this place seems to have on tap.

'The one with Victorine Meurent, posing as a prostitute staring at her client – who is you, the viewer. With the cat at the end of the bed.'

Paco stubs his cigarette out very slowly, still not looking at me, still shaking his head, and I start getting impatient.

'I don't know how you *can't* know it,' I insist. 'It's your wife's favourite painting. It's in the Louvre.'

He looks at me at last, raising his head very slowly. 'Look, Alicia,' he says as if with effort, as if he is endlessly weary. 'Carlotta and I are not Siamese twins, you know. We don't live in each others' pockets. We have our own lives.'

'I know you do,' I say meaningfully. But I give up without reminding him that Carlotta took him to see the painting in Paris not so long ago, or so she claimed. Paco is not giving anything away, and we're just going to end up fighting if I keep pushing.

Fortuitously, the champagne bottle has run dry, giving me a natural opening to call an end to the evening. When I stand up and push my chair back, however, Paco looks aghast.

'Where are you going?' he says.

'Home,' I tell him. 'I'm tired and –' I don't go on, can't tell him I won't sleep with him as long as I believe he's lying to me about the drawing. As long as I believe that there's something going on beneath the surface of all of this.

He stands up, pushes his own chair back and starts to march out. I follow.

'Why did you call me?' he says as he turns to me on the doorstep. 'You prick tease. Well, I don't need you, you know. I can get the best fuck in the world from my wife. Goodnight, Alicia.'

And with that he's off and I'm left standing here on the pavement, watching him stride away into the night, wondering again how I came to be involved in all of this.

Upstairs, my mobile rings and it's Carlotta, weepy and contrite. She's back at the hotel, she says, minus Jacqui and Michiko, regretting the whole unsavoury affair.

'I was only doing it to get attention, to make you jealous,' she sobs. 'You must see that, 'Licia. There no way ... I not even ...'

'It's OK,' I say. 'I understand. Listen, Paco just called me about some financial stuff and I know he's on his way back to the hotel so you'd better pull yourself together or he'll wonder what's wrong and you'll have some explaining to do.'

'OK,' she sniffs. 'Thanks. Listen, 'Licia. I know I not deserve it, but can I see you tomorrow?'

I can hardly refuse, given that her husband is paying for me to be her companion, but I'm very wary of Carlotta now. I'm not even sure how genuine these tears of hers are; I wish I could see her in the flesh, gauge how much she's putting it on. I was wrong, it turns out, to question her ability as an actress. She could give some of the Oscar winners a run for their money.

But however upset she is or isn't, I know one thing for sure – Carlotta is a control freak, and I would bet almost anything that her spot of frottage with the little Japanese waitress was intended not so much to make me jealous as to punish me for not obeying her, for not agreeing to a foursome.

'Sure,' I sigh. 'I'll pick you up at eleven, OK?'

'Whatever you want, 'Licia. I can't tell you how much you mean to me.'

'Goodnight, Carlotta.'

By the following lunchtime, we've walked right up through Regent's Park to the top of Primrose Hill to admire the views over London, and are about halfway back to the hotel, having butties and coffees in The Honest Sausage Cafe. I've lost count of the number of times Carlotta has apologised for yesterday, has declared her undying love for me. It's all making me feel a bit nauseous. Something rings false in all this.

I want to change the subject, but the other thing that's preying on my mind – the wonderful portrait she did of me – is out of bounds. Not just the fact that she lied about it, but just how bloody good it is. I want to ask her why she's dissipating her energies playing silly games in lesbian bars when she is so talented. But I can't because that would mean giving away what I've seen.

Carlotta must sense my *froideur*, for before long she suggests that she pay for me to have a long massage in the hotel spa to make up for her wanton behaviour. You know by now that I'm not one to turn down a freebie, and if Carlotta wants to splash out on a treatment for me to salve her conscience, I'm not going to protest. Thus it is that, twenty minutes later, I'm browsing the menu of treatments, trying to ascertain which is the longest and most luxurious. If it's the most expensive too, then all the better.

Carlotta waves to me as I'm ushered into a treatment room by a neat beautician, all scraped back hair and flawless skin and immaculate nails. She's perfect, and perfectly sexless. I'm relieved, was worried that my newfound appreciation of the female form might, when combined with a sumptuous massage, put ideas in my head.

In some ways, though, it's a shame: part of me would have loved to have got it on with my masseuse, would have loved to have had an oily romp on the treatment couch, just to get back at Carlotta. But that would be descending to her level. And in any case, I think I'm starting to get erotic burnout. The last thing I need right now is another fuck.

The masseuse, needless to say, is resolutely professional, and her fingers work their magic where they should – deep into my taut muscles, which soften like putty at her touch. My cunt doesn't stir at all, and I'm relieved to have some time off from its demands. For the last few days I feel its wants and needs have been dictating my life more than a little, more than is healthy. I need a pussy break.

Ninety minutes later, swaddled in a bathrobe and

smelling of lavender and ylang ylang, I go to find Carlotta. She told me she was having a swim while I was gone, and would wait for me on a lounger by the Jacuzzi. She's not there. I enter the changing room and peer inside the steam room and then the sauna. She's in the latter, naked on a towel, her damp brown skin gleaming in the orangey light. She's playing with her cunt, idly, lazily, eyes closed, a half-smile on her lips.

I'm about to back off, go get my clothes from the locker and get dressed, when she sits up, almost as if she's sensed my presence. *Come in*, she mouths, beckoning me with a hand. I sigh, pull open the door.

'How was it?' she smiles.

'Great.'

She stands up, steps towards me and pushes the robe off from my shoulders, then plunges her face into my neck. 'Mmmm, you smell *good*,' she says, her hand on my pussy, one finger already between my lips in search of my opening. I wish it wasn't, but it's already wet for her, and her finger slides in easily. I swoon back against the warm pine wall, look down as she falls to her knees. With her teeth she nips at my clit, while more and more fingers are pushed into my cunt until her hand fills it. She bunches it up into a fist, starts pummelling, looking up at my face for a reaction. I can see my juices dripping from her chin. I gasp, grab her head with both hands, amazed that I can accommodate so much of her, electrified by the combination of pleasure and pain, by the almost unbearable intensity of it all.

I start sliding down the wall, and then I'm lying on the ground and she's turning round and her cunt and arse come down on my face as she leans forward and continues going at me with her mouth, with both hands. At that moment something catches the corner of my eye and I turn my head and there's a figure standing in the door, indistinct behind the steamed-up glass. She – it's definitely a woman – looks to be wearing a swimsuit, and I wouldn't swear on it but I think as I watch that her hand slips into the bottom of it and she starts playing with herself as she observes us.

Carlotta looks up, follows my gaze, and the sight of the woman sets her off: she stands up, sits down on the bench right opposite the door, spreads her legs and gives our little friend a head-on view of her pussy as she brings herself off, whole body shuddering as she does so. The sight of her climaxing, in turn, has me reaching for my own cunt, and within seconds I'm slithering all over the floor as my orgasm whips through me like a tornado.

The woman disappears, seemingly without having come herself, though I imagine she's gone to the shower to carry on what she's begun. I look up at Carlotta, and we burst out laughing.

'You want go find her?' says Carlotta. 'Invite her up to the suite?'

My face falls. 'Carlotta,' I say, 'I thought you understood from yesterday –'

'OK, OK,' she says, hands up in a gesture of surrender. 'I know you not into that. I sorry.'

She stands up. 'I think I go for a Jacuzzi,' she says. 'You come?'

I shake my head. If Carlotta wants to stay down here for a while, I think I might take the opportunity to do a little more snooping.

'I need to pop upstairs,' I say, making a show of looking at my watch. 'I left my bag up there, and I'm expecting an important call from the States in about ten minutes. I'd better run and get it. I'll be right back.'

'Sure,' she says, pulling a towel around her and stepping out into the cooler air of the changing room. 'I not going anywhere. Here my door swipe.'

I enter the suite like a thief, breath held, on tiptoe, heart thudding away. It's ridiculous, when Carlotta knows full well I'm here, if not why I'm here. But I feel like I'm betraying her confidence in me, over a bunch of stupid suspicions.

The bedroom doors are open and I walk in, survey the scene for a moment. It's all neat and tidy: I wonder how Paco and Carlotta live at home, without a maid to clean up after them, to take their discarded underwear and empty glasses away. Or do they have a maid at home? Where, in fact, do they live? In a swanky modernist pad in the middle of Madrid, or on a country estate away from the paparazzi? I know nothing, I realise, about these people with whom, on the surface, I have become so terribly intimate.

I walk over to the bed, sit down. Perhaps, I think, there are some things that are better off not known. Perhaps I would be better just walking out of here right now, walking out of Paco and Carlotta's lives for good, paying them back the money for the days I haven't worked. Getting on with my wonderfully humdrum life, forgetting that our paths ever crossed. Yet something inside me is burning to find out the truth.

I lean forward and pull open the bedside drawer, and my mouth falls open. There, inside, alongside what I saw the last time, are a handful of photographs – photographs of me naked, on the heath with Carlotta yesterday, legs spread for her. Spread for her alone, or so I thought.

It's not me who's doing the betraying here. Carlotta told me she wouldn't even get prints of the pictures we took, that she would hide them away on a CD where no one would ever have access to them, for her own delectation. I'd never have posed for her if I'd known she'd do this. Anyone could see them – the maid, the butler – and I'd be a laughing stock. But I don't know them. I'm more worried about Paco. They're far from hidden from him. How much does he know about me and Carlotta? What *is* this weird little game that they're playing?

I call down to the spa, have the receptionist convey a message to Carlotta that I've had to leave on urgent business, will call her later. Outside, I cross Langham Place and walk briskly through Fitzrovia and into Bloomsbury. Despite my pace, I have no idea where I'm headed; all I know is that I need to walk, get some air inside me, give myself some space to think all of this through.

I thread through the University of London buildings and across Russell Square into 'Dickensland' – Dombey Street, Doughty Street and, further south, Lincoln's Inn Fields. There are few people about, and I grow more calm. I've always loved this part of London, the feeling of history and tradition pressing down on you. On a whim, I drop in at Sir John Soanes's Museum, where there's an eccentric collection of paintings, statues, furniture and other objects amassed by the late architect, in a maze of secret staircases, rooms within rooms, hidden panels and distorting mirrors. It's a universe unto itself, and for two hours I manage to lose myself entirely, forget all about Paco and Carlotta. When I come out, the early-evening sunlight dazzles me, and the thought of them returns with renewed savagery.

I walk back onto Kingsway and then I realise where I am and I walk down to Aldwych, follow that across the Strand into Lancaster Place, and with my back to

Waterloo Bridge stand and look up at the green dome that shelters the room in which Daniel and I had our first memorable encounter. In my head I hear the lyrics to one of my old favourites, 'Mood Indigo', written by Duke Ellington and sung by countless artistes, including Billie Holliday, Ella Fitzgerald, Nina Simone and Frank Sinatra. Breaks my heart whichever version it is.

Always get that mood indigo
Since my baby said goodbye
In the evenin' when lights are low
I'm so lonesome I could cry
'Cause there's nobody who cares about me
I'm just a soul who's bluer than blue can be
When I get that mood indigo
I could lay me down and die.

I wish so much I could wind time back, sort things out with Daniel, never have anything to do with Paco and Carlotta. Life was simple then: more boring, maybe, but at least nobody was messing with my head.

I'm certain, now I've walked and walked, that Paco and Carlotta know about my respective affairs with them. Worse, I think they may have even planned them, or colluded in them at the very least, as a way of titillating each other, keeping their passion alive. There's no way I can repeat these accusations to their faces, separately or together, but there must be a way of putting my theory to the test.

By the time I get back to my flat, I've given up trying to think of a way of outwitting Paco or Carlotta, of tricking them into revealing their intentions, and all I want to do is sit down and cry. So that's what I do. One hour, two G&Ts and several cigarettes later, all cried out, I've packed my holdall and am calling for a cab to take me to the station. Afterwards I telephone my mum, tell her I'll be in Brighton by eight, that I'm going to need to stay over for a night or two.

'Don't worry,' I say at her concerned tone. 'It's really nothing.'

I'm not sure why I'm going to Mum's, given that she's the last person in whom I would confide anything relating to my recent activities. She's always been pretty liberal, but I think there are certain things that parents are better off not knowing about their off-spring. All of a sudden, however, I just cannot bear to be in the same city as Paco and Carlotta, and Mum's place is within easy reach. Since she and Dad got divorced when I was fourteen, she hasn't remarried and still lives alone in what was my childhood home, which means that I am lucky enough to still have the bedroom I had as a girl. I suspect that part of the pull that 'home' is exercising on me right now is to do with the thought of sleeping in my old bed, surrounded by some of my most treasured possessions and old toys. I've lost my bearings and need to anchor myself in a comforting reality, to find my way again.

In the train, I doodle in the condensation on the window beside me with my finger, replaying in my mind everything that's happened over the last few days, trying to gain a new angle on events, to see things that I must have missed, to which all the sex must have blinded me. Is there something I could have done to stop all this? Sure, there were moments even prior to the incident in the Glass Bar when something Carlotta did surprised me, wounded me a little – most notably, the way she boasted to me of her and Paco's sessions after she'd taken me as her lover and knew that I might be hurt by her talk, even while it turned me on. If she *did* know that I was fucking Paco too, which seems increasingly likely, then this vaunting behaviour becomes something more sinister. Carlotta really was playing mind games with me. Yet is there any way I could have guessed that between them they were cooking something up, an unholy stew of which I was the main ingredient?

I think about Paco. Perhaps, I ponder, he more than Carlotta should have awakened my suspicions. The way he came onto me so forcefully, then backed off, summoning me but never really engaging with me even when, physically at least, our intimacy couldn't have been greater. That time after I went to his suite after being let down by Daniel, for instance – the sex couldn't have been more cursory, more devoid of emotion. The same goes of the time in the dressing room, now I come to think of it. It didn't occur to me at the time, but it was like his dancing on the stage just minutes before – physical fireworks but a failure to connect with the other party, with the audience, with me. Everything was happening in Paco's head, in Paco's body, and nothing else mattered to him. That he was staring into his own eyes in the mirror says it all.

No, I don't think Paco has ever really wanted me, and why should he? What have I got that a thousand groupies don't, that supermodels and actresses don't, that Carlotta doesn't? I was a fool to think there could be something. The only real attraction I have for him must be that I'm sleeping with his wife, so that when he's fucking me he can follow the traces of her on me. I'm a map of where Carlotta has been, a trail for him to follow, a new angle on a familar theme.

For Carlotta, I think the passion for me has been more real, more rooted. Either that or she truly is an outstanding actress. But I imagine that wasn't really part of the plan. Carlotta, I suspect, was the instigator of all this. She's a realist who knows how hard it is to keep your man, especially in showbusiness circles, where beautiful rivals are throwing themselves at him day and night. She's been keeping things spicy by introducing a new element into the game, a fiery pinch of chilli with which they could tickle each other's taste-buds. Who's to say I'm the first to have fallen into this role?

At Brighton I head out to the station forecourt, look-ing for Mum's battered old Mini Cooper. It's well over-due for the scrap yard, but she doesn't really use it for anything more than trundling around Brighton these days, so I suppose it may last her a couple more years. She's not well off, bless her – she works as a paediatric nurse and, after Dad buggered off to Australia with his bit on the side, she struggled to bring me and my brother up without any help. I'm not sure I've ever really thanked her enough for all the sacrifices she made. As I climb into the passenger seat and lean over for a hug, I wonder if I should maybe buy her a ticket to the Caribbean with me.

She runs her hands over my hair, then brushes it back from my face. 'You look tired,' she says. She'll try to worm it out of me rather than ask any direct questions.

I nod, avoid her eyes. 'I've been overdoing it,' I say as she turns away and starts up the engine. It wheezes and whirrs like a a bronchial old man. 'Took too much on.'

'Sounds like you need a holiday.'

I smile. 'I've been thinking the same thing,' I say. 'I just need to recharge here for the night. If I'm at my flat, I can't get away from the telephone, from my emails, from the long list of things that need doing. A good night's sleep and I'll go back and clear the decks and book a holiday.'

I might be avoiding the subject, but as I'm speaking it becomes clear to me that I'm talking sense. Tomorrow I am going to sort my life out – excise the cancer of Paco and Carlotta, and spend the remaining week of their booking frying on some tropical beach. If Paco – or his lackey Fenella – make me pay back the money for the days I won't have worked, then so be it. I'll sling it on my credit card and worry about it later.

On the way back to her house, Mum pulls up by a row of shops and jumps out, returning a couple of minutes later with two steaming newspaper wraps of fish and chips. The acrid smell of vinegar wafts up, piquing my eyes and nose, making me realise that I'm ravenously hungry. I haven't eaten since this morning in the park with Carlotta. Mum selects first gear and the Mini lurches away from the kerb with effort, but we don't go far – she finds a parking spot further up the road, and we sit eating our supper with our fingers in the darkness of the car, looking out at the waves churning in the night.

We talk about my brother, about my gran, who's been in a nursing home since losing her marbles a couple of years back, about some trouble Mum's been having at work with a new manager. As I listen to her small everyday concerns, I feel the universe resume its familiar contours around me. Life has been continuing as normal while my own existence was ambushed by chaos. There's an ordinary world still out there, just waiting for me to rejoin it.

A shrill noise from my mobile makes us start. I look at the little screen. It's the witch. I narrow my eyes. It's as if she was tuning into my thoughts. Oh no you don't,

I almost hear her say. She's not going to let me escape her clutches that easily.

I don't want to give Mum food for thought by killing the call without answering, so I bring the phone to my ear and press the green button. 'Hello?' I say, in as composed a tone as I can manage.

''Licia, where *are* you?' says Carlotta.

'Oh hi,' I reply coolly. 'Didn't you get my message?'

'Yes, but I thinking you would have called by now. It's been hours.'

'I know, I'm sorry. I got a bit bogged down.'

'Hmmm,' she says sulkily. It sounds to me like she's bored.

'Wasn't Paco supposed to be coming back early tonight?' I say.

'Yeah,' she sighs. 'But then he get a dinner invitation.'

'Didn't you want to go too?'

'No. I hate all that. All the flattery, the ass-lickers.' I hear her light a cigarette, take a sip of something. 'So what we do tomorrow?' she says. 'How about those galleries we not get to?

I hesitate. 'Look, Carlotta,' I say. 'Something's come up. I've had to go to my mum's place and I won't be back in London before tomorrow evening.'

She doesn't lose a beat before saying, 'Where your mother live? I join you there in the morning. That will be fun, no?'

It seems I say 'No' a little forcefully, because there's both a stunned silence at the end of the line from Carlotta and, I see at the edge of my vision, a surprised glance from my mum.

'I'm sorry,' I say more softly. 'There's are just things I need to attend to. Personal matters.'

I'm shocked to hear Carlotta's voice take on an aggressive undertone. 'You forget,' she says, in a way that suggests she's containing some kind of rage, 'that my husband paying you to spend the day with me? You cannot just go away –'

'I wouldn't if I couldn't avoid it,' I say placatingly, trying to keep a lid on the anger I can feel bubbling away inside her. 'I'll refund Paco via Fenella. You don't have to worry about that.'

'Fine,' she snaps. 'So, I see you after tomorrow.'

With that she hangs up, and for the first time I wonder about her real feelings for me – she didn't even ask if I was OK, if the family matters I alluded to are anything serious. Not that I would have liked her prying even if there was something wrong. But it would have been nice if she'd shown some kind of concern, rather than just try to muscle in on my absence as a way of getting out of the city, having some fun in a new place. As just another adventure. I stare out at the sea, my mood sombre once more.

'That sounded a bit fraught, love,' says my mum, and I feel her hand on the back of mine. 'Anything you want to talk about?'

For one mad moment, I consider laying my head on my mum's lap and letting it all spill out – Paco, Carlotta, the whole damn mess. I'm sure she'd have some wise words to impart. But I'm frightened of hurting her. In some part of her I'm sure I'm still the baby girl she nurtured inside herself for nine months, she held in her arms for untold hours, vowing to herself that she'd protect her against everything the world would throw at her, even as she knew that that was impossible. I don't want her to know how I have sabotaged my own happiness, perhaps even my sanity, for fleeting sexual delight in the arms of strangers.

'No,' I say, turning my palm upwards and winding my fingers through hers. 'Just a bit of a stroppy client. Nothing I can't handle.'

The look Mum gives me shows me she's not convinced, but she turns the key in the ignition and the Mini cranks into life again. Reversing out of the spot, she does an illegal U-turn and we start heading towards Preston Park, where she lives. After a few minutes she leans forward to switch on the radio, fiddles with the dial and then starts singing along to some chart hit that's being played.

Before long we're stepping into her hallway and shrugging off our coats.

'Cup of tea?' says Mum over her shoulder as she heads for the kitchen.

'No thanks,' I say. 'Mind if I fix myself a drink?'

'Course not, love. You go ahead. Make yourself right at home.'

I open the 1970s drinks cabinet that's occupied the same corner of her living room for the last thirty-odd years, pour myself a gin and tonic. In among the supermarket bottles of booze are the chunky cut-glass decanters in which Dad stored his various whiskies. Mum never got round to chucking them out. I wonder if she still thinks about him, in bed at night. There have been a handful of boyfriends over the last fifteen years, but no one has ever lasted the distance. I'd love it if she could find someone who made her happy, with whom she could share her old age. She deserves it. I hate to think that she's lonely.

'Got any lemon?' I say, strolling into the kitchen behind her, and she opens the fridge door, takes one out and carves me a slice.

'Want some company,' she says, 'or do you need to be alone?'

She knows me so well, understands that I don't want to talk about it, or not yet. I love the way she can read me like this, the way she leaves me be and never pushes when she senses I need time to myself. I empty my glass, stand up to make another drink. I really should go to bed, I tell myself; get the rest I promised myself. But another voice tells me that there's no chance of sleep.

I shake my head, smile sadly.

'Night then, love,' she says, and she's gone.

In the dim light of the living room, with a single lamp burning in the corner, I sit watching the minute hand travel around the face of the clock on the mantlepiece over and over. After a long time, I stand up and go back into the kitchen. As I'm popping ice cubes out of the tray into my glass, I scan Mum's cork pinboard with my eyes. In amidst the money-off supermarket vouchers are snapshots of me and my brother Jake taken on holidays in Scotland when we were little, of Gran in younger, happier days, sometimes with Grandad. Memories of life before it got so bloody complicated. Heading back into the living room, I pour myself another drink, wondering why things have to change, why the carefree joy and spontaneity of childhood have to go. Why sex has to come along and mess everything up.

Even the first time, things had been complex, confusing, riven with misunderstanding, betrayals and ambiguities. Every summer since I was fourteen, I spent two weeks at my French penfriend Aude's house just outside Paris, and I'd always had a thing about Eric, the boyfriend of Aude's best friend Natalie. He wasn't the best-looking of guys by any stretch of the imagination, but he did have an undeniable Gallic charm. And although he was spoken for, I'd frequently caught him looking at me from behind a cloud of Gauloise smoke as we hung out in the village square, or opened my eyes to find him admiring my tits as we sunbathed at a nearby lake. Even after I'd left for home, I'd often found myself thinking about him as I lay in bed, discovering myself.

One night, the last year I went there – the year of my A levels – Aude and I had heard Eric and Natalie banging away one night as we'd walked down her lane. The window to her bedroom on the ground floor had been flung open to the summer night, and from behind the fluttering voile we could hear her whimpering.

'Encore, encore,' she had started to beg him, and the bedsprings had gone crazy, the iron bedstead had clanked against the wall behind it, and we'd stood in wonder, listening to their wild, hooting climaxes. Then we'd fallen prey to a giggling fit and had to leg it down the track before either of them heard us. I don't know about Aude, but that night I came for the first time, alone in my room, thinking about Eric and Natalie pleasuring each other.

After a late breakfast of madeleines and hot chocolate the next morning, Aude suggested we bike out to the lake and spend the morning swimming. Within an hour we were spread out on our towels on the soft greyish sand, talking about what had happened in our lives since we'd seen each other the previous year. Aude, I soon discovered, had lost it to one of her brother's friends after going to visit him at university in Poitiers.

'What was it like?' I whispered.

She wrinkled up her nose. 'It hurt a little bit,' she said, 'the first time. I think I needed to relax, but, well, you know ... anyway, when it was over, we went to sleep and then I woke up in the morning and he was licking my pussy and it was heaven, and he put it inside me again and it felt wonderful.'

'Did you have an orgasm?'

'I don't think so. I suppose if I don't think so, then I couldn't have done. But it felt lovely and tingly inside, more and more so, and maybe I was on the way.' She turned her head to look at me, shielding her eyes from the glare of the sun. 'Eric is aching for you, always has,' she said.

I looked at her. 'But he's with Natalie.'

She smiled, a secretive, knowing smile. 'No matter,' she said. 'He's yours, if you want him. She doesn't need to know.'

'But she's your friend.'

'So are you. And I want you to have a good time. Why don't you take advantage?'

I leaned back against the sand, head spinning. I wanted Eric; he had always done it for me. Would I regret it more if I didn't give into my desire, even though I knew I'd probably never see him again? Afterwards, I'd go home, and he'd go off to college, or to a new life in a big city, and our paths would probably never cross again. He probably wouldn't stay with Natalie either, so it was foolish to resist on that count. It's the way it was. We were all birds about to fly the nest.

In the growing heat, my brain started to feel like melting brie, and after a while I stopped thinking and just lay there baking, letting the gentle lap of the water on the shoreline carry me away to a place where there was nothing beyond the slow pulse of my veins, the red wash of blood behind my eyelids. I drifted, just a body now, and nothing mattered any more.

I was wakened by the angry buzz of moped engines and opened my eyes to see Eric and two of his friends raising dust as they braked sharply on the little path leading down to the lake, looking over at us. They thought they were too cool to wear helmets, and in the sunshine reflecting off the water I could see Eric's eyes sparkling like clusters of gems. Like I said, he was no oil painting, but sometimes even a downright ugly man can make a girl cross her legs and squeeze hard. Eric's floppy brown hair could have done with a wash, and his crumpled face suggested he'd gone a few rounds with a local thug, but in his own dishevelled, slightly grubby way, he was sex on a stick.

Aude stood up, walked over to them, hips sashaying in a little pink and white sarong she'd brought along, and spoke with them for a while. Then she came back over and looked down at me, the sunlight a halo around her head

'We've been invited for lunch,' she said. 'Eric's house-sitting for his brother while he's on holiday. Wanna go?'

Yes and no, I felt like saying. All at once I was afraid. But short of pretending I suddenly felt unwell, there was no way of getting out of it. I stood up, picked up my towel. I glanced over towards the boys and my tummy cartwheeled. Eric was staring right at me, a weird smile in his eyes. I looked at my feet.

Dressing quickly, Aude and I walked over to the mopeds, where she hopped onto the back of Eric's friend Stefan's. Eric, now smiling with his mouth as well as his eyes, slung his leg over his own, looked at me and patted the rear seat. I climbed aboard, put my hands around his waist. Immediately I felt my pussy start to throb as my clit pressed up against his backside through my jeans. I tightened my grip as we span in the dust and sped away, afraid that in my dizziness I might lose hold.

It wasn't far to the house, set apart from the rest of its village on the edge of a small wood. Outside, a wooden table and chairs took up a little patio area, and Eric invited us all to make ourselves comfortable there while he fetched us some beers. He disappeared into the house and after a moment loud music began to pump away. I recognised it as The Prodigy, 'Firestarter'.

We sat on the sun-drenched terrace, smoking and chatting and enjoying our cold beers, as Eric flitted in and out of the kitchen before finally materialising with plates of *steak frites*.

'*Voilà!*' he said with a flourish, and I blanched as I looked down at the plate he set before me. Blood oozed from the barely cooked meat. It could barely have touched the pan. I might as well be taking a bite directly from a cow's arse.

However, at that impressionable age I was highly conscious of drawing attention to myself. Not only that, but I was still of the opinion that anything French was sophisticated and chic. So without a word, I took up my steak knife and fork, cut myself a piece of flesh and sunk my teeth in.

It was, for all I say above, delicious, as were the thin *frites* and cheap red plonk we washed it down with. As we all ate, and The Prodigy continued to belt out from the living room, I listened to them chatter but spoke little. I was pretty proficient in French by now, but when lots of people were speaking it together, and using lots of slang, I sometimes found it hard to keep up. Mixed with that was my natural shyness, and my nervous anticipation of how things were going to turn out with Eric.

As I finished my meal, I became aware that Eric had also fallen quiet, and when I finally dared glance over at him, I found he was looking at me too. He smiled when our eyes met, a slow, soft smile, not at all predatory. The moment had come, I realised. It was now or never.

'Where's the toilet?' I asked him, and he waved back towards the house. I stood up, walked around the end of the table, and as I passed him he stood up.

'It's upstairs,' he said. 'I'll show you.'

As we moved away from the others, his hand was in the small of my back. At the bottom of the stairs, I stopped and turned to face him, and he put his arms around my buttocks and pulled me up towards him. I folded my legs around his back, and as he lowered me down to the staircase, our teeth were clashing in the savagery of our first kiss.

I was losing it already, gasping and uttering little sobs as our bodies adjusted themselves against each other, tried each other out for size. My T-shirt had ridden up as Eric reached inside to clasp one breast in his sweat-moistened palm, and as he moved up and down against me, I felt the weight of his cock as it strained at the heavy fabric of his jeans, as it pressed against my belly.

'Baise-moi,' I commanded.

He responded to my order by lifting me up in his arms and carrying me upstairs. At the top, he pushed a door with his foot and it swung open to reveal an unmade bed surrounded by balled-up clothes, which I gathered to be his. His guitar, with which he had sometimes serenaded us in the village square after nightfall, rested next to the bed.

Marching over, he threw me down on it. 'I've wanted you for so long,' he muttered as he tore his clothes off.

195

'If only you knew how many times I've dreamt of this moment.'

'I know,' I said, slithering out of my jeans and knickers, then spreading my legs for him, emboldened by sheer lust. 'Look how much I want you,' I said, awestruck. I dipped my fingers into my sweet sap, held them out to him. He took them in his mouth, closed his eyes. Beneath him I reached for his prick, and marvelled at the hot handful that accepted my caress so willingly. As I start to pump him, I groped beneath him again with my other hand, cupped his lightly furred balls, squeezed and then relented several times over until his breath was coming jagged on my neck as he gnawed at me with his teeth.

I couldn't hold out a moment longer. Taking him by the shoulders, I shunted him round and pushed him down on the bed, then climbed on top, slotting myself down over his dick. Then I leant down to kiss him, hair trailing down onto his face as my lips sought his, breasts crushing against the mohair of his chest. His hands on my buttocks, Eric guided me on and off him, helping me to gain a position and a motion that had us both bordering on orgasm within moments.

'*Attends*,' I whispered urgently. '*C'est la première fois*. First time. Go slow. *Doucement*.'

He eased me up off him, rolled me over and brought his face down to my cunt, where he slurped at me, making satisfied little noises like a cat awarded its ration of cream. I giggled uncontrollably, confused by the simultaneous urge to throw him off me and to pull his face tighter into me, to mash my pussy against his jaw. His tongue flicked in and out of my hole, and his stubble grated, not altogether unpleasantly, at the plump skin surrounding my arsehole. I could see his hand busy between his legs, keeping himself primed for me. Gripping his upper arms, I pulled him up towards me again and he dipped back inside me.

This time there was no way of holding things back, of putting on the brakes. Our bodies met like old friends, and he went deep inside me, then, though I thought it couldn't happen, deeper still, until I felt so full, so complete, I knew that I would always be seeking to find this feeling again, wherever I went, whoever I became. My clitoris, lost inside the soft pile of Eric's pubic hair, was kneaded by his weight. Complemented by his movements inside me, it had me snatching for breath as wave after wave built up, crashed down, retreated and then came back to bowl me down.

Eric held on, fought valiantly, and my contractions were ebbing away when his own climax bore down on him, and he pulled away from me and gripped his dick in his fist as his white jelly rained down on me.

By the time we got downstairs, the others were gone; a note on the wooden table informed us they had returned for a swim. We climbed on the bike and set out for the lake, and as darkness stole over us we all sat by the water smoking and talking. Others arrived, and soon there was a large gang of us. Among the newcomers, I soon realised, was Natalie. I moved away from Eric, located Aude and sat down beside her.

'How did it go?' she whispered.

I smiled at her. 'Natalie's here,' I said.

'Don't panic,' she said. 'Nobody's going to say anything, I promise you. So, how was it?'

I leaned in towards her. 'Amazing,' I breathed. 'It was amazing. I feel – I don't know how to describe it. Life will never be the same again.'

'I'm so happy for you,' said Aude, pulling her sweater up over her head. 'Look,' she pointed.

I followed her gesture, saw figures moving into the water, naked flesh glowly faintly in the light of the crescent moon.

'You coming?' she said.

I stripped off, followed her into the lake. The skinny-dipping bug took hold quickly and before long there were twenty or so of us floating around in the water.

I don't know how much time had passed when Eric appeared beside me, the water level at his chest where it reached my shoulders. Looking around anxiously, unable to see Natalie anywhere nearby, I knew this was my last chance – I was flying home the following evening. I put my arms around Eric's neck, encircled his waist tightly with my legs and kissed him, feeling my hardening nipples press against his chest. I felt so grateful for what he had given me that afternoon, I would have done anything for him at that moment.

His tongue wrestling mine, plunging far inside my mouth, he slipped one hand around my buttock, supporting my weight with the other, and shot one finger up inside my cunt. Finding me wet and ready for him, he took it out and, prising my bum cheeks apart, entered me with an almost bestial grunt of pleasure. I looked around to see if the others had heard, but the light had died and I could see no one save a few stragglers on the shore, and even them I could only make out by the orange flare of their cigarettes. But even had Natalie been standing there watching us, even if she'd been striding out into the lake to tear us apart from each other, I don't think I'd have been able to stop. I was so far gone, not taking this all the way was not an option.

I turned back to Eric, started to eat at his face again.

'*Je t'adore*,' I said when I pulled away, and in that moment I really meant it. His fingers tightening on my arse, driving into my flesh, Eric responded by pushing himself even harder into me, burying his face in my tits. When he sensed the dam ready to burst in me, he walked me back and laid me on the shore, where he rode me as I spasmed violently beneath him, tears rolling down my face. Then he kissed me long and hard, into the night. It was, we both knew, our farewell kiss.

So it wasn't bad, for a first time. In fact, it was pretty damn wonderful. But I left France, and I left Eric, without any real regrets. Like Aude had said, we were young adults, on the threshold of new lives that would take us far away, in directions and to places we couldn't predict. It had been brewing up between us for several years, and the air had finally been cleared by one almighty storm that neither of us would ever forget. That was worth a lot.

Back in Brighton, I was a different person – a woman, I thought, at last. I walked differently, I talked differently. I cut my long straight hair, and I took down my old pop posters. The old Alicia was gone, and an enormous sense of freedom and potential washed over me. A new life was beckoning – a life in which the potential for pleasure was only limited by my imagination.

14

The following morning Mum brings me breakfast in bed after coming home from her shift, and I lie in until lunchtime, taking the train back to London in the early afternoon. On the way I decide that I do need to get away, and soon. But I know that if I leave without confirming my suspicions, without finding out what has really been going on with Paco and Carlotta and how much they know of each others' activities with me, I'll always be wondering if I overreacted, if I misjudged them. There are things I need to do before I head off into the sunset.

I call Jess, and after I've listened to her remonstrations about not having returned so many of her calls, manage to sweet talk her into meeting me for a drink at the Moroccan bar. Within an hour she's there, smoking like fury, gesticulating with her arms as she tells me about her new conquest.

'His dick was like this,' she says, bending her arm at the elbow and drawing her finger the whole length of her forearm.

I laugh. 'And just as thick, no doubt.'

'No kidding, Al – I could hardly walk the next day.'

'So what happened after that first night?'

She leans in to me over the table, a wild look in her eyes. 'I picked him up after work the following evening,' she said, 'and we drove out of town.'

'Where did you go?' I imagine Jess in her red convertible, whipping along at some fantastical speed, auburn hair flying out behind her like flames, the gorgeous barman beside her, one hand on her thigh, the other on his cock.

'Out into the sticks,' she said. 'Who knows? It doesn't matter. It was dark, and we got into the back seat and he went down on me and I was wailing like a banshee with no one around to hear me, just the owls.'

She takes a long drink, readjusts herself a little in her seat, which I take to be a sign that she's getting just a little bit moist down below. She grins.

'I let him drive home,' she says. 'And we hit London at 100 miles an hour. I straddled him all the way along the Westway. He came just as we reached the Marylebone flyover, struggling to keep hold of the wheel. I thought we were going to take off, go out in a blaze of glory.'

They were an item now, she told me, and she was blissfully happy. She thought she'd been fucked in her time, but she creamed her pants just thinking about this guy and what he was going to do with her at the end of each day. She couldn't concentrate on her work, could barely eat. She was even thinking it might be love.

At the dreaded L word, we both grow silent, pensive, until at last Jess looks up at me through her fringe, all serious now, and says:

'So you're still sleeping with Paco, I guess. That's why you've not been in touch, isn't it?'

I feel myself slump down in my seat. 'It's a fuck of a lot more complicated than that,' I tell her, and she raises her eyebrows, leans back and lights a cigarette, and just listens, as real friends do, while I unravel the whole sorry tale.

'You and your appetites,' she says at one point. 'You're always letting them get you into trouble. It's like … I don't know. It's like you have to have the danger to get you going. It's like your little drug.'

'That's not true,' I protest. Sure, it was most likely true of Eric, it's true of Paco and Carlotta, and of a whole lot of people in between. But it wasn't true of Daniel. Perhaps that's why meeting him was such a revelation for me, why the comedown was so bloody hard.

I carry on with my story, and at the end of it all, when I get to the discovery of the photographs of me in the bedside drawer, Jess lets out a low whistle between her teeth.

'Jeez, Ally,' she says. 'Moving swiftly over the shock revelation that you've been batting for the other side, I don't think it takes a genius to see that these guys seem to be really playing you for all you're worth.'

'I know that,' I say, suddenly awash with self-pity and a feeling of helplessness. 'But what the hell do I do to prove it?'

We sit thinking for a minute, and then suddenly Jess is grinning madly.

'You hide in their room,' she says, as if it's the most obvious thing in the world. 'You find a time when you know they're going to be there together, and you wait and see what happens.'

'But I won't be able to understand them. They speak in Spanish.'

'Yes, that's a bummer. But I'll bet my bottom dollar you'll see or hear something very enlightening with regard to your predicament.'

'And how do you propose I go about getting in there and hiding without either of them knowing?'

Jess taps the side of her nose. 'You just leave the finer details to me,' she says with a wink.

* * *

The plan goes into action back at my flat, over a nightcap. Jess has me call Carlotta and apologise again for my sudden departure from the hotel and subsequent disappearing act.

'Somebody had sent me an urgent email about flight changes, and I had to get back to the flat,' I say coolly, with Jess nodding approvingly. Suddenly, with her by my side, I feel brave, able to cope with all this. 'Then my mum called about some problems with my brother and I had to rush down there.'

'No problem, baby,' says Carlotta. 'I just glad you back.' Her voice has an undertone to it, and I wonder if she didn't take advantage of my disappearance from the hotel to find the woman from the sauna, to attend to her own unfinished business. Not that I care anymore. She can screw whosoever she wants. I'm out of it.

'You want to do something tomorrow?' I go on. 'What are your plans?'

'Well, Paco isn't performing, so we thought after he get back from some meetings late afternoon we chill at the hotel, order room service and a movie. We not spent any proper time together lately.'

I seize the opportunity. 'Well, how say we go to the British Museum, take in some culture?' I say. It's a inspired plan because her hotel is between the museum and my house, and I should easily be able to think of an excuse to come up to her room for a few minutes on the way home. Then Jess can find some way of distracting her while I stake out a hiding place.

'Cool,' says Carlotta. 'I book some beauty treatments in the morning, so how about you pick me up around lunchtime – one o'clock?'

'Fine, see you then.'

I put down the receiver and Jess proffers me a cigarette. 'Attagirl,' she says.

We start with strawberry tarts at the restaurant in the Great Court of the museum, where I confess to Carlotta that I'm utterly bamboozled by where to begin, the place is just so huge. She's seen enough paintings of late, she says, even for an aspiring artist, so in the end we agree to join one of the Eyeopener tours, the one about the classical world, about which we both confess to know little.

As we're talking, I sit and look at her, with her fake blonde hair streaming down over her fake-tanned shoulders, taking little bites of her strawberry tart with her cosmetically whitened teeth. She stands out like a sore thumb here, in her black leather mini skirt and white and orange striped low-cut top, in her seamed stockings and silver ankle boots. The queen of trash in this great storehouse of culture. And yet in spite of everything, I ache for her. She exudes sex from every pore.

And then there's the fact that beneath this brashy exterior is a brilliant artist and a sensitive soul with a profound knowledge and understanding of art. I feel that if only I could talk to her properly, tell her what I've seen of her work, tell her that Paco really isn't worthy of her, then maybe she could break free of this siren's role she has created for herself, and that has become her prison. But that would be overstepping the mark. Besides, it's not my responsibility if she wants to squander her life. If her art meant that much to her, she'd fight him for it. She must know, deep down, how good she is.

It's time for the tour, and we spend fifty minutes

following a guide around some of the greatest treasures of the classical world. Carlotta hangs on his every word, studies each piece we are shown with great intensity, as if she's trying to commit every aspect of it to memory. I find myself wishing I could read her mind. Then I might really know this frustrating, enigmatic, contradictory creature.

Afterwards, when the tour is over, Carlotta takes my hand and leads me back through a labyrinth of rooms to something, she says, that has caught her eye. It turns out to be a Roman version of a Hellenic Greek statue of Aphrodite/Venus, naked, crouching at her bath, placed in the centre of one of the smaller galleries. From the souvenir guide that I brought on our way in, we learn that the original statue was an important innovation in classical sculpture, since until then the female form had always been covered by some kind of loose drapery hiding the rude bits.

Carlotta is gazing up at it. 'The way she try to hide her pussy and tits with her arm and legs,' she says, 'actually just draw our attention to her nudity, no? For me that is most erotic thing. I love her look of surprise at being seen washing herself – the most intimate thing of all, no?'

'You think so?'

'Maybe,' she says. 'OK, Paco fuck me up the arse, but I no let him see me washing it.'

Again, I'm floored by her insights, her almost brutal honesty when it comes to physical matters. I only wish she were so forthright when it comes to matters of the heart. Then, perhaps, this thing that took seed between us could blossom into something true, something strong. Something that goes beyond the fact that she is married to Paco, that rises above it.

She's standing against me now. 'I *have* to have you,' she says simply but authoritatively. 'Let's go back to the hotel before Paco get home. Come on. We have time.'

She doesn't even give me the chance to answer before turning and making for the door. I follow, happy that my access to the suite has been made so easy but more than a little repulsed now by the imperious way in which she acts and speaks. It's funny how something that was a turn on not so long ago has become offensive to me.

In the taxi, I tell her I'm sending a message to my friend Jess about meeting her later. I don't tell her the text actually reads:

ON WAY TO HOTEL WITH C. BE ON STANDBY.

She has her hand on my thigh as I'm tapping in the letters; she's looking out of the window but squirming around in her seat. She's obviously gagging for me. I try not to feel too guilty. She shouldn't have made the prints without telling me first, whatever their purpose, whoever looks at them. She told me she wouldn't and she did, and now she is going to have to face the consequences.

We climb out, and I follow her as she stalks up the stairs into the reception hall. I feel I'm almost on first-name terms with the doormen now, I've been in and out of here so many times over the past few days. We get in the lift, and as soon as the doors close Carlotta turns round, shoves me into the corner and, pulling up my shirt, buries her face in my tits.

'God,' she's moaning. 'Oh God. I can't wait. I have to have you now.'

She's turning round, fumbling for the button to halt the lift.

'No, Carlotta,' I breathe. 'Not here. We'll be there in a minute. I want you on the bed, *your* bed.' By which I mean the one Paco has always kept me away from, as if by not fucking me on the bed he shares with his wife he were not really cheating on her. If I'm going to do it one last time with Carlotta, and it's looking increasingly likely that I am, then it's damn well going to be on their own bed. I'm not some kind of leper, some taint.

We make it to the suite, against Carlotta's will, but as soon as I'm over the threshold and we're moving bedwards I get cold feet. I do not want to fuck this woman who's been feeding me a tissue of lies. I will not fuck her. Not until I know what the photographs are all about.

'Whoa,' I say, pulling myself away from her, clothes dishevelled. I sit down on the bed, look up at her. 'I can't do this,' I say, stalling for time. 'I – I'm worried that I'm getting in too deep, that I'm getting too attached to you. In a few days you're leaving, and I'm afraid of being hurt.'

Carlotta kneels down in front of me, takes my face in her hands. ''Licia, 'Licia,' she says, over and over. It's like a chant or an invocation, and I wonder if she's trying to hypnotise me into bed. There's nothing I wouldn't put past this woman.

'Listen to me, 'Licia,' she continues, her big blue eyes penetrating mine. She *is* a witch, I think, to myself. Resist. Resist.

'I love you, *nene*, and you no worry about a thing. I don't want this to end when I go, and there is no reason why it will end.'

'What are we going to do, then?'

'Well, you come see me in Madrid, of course. I pay for you to stay in best hotel, and I come and see you there, bring you presents, chocolates, sexy underwear.' She giggles. 'You be my concubine.'

I smile nervously. She's mad, I've realised. Mad as well as devious.

'And we see each other in London too,' she goes on. 'Paco come here often, and you know how busy he get. I can even get him to pay you again to keep me company! And maybe next time,' she adds, a touch mockingly I feel, a little condescendingly, 'you let me see your little nest.'

'Maybe,' I say, trying to smile. Then I excuse myself, and in the bathroom I type a hasty text to Jess, who's hopefully waiting in the corridor just outside the suite.

READY WHEN YOU ARE, it says. I've turned the volume down, but I see a message flash right back:

THUNDERBIRDS R GO.

I head back into the bedroom. Carlotta is on the bed now, head turned towards me, eyes watchful, calculating. No doubt she's trying to think of the best way of getting me to take off my clothes and fall into her arms. She's tried 'I love you', and that old chestnut didn't work. Perhaps she'll come up with something a bit more subtle if given time. But I won't give her time.

'Carlotta,' I say, clutching my head. 'I feel really bad. I'm just so tired and freaked out by all this. I need some space. I'm an emotional wreck.'

She sits up, looks at me squarely. 'You love me?' she says, and there's an undertone of aggression there. God help you, it seems to say, if you don't.

But I won't say it, not even to placate her, and she falls back onto the bed, looks away from me.

'Go then,' she says. 'Find someone half as good as me who fuck you.'

I stare at her. She and Paco are made for each other, with vicious tempers like that. They're both children, quick to flare up when the world doesn't go their own way. They deserve each other.

I start walking out, through the drawing room and down the hallway, past the prismatic glass sculpture that she used to taunt me, to make me choose between cocks and cunts. I get to the doorway, turn round and shout 'Bye, Carlotta!' Then I open the main door to the suite, clock Jess standing outside, and close it again. Listening out for Carlotta for a moment, I run back along the hall and dart around the corner and into the butler's kitchen. Then I hold my breath and wait for Jess to take over.

Right on cue, the doorbell rings and I hear Carlotta swear in Spanish. A few seconds later she's padding out of the bedroom, past the sofa and into the hallway, calling out 'Who is it?'

I poke my head out from my hiding place, watch the gentle sway of her hips as she walks barefoot, see the smoke from her cigarette wafting up, wreathing her like a phantom. She opens the door.

'Yes?' I hear her say.

'Oh, *I'm* sorry,' I hear the familiar voice of Jess say. 'I must have the wrong suite. I was looking for my friend Pollyanna Hargreaves-Smythe.'

I giggle into my hand. Trust Jess to think of some comedy name at a moment like this. I stay where I am, listening to her drawing out the conversation, trying to get Carlotta to give her directions. And I don't suppose it's with any real surprise that I hear Carlotta's voice softening as she replies, as she notices that Jess is actually really rather lovely. Jess is like a far better version of me, really – a bit taller, a bit more auburn, a bit less freckly. People have often mistaken us for sisters, in fact. Perhaps, it strikes me now, that's the real reason I never came onto her – the element of incest. The taboo of fucking your kin, or even – God help me – your own image. Narcissus eat your heart out.

'... come in for a drink...' I'm sure I hear Carlotta

say at one point, and I suddenly realise that Jess isn't going to be able to keep going for much longer, that short of being lured in by Carlotta, she's going to have to make a break for it. I don't have much time. I stand up, have just the time to glimpse Carlotta standing in the doorway, one hand on hip, back slightly arched, thrusting her boobs out at Jess, who – I can tell from this distance – is trying not to laugh, before I'm across the hallway and into the bedroom.

I head for the left, into the men's dressing room, which I imagine will see less traffic than Carlotta's once they're back. I leave the door ajar, otherwise I won't be able to hear a thing. At once I'm bathed in light. Shit, I think – I wasn't counting on movement-sensitive lighting. Perhaps it will turn itself off if I get inside the wardrobe itself.

I open the walnut doors with their distressed mirrors, climb inside, leaving just a small opening through which I hope to be able to hear what goes on between Paco and Carlotta when he gets back. Inside it positively reeks of Paco – that sexy *mélange* of sweat and Hugo Boss eau de cologne. I push my way to the back, through his suits and trousers and jeans and shirts, and huddle there. Outside I see the light die, heave a sigh of relief.

My breath rasps in my throat and I struggle to contain it, anxious not to miss any sounds from the rest of the suite. Blood is beating in my veins. It's amazing what a noisy contraption the body is when you don't want it to be. I inhale deeply, practise a few yoga techniques to quieten me down.

It seems to work: I hear the front door slam, hear Carlotta pacing back into the drawing room, muttering in Spanish. A moment late the words have been replaced by moans, which lengthen and deepen until I'm sure that she is having a wank, sprawled out on the sofa, satisfying the itch that neither I nor Jess would scratch. I wonder which one of us she is thinking of, or whether her mind is filled with Paco.

I stay where I am, listening to her moans fade and then her voice return to normal as she chats to someone on the phone in Spanish. Then she's walking through the bedroom, heading for the bathroom past the door to the dressing room, turning on the shower. There's a part of me that so wants to climb out of the wardrobe and go and watch her soap herself up, but I daren't risk blowing my cover. Instead, taking advantage of the noise of the jets, I phone Jess.

'Where are you?' she says.

'In the wardrobe,' I whisper. 'Was I imagining it or did she come onto you?'

'You didn't imagine it,' she says. 'She really did.'

'God, she's like a bitch on heat,' I say. 'It's really very insulting to find out she'll fuck anything that moves.'

'Thanks a lot,' laughs Jess.

'Oh, you know I didn't mean it that way, babes.'

'Course not. She's pretty highly sexed, isn't she? And with that body she can't go short.'

'You think she's attractive?'

'God, Al – understatement of the year.'

'Don't tell me *you* were tempted?'

'Let's just say –' She pauses, and when she speaks again there's a coyness comes into her voice that I haven't heard before. 'Let's just say if I was that way inclined . . .'

'Well, I never thought I'd hear the day,' I say. 'You don't think she's a bit, I don't know, trashy?'

'God yeah, but that's what's sexy about her, in a way. I mean, I'm sure she'd be very sexy as she is, *au naturel* and all that, in jeans and a sweatshirt. But the way she presents herself – you've got to have a hell of a lot of self-confidence to do that. And it's a turn-on, someone who knows they're hot enough to carry that off.'

As usual, Jess has it in a nutshell, from having spent just a few minutes with Carlotta. In a way, I'm glad she sort of fancied her, even if she'd never do anything about it. It validates all this drama, all this trouble that's come from me having fallen into Carlotta's arms, into her bed. She doesn't blame me, can see how I got into the mess that I have, and that's important to me.

I'm just having a little moan to her about how hurt I am by the lies Carlotta's been feeding me – about love, about us carrying on after this, about me being her bloody *mistress* – when I hear the main door open again and have to hang up quick. It's Paco, I realise, as I hear him calling for Carlotta. She comes through from the bathroom, goes to greet him in the drawing room. I listen to the drone of their chat, then hear Paco head through the bedroom, past the door to the dressing room, and switch on the shower again. There's no sound from the drawing room; I have no idea where Carlotta is or what she's doing.

In a couple of minutes the shower is turned off and Paco strolls through into the bedroom. The light in the dressing area flashes on, and I shrink back in the wardrobe. The worst possible thing happens next: one of the doors opens and a hand reaches in and starts groping around among the shirts and jackets. I flatten myself against the back of the wardrobe, hold my breath. I need a piss, I suddenly realise, and short of wetting my pants there's no chance of relieving myself. What the fuck am I doing here?

The door closes again and Paco goes back into the bedroom. For a while I hear nothing. After five minutes or so I have to risk it: my bladder is bursting. I step out of the wardrobe, approach the door between the dressing room and the bedroom and peep round. All clear. They are in the drawing room. I run into the bathroom, let forth a stream of hot urine. Too late I realise I can't flush the loo without them hearing it, so I put the lid down and hope that neither of them comes back in.

I trot back into the dressing room, stand listening at the door. I can hear low voices, and then I hear a knock on the door. It's the butler, it transpires, bringing in room service. My tummy growls. I wish I had eaten more before beginning my vigil.

The front door closes again, and feeling brave now I know they are probably sitting eating at the table, I move back out into the bedroom and towards the doorway to the hall. From there I can hear that they are watching a movie in Spanish in the drawing room. I sit down on the chair on which Paco fucked me that first night, that night when it all started. Part of me wishes I could go back and decline his invitation to come back to his suite, but there's another part of me that wouldn't change a thing, in spite of all the hurt and confusion. I've learnt so much about myself this last week. Some bad things, maybe, but some precious things too.

The film goes on, and I hear nothing from Paco and Carlotta. I start to get bored. Why am I not at home, booking a last-minute flight, packing my case? I pick at my nails, let my mind wander. Eric plays through my thoughts. Again, I think, I wouldn't change a thing. Whatever happens in my life, I will always have that first time with him to think about.

My meandering thoughts are interrupted by a moan. It's Paco. I sit up straight, strain an ear towards the door. I hear several more moans, even longer and deeper than the last, but nothing from Carlotta, which leads me to think she must be going down on him. I'm just sneaking through the bedroom doorway to risk a glance when I hear Carlotta's voice and some general movement. I hotfoot it back to the dressing room, leaving a gap in the door through which to peep.

I was right in thinking they were heading for the bedroom; through the slot I see them cross the room towards the bed. Paco is already naked, his cock proud and erect, wobbling in front of him as he walks. Carlotta follows, still fully dressed. As her husband climbs onto the bed, she walks around to one side of it, loosens the tie on the silk curtain and draws it. Then she crosses to the other side and does the same. At the end of the bed, she sits down on the footstool and kicks off her shoes, rolls down her hold-up stockings with their lacy tops and then pulls her dress up over her head. She was wearing no underwear I see, and her breasts bounce forth gleefully. I feel a stab of pleasure in my groin.

She turns around, on her knees on the stool now, and nuzzling her head through the curtains crawls into the little den she has created, like a lioness going in search of her prey. I hear Paco let out another low drawn-out moan, then for a few minutes I hear them purring at one another in rapid Spanish. After a minute I hear a little knock, and I wonder if one of them has bashed an ankle or wrist against one of the bedposts.

It's only after a while that I start to imagine I'm hearing my own name crop up every so often. I listen more attentively, and I'm right. 'Alicia', I keep hearing, uttered by each of them at various points.

'Oh Paco ... mi amore ... si, 'Licia ... si, es bueno ... Si, si ...'Licia ...' The words tumble forth, but as things heat up in their love nest they all start to blur into one sound and I can understand less and less. The sound rises in pitch, little by little, until all I can hear is one scream as they share a climax. Then, for a moment, it goes deathly quiet. I lean back against the wall, heart racing with a mixture of fear and longing.

After a few minutes I hear one of them pull back the curtain and pad over towards the bathroom. The sound of rushing water tells me he or she is running a bath. I wait, holding my breath, spying out, and when I see Carlotta, hair bedraggled, appear from behind the curtain and cross the room, I give it five minutes and then I tiptoe out. I make one wide soundless step towards the bathroom door and glance around. Paco is in the bath, leaning back, eyes closed. Carlotta is standing over him, bringing her pussy towards his face.

I'd like to watch him apply his mouth to her, investigate the treasure chest of her cunt, her infinite riches, but I can't waste a moment. I dash over to the bed, pull back one of the curtains, and stare inside. What I see makes my heart leap up in my throat.

There, on the mussed-up sheets, are the nude pictures that Carlotta took of me on the heath and that I found in her bedside drawer. Everything I suspected is true. Paco and Carlotta have been using me, getting off on the fact that each of them was sleeping with me without my knowledge, using me as some kind of sex toy, or marital aid. God help them, I think, if they need pictures of me to spark the flames.

My first instinct is to tear the photos into little pieces, run away. Then something deeper, murkier, takes hold. I pick up the snapshots, shuffle them together and slip them into my pocket. Then, slowly, I take off my clothes.

When Paco pulls back the curtain and sees me lying there butt-naked on his and Carlotta's bed, he looks so exquisitely taken aback, I regret not having a camera to hand.

'Hi Paco,' I say sultrily, and I hear Carlotta squawk in surprise before she comes running out of the bathroom.

''Licia!' she exclaims. 'What you doing?'

'The maid let me in,' I say. 'I'm going away tomorrow. I wanted to give you both a parting gift.'

Paco is still frozen still in the centre of the room, but Carlotta moves forwards towards me. Her lush body still shines with water from her bath. She smiles, a smile full of lust. As she steps onto the footstool and then starts to come to me over the bed, Paco seems to awaken as if from a dream and follows her. Carlotta glances back at him, eyes flashing some secret message that I'm not equipped to decipher. I might have fallen for her, fallen hard, but I know her so little. It takes a mind as devious and conniving as hers, I realise, to understand her. Maybe that's why she and Paco are so drawn to one another. They are like twins, dark conspirators.

Though it is me who, ostensibly, has bidden them, it is Carlotta – unsurprisingly – who takes charge. I decide to let her. My sense of betrayal is dissolving like vapour trails across the sky, and I'm interested to see where she wants to take me, where she wants to take us. As I said before, I knew when I returned from France that my erotic life was only going to be limited by my imagination, and what has happened between Carlotta and me has extended my boundaries like nothing before.

For a moment there I wanted revenge; for a moment my mind even turned to the cufflinks, and to more photographs – only photographs taken by me this time. But then I thought I might as well milk this for all it's worth, while I still can.

Flinging one leg out to the side and over me, Carlotta pins me down with her pussy, presses it into my own mound. Then she leans forwards, takes a mouthful of soft, doughy tit and munches down hard on it. I stick my head out to one side and see that she has Paco's cock in one hand, is directing it towards her displayed rump. Paco's forehead is beaded with sweat; no doubt he can't believe his luck. Part of me would have liked to have refused them what they have wanted all along but probably never really believed they would get. But my confounded appetite won't let me – the two of them apart were magnificent enough. Together, they are going to take me into the stratosphere.

Paco's inside Carlotta now, and I can feel the rhythm of him in her body against mine. Then she kneels up on all fours, all the while looking down at me, laughter in her eyes. It's infectious, the pleasure she's taking in all of this, the way she's getting off on it. It must be something she's been hoping for for a long time. Perhaps that's even triumph in her eyes, along with the joy.

My head is up now; I'm sucking on her tits, encircling her dark areola with my tongue. I edge myself down so I'm lying directly beneath her, legs wide apart, pussy gaping, sodden with the desire for someone to enter me. Over her right shoulder I can see Paco's hair; he's burying his face into her brown flesh as he bounces in and out of her, groaning with the effort to stop himself coming too soon. Carlotta is quick to see that I've opened like a flower for her and penetrates me deeply with four fingers of one hand, keeping her thumb pressed firmly on my clit. New juices flow forth from me.

'Make me come,' I beg, helpless, even though I know it's too soon. I don't want the spell to break, but my body has its own dictates, its imperious demands.

'My turn,' moans Paco, and I see him back up and away from Carlotta.

'No,' she whispers, 'Paco, *por favor.*'

But it's too late; already he's dipped below her and, pulling her hand from between my legs, enters me. Carlotta moves her fingers quickly to my clit, but I brush them away. I'm on the edge of madness again, but if I give in to the orgasm that's about to explode inside me, I won't be able to carry on.

'The vibrator,' I gasp hoarsely, and Carlotta smiles.

'You a woman after my own heart,' she says, arching her sublime torso over to one side, reaching for the bedside drawer. Taking out the dildo, she separates it from the harness, which she then threads around my hips. When it's fastened, she slots the dildo back in through the aperture. She looks back over her shoulder at Paco; he nods silently, puts his hand under my knees and pulls me down the bed without taking his cock out of me, lowering himself to his knees. My hips are on the edge of the bed, so that he can continue fucking me from his new position.

For a moment Carlotta is still, surveying the scene then she smiles again, that charming, almost childlike little smile of hers, and she climbs aboard, impaling herself on me. And there I am, being fucked by Paco as he kneels with his arms around his wife right in front of him, her breasts clamped tight in his hands. His wife, in turn, is circling her hips, on top of mine, looking for all the world like she's going to pass out as I massage that fat, insatiable clit of hers. Returning the favour, she is kneading mine with the pads of her fingers.

It would be too much to hope for that we all come together, but Carlotta and I do, at least, gazing into each other's eyes as our faces contort in both ecstasy and shock – shock, I think, that anything could ever be this good. And as her husband pulls out of me with a roar, we're still staring into each other's eyes, almost utterly oblivious to him.

They're both still sleeping when I awake. Taking the photographs out of my pocket, I shred them and, in one last self-consciously dramatic gesture that I don't feel embarrassed by in this setting or in these circumstances, I sprinkle the bright confetti over the lovers before turning on my heel. I stop only to open the bedside drawer and take two last items. I stop myself looking at Carlotta on the way out; if I do, I know that I'll cry, and I'm determined not to do that.

In the taxi I put the CD of photos in my bag and then I look at the drawing of myself. It's great; there's no doubt in my mind that Carlotta is a true artist who, for various reasons, has lost her way. I hope she will stop playing games with people, including herself, and return to something she is good at, something meaningful, something with the power to change the world. As we pull up outside my apartment block, I'm thinking I might write her a letter to say as much. Not now, but one day.

Jess is waiting for me at the flat, dying to know what happened. I fill her in, over a few drinks, and as we talk all the hurt dissolves like smoke and we laugh about Paco and Carlotta, decide that I should put it all down to experience.

Afterwards, I tell her about my email exchange with Daniel Lubowski, about my rude message and how much I regretted having been so hard on him.

She smiles at me a bit tipsily. We've had a couple too many by now.

'Just get back online and tell him you've had a cancellation,' she says. 'If what happened really means that much to you, you should give it one last shot.'

15

Daniel and I find each other again – where else? – in the Dome Suite, from which we barely emerge for a week. He's not changed since we last met, or not to my eyes. I wonder if I have to his. It's surely not possible that I can have emerged unscathed from all I've been through.

I'm so nervous when I arrive the first day, after getting the message that he's on his way from the airport and that I'm to check in before him if I'm not busy. The suite, of course, is the same; kicking off my shoes, I collapse back onto the sofa and enjoy a glass of champagne, staring through the double doors into the dome room itself, with its large round mahogany table. And all of a sudden it's as if no time has passed, as if the intervening months – with Kip, and Paco and Carlotta – have been some kind of weird dream from which I have finally awoken into real life. I am being transported back in time, given a second chance.

The door opens; I can hardly bear to turn my head, my heart is thudding so loudly inside me, like a captive bird.

'Alicia,' says a familiar voice.

I stand up, hand at my throat. 'Daniel,' I reply.

He advances, unsurely, even now I'm here, even though he's flown all this way, taken time out of his loaded schedule, to be with me.

I smile what I hope to be a reassuring smile, realising he's as nervous as me. He takes my hand.

'Let's go to bed,' we say at the same time, and the ice is broken, laughter tinkling in our throats like crystal.

I live in Hollywood these days, walking my dog in the hills, swimming in my pool as dusk settles over the city like a cloak, although the so-called glamour of showbiz life no longer fascinates me now that I've seen its dark face. I still have my little flat in London, to which I return a couple of times a year to do research. I've written a series of guidebooks to the city: *Erotic London*, *Romantic London*, *London for Lovers*. All of them are bestsellers.

I never did get to the Caribbean, but I bought a ticket for my mum instead, and was thrilled when I got a postcard telling me that she had met someone she liked. His name is Freddie, and he runs a beach bar near the hotel where she was staying. Two years and four visits later, she's considering moving out there and marrying him. As for Jess, she still lives in London, but she comes and stays often, and Dan and I chuckle together when we hear her and her barman, Luke, bumping and grinding the morning away in the spare bedroom. We laugh, too, about the drawing of me that hangs above our bed. Dan and I have no secrets from one another.

I never did write that letter to Carlotta, although I do see pictures of her from time to time, in the glossies, on Paco's arm, and then the memories unfold like the petals of a flower at dawn. I still sting a little from the whole affair, but I can't help but retain some affection for her too. She opened up a whole side of me that I didn't know existed, but without which I wasn't complete. Without her I wouldn't have lived as deeply, as richly, as I do.

Daniel knows when it's happening, when a curvy blonde waitress in a diner or a redhead surfer chick on the beach catches my eye, raises the hairs on the back of my neck, and he knows equally that there'll come a day when I'll bring one of them home. And Dan's ready for whatever role I want him to play in that – if I want him to be involved at all, if I don't keep her all to myself. He knows it's part of me now, and always will be. But we share one another's fantasies, and that's what makes it so exciting. That's what's important. That's what keeps it alive.

Visit the Black Lace website at
www.black-lace-books.com

LOOK OUT FOR THE ALL-NEW BLACK LACE BOOKS – AVAILABLE NOW!

All books priced £7.99 in the UK. Please note publication dates apply to the UK only. For other territories, please contact your retailer.

DIVINE TORMENT
Janine Ashbless
ISBN 978 0 352 33719 1

In the ancient temple city of Mulhanabin, the voluptuous Malia Shai awaits her destiny. Millions of people worship her, believing her to be a goddess incarnate. She is, however, very human and consumed by erotic passions that have no outlet. Into this sacred city comes General Verlaine – the rugged gladiatorial leader of the occupying army. Intimate contact between Veraine and Malia Shai is forbidden by every law of their hostile peoples. But she is the only thing he wants – and he will risk everything to have her.

Coming in September 2007

THE TEMPLAR PRIZE
Deanna Ashford
ISBN 978 0 352 34137 2

At last free of a disastrous forced marriage, Edwina de Moreville accompanies Princess Berengaria and her betrothed, Richard the Lionheart on a quest to the Holy Land to recapture Jerusalem from the Saracens. Edwina has happily been reunited with her first and only love, Stephen the Comte de Chalais, one of Richard's most loyal knights but, although their passion for each other is as strong as ever, the path before them will be far from easy.

After surviving a terrible storm at sea, Edwina and the princess fall into the hands of the cruel, debauched Emperor of Cyprus, Isaac Comenius. He has even more frightening plans for Edwina but, with Stephen's help, she and the princess escape. However, Stephen has an enemy he is unaware of Guy de Lusignan, the King of Jerusalem, who also desires Edwina.

When they reached the besieged city of Acre, their situation becomes more perilous. Guy lures Stephen away from the Christian lines and, with the help of a group of renegade Knights Templar, has him imprisoned in their fortress. When Edwina tries to pursue Stephen, she is captured and enslaved by a Saracen nobleman who desires her for his harem. In the end only one man can help them escape their destiny, the great Saracen leader Saladin. But he also is in danger from the strange sect of assassins, the Hashshashin.

THE CAPTIVATION
Natasha Rostova
ISBN 978 0 352 33234 9

In 1917, war-torn Russia is teetering on the brink of revolution. A Russian princess, Katya Leskova, and her family are forced to leave their estate when a mob threatens their lives. Katya ends up in the encampment of a rebel Cossack army; the men have not seen a woman for months and their libidos are out of control.

When the Cossack captain discovers Katya's privileged background he has no intention of letting her leave the camp. Against the turbulent background of a country in turmoil, Katya and the captain become involved in an erotic struggle to prove their power over each other.

Black Lace Booklist

Information is correct at time of printing. To avoid disappointment, check availability before ordering. Go to www.black-lace-books.com. All books are priced £7.99 unless another price is given.

BLACK LACE BOOKS WITH A CONTEMPORARY SETTING

☐ ALWAYS THE BRIDEGROOM Tesni Morgan	ISBN 978 0 352 33855 6	£6.99
☐ THE ANGELS' SHARE Maya Hess	ISBN 978 0 352 34043 6	
☐ ARIA APPASSIONATA Julie Hastings	ISBN 978 0 352 33056 7	£6.99
☐ ASKING FOR TROUBLE Kristina Lloyd	ISBN 978 0 352 33362 9	
☐ BLACK LIPSTICK KISSES Monica Belle	ISBN 978 0 352 33885 3	£6.99
☐ THE BLUE GUIDE Carrie Williams	ISBN 978 0 352 34131 0	
☐ BONDED Fleur Reynolds	ISBN 978 0 352 33192 2	£6.99
☐ THE BOSS Monica Belle	ISBN 978 0 352 34088 7	
☐ BOUND IN BLUE Monica Belle	ISBN 978 0 352 34012 2	
☐ CAMPAIGN HEAT Gabrielle Marcola	ISBN 978 0 352 33941 6	
☐ CAT SCRATCH FEVER Sophie Mouette	ISBN 978 0 352 34021 4	
☐ CIRCUS EXCITE Nikki Magennis	ISBN 978 0 352 34033 7	
☐ CLUB CRÈME Primula Bond	ISBN 978 0 352 33907 2	£6.99
☐ COMING ROUND THE MOUNTAIN Tabitha Flyte	ISBN 978 0 352 33873 0	£6.99
☐ CONFESSIONAL Judith Roycroft	ISBN 978 0 352 33421 3	
☐ CONTINUUM Portia Da Costa	ISBN 978 0 352 33120 5	
☐ COOKING UP A STORM Emma Holly	ISBN 978 0 352 34114 3	
☐ DANGEROUS CONSEQUENCES Pamela Rochford	ISBN 978 0 352 33185 4	
☐ DARK DESIGNS Madelynne Ellis	ISBN 978 0 352 34075 7	
☐ THE DEVIL INSIDE Portia Da Costa	ISBN 978 0 352 32993 6	
☐ EDEN'S FLESH Robyn Russell	ISBN 978 0 352 33923 2	£6.99
☐ ENTERTAINING MR STONE Portia Da Costa	ISBN 978 0 352 34029 0	
☐ EQUAL OPPORTUNITIES Mathilde Madden	ISBN 978 0 352 34070 2	
☐ FEMININE WILES Karina Moore	ISBN 978 0 352 33874 7	
☐ FIRE AND ICE Laura Hamilton	ISBN 978 0 352 33486 2	
☐ GOING DEEP Kimberly Dean	ISBN 978 0 352 33876 1	£6.99

☐ VILLAGE OF SECRETS Mercedes Kelly	ISBN 978 0 352 33344 5	
☐ WILD BY NATURE Monica Belle	ISBN 978 0 352 33915 7	£6.99
☐ WILD CARD Madeline Moore	ISBN 978 0 352 34038 2	
☐ WING OF MADNESS Mae Nixon	ISBN 978 0 352 34099 3	

BLACK LACE BOOKS WITH AN HISTORICAL SETTING

☐ THE AMULET Lisette Allen	ISBN 978 0 352 33019 2	£6.99
☐ THE BARBARIAN GEISHA Charlotte Royal	ISBN 978 0 352 33267 7	
☐ BARBARIAN PRIZE Deanna Ashford	ISBN 978 0 352 34017 7	
☐ DANCE OF OBSESSION Olivia Christie	ISBN 978 0 352 33101 4	
☐ DARKER THAN LOVE Kristina Lloyd	ISBN 978 0 352 33279 0	
☐ ELENA'S DESTINY Lisette Allen	ISBN 978 0 352 33218 9	
☐ FRENCH MANNERS Olivia Christie	ISBN 978 0 352 33214 1	
☐ LORD WRAXALL'S FANCY Anna Lieff Saxby	ISBN 978 0 352 33080 2	
☐ NICOLE'S REVENGE Lisette Allen	ISBN 978 0 352 32984 4	
☐ THE SENSES BEJEWELLED Cleo Cordell	ISBN 978 0 352 32904 2	£6.99
☐ THE SOCIETY OF SIN Sian Lacey Taylder	ISBN 978 0 352 34080 1	
☐ UNDRESSING THE DEVIL Angel Strand	ISBN 978 0 352 33938 6	
☐ WHITE ROSE ENSNARED Juliet Hastings	ISBN 978 0 352 33052 9	£6.99

BLACK LACE BOOKS WITH A PARANORMAL THEME

☐ BRIGHT FIRE Maya Hess	ISBN 978 0 352 34104 4	
☐ BURNING BRIGHT Janine Ashbless	ISBN 978 0 352 34085 6	
☐ CRUEL ENCHANTMENT Janine Ashbless	ISBN 978 0 352 33483 1	
☐ DIVINE TORMENT Janine Ashbless	ISBN 978 0 352 33719 1	
☐ FLOOD Anna Clare	ISBN 978 0 352 34094 8	
☐ GOTHIC BLUE Portia Da Costa	ISBN 978 0 352 33075 8	
☐ THE PRIDE Edie Bingham	ISBN 978 0 352 33997 3	
☐ THE TEN VISIONS Olivia Knight	ISBN 978 0 352 34119 8	

BLACK LACE ANTHOLOGIES

☐ BLACK LACE QUICKIES 1 Various	ISBN 978 0 352 34126 6	£2.99
☐ BLACK LACE QUICKIES 2 Various	ISBN 978 0 352 34127 3	£2.99
☐ BLACK LACE QUICKIES 3 Various	ISBN 978 0 352 34128 0	£2.99
☐ BLACK LACE QUICKIES 4 Various	ISBN 978 0 352 34129 7	£2.99
☐ BLACK LACE QUICKIES 5 Various	ISBN 978 0 352 34130 3	£2.99

☐ BLACK LACE QUICKIES 6 Various	ISBN 978 0 352 34133 4	£2.99
☐ MORE WICKED WORDS Various	ISBN 978 0 352 33487 9	£6.99
☐ WICKED WORDS 3 Various	ISBN 978 0 352 33522 7	£6.99
☐ WICKED WORDS 4 Various	ISBN 978 0 352 33603 3	£6.99
☐ WICKED WORDS 5 Various	ISBN 978 0 352 33642 2	£6.99
☐ WICKED WORDS 6 Various	ISBN 978 0 352 33690 3	£6.99
☐ WICKED WORDS 7 Various	ISBN 978 0 352 33743 6	£6.99
☐ WICKED WORDS 8 Various	ISBN 978 0 352 33787 0	£6.99
☐ WICKED WORDS 9 Various	ISBN 978 0 352 33860 0	
☐ WICKED WORDS 10 Various	ISBN 978 0 352 33893 8	
☐ THE BEST OF BLACK LACE 2 Various	ISBN 978 0 352 33718 4	
☐ WICKED WORDS: SEX IN THE OFFICE Various	ISBN 978 0 352 33944 7	
☐ WICKED WORDS: SEX AT THE SPORTS CLUB Various	ISBN 978 0 352 33991 1	
☐ WICKED WORDS: SEX ON HOLIDAY Various	ISBN 978 0 352 33961 4	
☐ WICKED WORDS: SEX IN UNIFORM Various	ISBN 978 0 352 34002 3	
☐ WICKED WORDS: SEX IN THE KITCHEN Various	ISBN 978 0 352 34018 4	
☐ WICKED WORDS: SEX ON THE MOVE Various	ISBN 978 0 352 34034 4	
☐ WICKED WORDS: SEX AND MUSIC Various	ISBN 978 0 352 34061 0	
☐ WICKED WORDS: SEX AND SHOPPING Various	ISBN 978 0 352 34076 4	
☐ SEX IN PUBLIC Various	ISBN 978 0 352 34089 4	
☐ SEX WITH STRANGERS Various	ISBN 978 0 352 34105 1	
☐ PARANORMAL EROTICA Various	ISBN 978 0 352 34132 7	

BLACK LACE NON-FICTION

☐ THE BLACK LACE BOOK OF WOMEN'S SEXUAL FANTASIES Edited by Kerri Sharp	ISBN 978 0 352 33793 1	£6.99

To find out the latest information about Black Lace titles, check out the website: www.black-lace-books.com or send for a booklist with complete synopses by writing to:

Black Lace Booklist, Virgin Books Ltd
Thames Wharf Studios
Rainville Road
London W6 9HA

Please include an SAE of decent size. Please note only British stamps are valid.

Our privacy policy
We will not disclose information you supply us to any other parties. We will not disclose any information which identifies you personally to any person without your express consent.

From time to time we may send out information about Black Lace books and special offers. Please tick here if you do <u>not</u> wish to receive Black Lace information. ❑

Please send me the books I have ticked above.

Name ....

Address ....

....

....

....

Post Code ....

Send to: Virgin Books Cash Sales, Thames Wharf Studios, Rainville Road, London W6 9HA.

US customers: for prices and details of how to order books for delivery by mail, call 888-330-8477.

Please enclose a cheque or postal order, made payable to Virgin Books Ltd, to the value of the books you have ordered plus postage and packing costs as follows:

UK and BFPO – £1.00 for the first book, 50p for each subsequent book.

Overseas (including Republic of Ireland) – £2.00 for the first book, £1.00 for each subsequent book.

If you would prefer to pay by VISA, ACCESS/MASTERCARD, DINERS CLUB, AMEX or SWITCH, please write your card number and expiry date here:

....

Signature ....

Please allow up to 28 days for delivery.